Memories
of
Heather
House

BOOKS BY REBECCA ALEXANDER

WILDFLOWER SECRETS SERIES
Secrets of Foxglove Cottage

THE ISLAND COTTAGE SERIES
Secrets of the Cottage by the Sea
Memories of the Cottage by the Sea
Dreams of the Cottage by the Sea
Coming Home to the Cottage by the Sea
Second Chances at the Cottage by the Sea
The Girl in the Cottage by the Sea

Rebecca Alexander

Memories
of
Heather
House

Bookouture

Published by Bookouture in 2025

An imprint of Storyfire Ltd.
Carmelite House
50 Victoria Embankment
London EC4Y 0DZ

www.bookouture.com

The authorised representative in the EEA is Hachette Ireland
8 Castlecourt Centre
Dublin 15 D15 XTP3
Ireland
(email: info@hbgi.ie)

ISBN: 978-1-80550-073-5
eBook ISBN: 978-1-80550-072-8

To Russell

1

PRESENT DAY, FEBRUARY

Ruby gazed at the moorland stretching away from the old house. Snow touched the peaks far away, the tors jutting into the cloudy sky. It was both familiar and alien, because she hadn't lived in the house for so long. She turned and looked up at the old building, the grey light reflecting off the windows, making it look shuttered. Or derelict. A covering of slush and ice on the front garden was melting. Blackened stems reached over the gravel drive like a barbed-wire fence. A few cars were already here, more were parked on the verges along the road below the house. She just wanted to walk across the road, hike up to one of the tors and breathe. The last few weeks had scoured her of tears, of any feelings except this coldness, this emptiness. She wondered whether she would ever feel warm again.

She took a deep breath and steadied herself against the ornate door frame. This was the last thing she could do for her mother, Fiona. The funeral was over. Only Fiona's closest friends had come back to the house that loomed over her, the property she had promised to leave to her daughter. Ruby noticed the peeling paint, the window frames that were split and cracked, the sagging guttering. The front door was large and grand, but was bleached by the sun and covered in dust. She walked into the wide hallway, lit by a few bulbs hanging from the high ceiling, one broken. Unshed tears compressed her chest and restricted her breathing as she realised she didn't know how to talk to the mourners gathered in the dining room.

Instead, she pushed the door open into the empty drawing room, the grandest room in the large Victorian house, and slipped inside. She had wondered if she would feel Fiona there, but it was echoing and empty as she walked over to the shutters and folded them back. The light showed the extent of the water damage. The centre of the room had had a leak coming through the floors above, dripping onto the sofa, its purple faded to lavender and grey. Mice had left droppings in the torn creases of the velvet, and a riot of feathers had erupted from one cushion. Part of her wanted to drag it outside into the yard and burn it, but she knew she couldn't, not if there were baby mice still living inside it. She sat on the driest corner. A pile of horsehair and plaster from the waterlogged ceiling sat on the blackened and rotting oak parquet. She turned to a shuffling sound in the doorway.

'Hello, Ruby Roo.' The voice was reedy and small, coming from a woman bent almost in half by age, her glasses slipping down her nose under long strands of white hair. Her eyes were milky – she had never had her cataracts treated and now it was probably too late. 'Good funeral. I'm glad you did it in the village. Father Leon was good, wasn't he?'

'Hello, Pony.' She moved up to make room for the old lady to hobble across and sit down, a cane in each hand. The sticks were gnarled, probably taken from the contorted local trees, deformed by the endless winter winds into stunted shrubs. Her hair was so thin Ruby could see age spots on her scalp. 'I think he cried as much as we did,' Ruby said.

'Well, he used to visit quite a bit. I thought I'd be first to go,'

Pony – Penelope – said. Ruby had never been able to say her name when she was a toddler, and as she was horse mad, the name stuck. 'And that Fiona would go on to a hundred.'

'So did she,' Ruby said, her voice catching in her throat. 'She didn't even make it to eighty.'

'So, what are you going to do with the house?' Pony said, looking up at the hole in the ceiling. 'It needs a lot of work.'

'I don't know what to do. I'm not even sure Mum left a will, not with a solicitor, anyway. Who came back to the house?'

Pony patted her hand with fingers as gnarled as her sticks. The bones were twisted into knots at each knuckle and at the wrists. She looked like she was growing into a Dartmoor tree too. 'Your mum's friends, of course. The vicar's here with his wife. Fiona's solicitor is here, and another man, I thought he might be a lawyer, too. An American.' She made it sound like he was an exotic bird.

'I don't know who that could be. I didn't invite anyone else.'

'There was an American who made contact with Fiona last year. I don't think they met in person – she was diagnosed around then.' Her mother had so many friends, Ruby had never tried to keep track. But she had hoped that her father might be among the mourners. Fiona had never told her who he was, and this might be the last chance to find out.

She stood up and turned to look at the dominant painting on the back wall. The familiar picture of Clara – Fiona's sister – as a baby, smiled down at Ruby from several hay bales, arranged to form a seat. The painted surface was shrouded in dusty cobwebs. Her bright green eyes looked greyed, her white dress dulled. Maybe she was six, eight months old; Ruby could never guess the age of babies. She had blonde curls which gleamed through the dust, and fat bare feet. Beside her was a huge dog. Ruby had tried to identify it once; maybe it was a Rottweiler as it had a black and tan face and grinning mouth. Clara had been her mother's glamorous older stepsister. The picture had been painted by her own grandmother, a famous painter in the twenties and thirties.

The bleached wallpaper around the picture, probably close to a hundred years old, bore squares of deeper colour where previous art had been sold off. But never this one, which Ruby was happy about. If they couldn't save the sagging, broken-down manor house, perhaps she could keep the painting, although where it would go in her modern apartment would be a challenge. Her mother had disapproved of the city flat with sea view over Plymouth Hoe when Ruby bought it, declaring it conventional and soulless. But she had come to appreciate it when she became seriously ill and had to move in with Ruby. It made trips to the hospital much easier too, and in time, moving to the hospice. It seemed impending death had mellowed Fiona more than anything had done before, as if the fuse that lit the firecracker was gone.

'Should I talk to him? The American?' she said, staring up at the baby. 'I suppose we ought to find out what Mum wanted.'

'She wanted you to have it all,' Pony said, struggling to her feet. 'She thought you could just carry on as she did, when she inherited. But I don't think she even wrote a will.'

Ruby was startled. 'Surely it's left between you and me? Maybe even Maxwell?' Fiona had long counted the other artists living at the house as family, sometimes choosing them over her own daughter. 'There *must* be some sort of instruction?' She had always assumed there would be, as Fiona had spoken to her solicitor several times before she died.

Pony shook her head. 'She thought we'd be long gone, so she didn't worry about us, and we're not *technically* family. You're her daughter, she wanted to leave it all to you.'

'I don't know if I *can* look after the house,' she said, staring up at the hole in the ceiling. 'It would cost a lot just to get it watertight.' *My responsibility.* 'How much is the roof going to cost to fix?'

'The last estimate was forty, fifty thousand,' said Pony, wheezing towards the door. 'More if there are bats, they're protected.' Pony pulled out a tissue and coughed, looking around. 'I don't come in here much, too dusty and mouldy. I first moved to the house when the old gals, your grandmas, were still running the place. I first met your mother when she was a teenager. I didn't think I would see her die.' She stared off into space for a moment, then shook herself. 'It's a bit draughty in here, isn't it? There are a couple of holes in the front windows.'

Half the six-over-six panes were cracked and a few had corners missing, allowing cold air to trickle in. 'Pony, did Mum have any idea how she was going to make the repairs?' She ran through her resources, which probably ran to a few thousand in her savings account and the equity in the flat. Which she loved and was close to her job. Ruby pulled her jacket around her shoulders and stared at the windowsill. 'Maybe Mum had a bit of money tucked away.'

'I'm always broke, but Max has got a bit in the bank. He might be able to help, at least with the roof.' Maxwell and Pony were the last of the original owners' artistic community. He was now in his nineties. He had filled the barns with the decaying carcasses of cars, tractors, even the back end of a boat, with which he created his exquisite, industrial sculptures of intermingled figures, human and animal, but he hadn't worked for a couple of decades. One remaining statue, Zeus and Leda, stood out in the front yard, although the metallic queen looked like she was winning against the lustful bird.

'He could sell Leda,' Pony said, cackling with laughter. 'We've talked about buying one of those retirement cottages in the grounds of a care home. It would be nice to be comfortable. With good central heating and hot water,' she said, her chuckle turning into a cough. 'Maybe we could stick Leda out the front.'

Ruby smiled at the thought of the nine-foot sculpture parked in front of a tiny cottage. 'I'm not sure everyone would appreciate that. And I know you wouldn't want to be in a retirement home.'

There was a long silence while Pony caught her breath. 'It would be a big job to fix it up,' she said. 'But it's been our home, all of us. It's got so many ghosts, too many memories. Lots of secrets and sadness.' She coughed again. 'You could sell the painting of Clara, that must be worth a bit, that might help with the repairs.'

'I'd really like to keep it,' Ruby said, staring into the depths of dust. The baby was looking straight at her.

'It's the best picture in the house,' Pony said. 'It was Marissa's favourite, too.'

Lady Marissa had worn black for the last decade of her life, wandering from one room to another. She used to stare at the pictures, dusting them, stroking them so much a few had been damaged. Sometimes she talked to Clara, chiding her for not being alive.

She had once been a well-known photographer, a stately old lady who Ruby knew as one of her grandmothers. Marissa and Alice – Ruby's biological grandmother – were lovers, partners. Marissa, while loving, had been the more stern, serious of her grandmothers, whereas one of Ruby's abiding memories of Alice, an accomplished painter, was of her sweeping Ruby up in a flurry of chiffon and a cloud of perfume for a kiss. After her death, Marissa hadn't let go of one of Alice's works, but in the years since Marissa's death, Ruby's mother had had to sell many of them.

'There aren't many finished paintings left,' Ruby said. 'Except the baby. There are a few sketches and studies in the bedrooms. There's a nice one of the tor in my room. It's just a drawing, though.'

Pony looked back. 'They are all valuable. The baby picture must be worth a packet. Enough to fix the roof and windows, I would have thought.'

'It isn't signed,' Ruby said, feeling a tight resistance in her chest at the thought of letting it go.

'It doesn't matter. Alice painted that here, and it would be her granddaughter selling it – that's all the provenance you need. It's gloomy in here now, isn't it?'

The light was going, the clouds tinged with purple. It felt as if the draughts were whispering tiny grey thoughts.

'I'd really like to keep the picture,' Ruby said again. The baby was gazing straight at her, with jade-coloured eyes, and it looked like she was laughing. 'Clara was Mum's sister.'

'Not biologically,' Pony said. 'By Marissa and another mysterious missing father. And twenty-odd years apart.' Pony took her sticks firmly in each clawed hand. 'You can see it was painted in front of the hay barn, where Marissa kept the dogs. Before Max turned it into his giant storeroom.'

'Do you know anything about the picture? When it was painted?'

'It's always been here. Alice painted that before my time. I came here in the sixties. Actually, neither of them talked about it. I assumed it was too difficult after Clara died. Another one of the mysteries we weren't allowed to question. Come and talk to this American chap, he was looking for you. And your solicitor wants a word.'

Ruby guided her with a hand under her elbow around the blackened mess of plaster in the middle of the room and into the hall. An ancient door on the other side led to the 'west wing', previously designated as the scullery and stores with lower ceilings beside the big kitchen. A large building housing three art studios stretched back behind it.

Out of long-established habit, Ruby brushed the huge photograph of Giles Ashton-Wilson, air ace. He had once been engaged to the fascinating Clara, daughter to the owners of the house, herself a brilliant pilot. Her fingers left smears on the dusty glass as she remembered the romantic fantasies she had made up around the couple. A murmur of voices came from the dining room, and she had to steel herself to face them.

The old table was covered in clean cloths, with trays of food provided by a local café. The caterer, Zosia, was discreetly carrying a tray of drinks around, and smiled at Ruby. Finger sandwiches, tiny cakes, little doughnuts. A few of their neighbours were gathered; her family's solicitor nodded to her, and the funeral director had stayed as he knew Fiona personally. Half a dozen artist friends from the moorland community had come, too. So many people loved her, Ruby realised, with a dull pain in her chest. Grief was exhausting, and she felt a pull towards her old bedroom to lie down. The vicar was sitting at one end of the table speaking to a stranger, and he stood up when he saw Ruby.

'Here she is. This is Jake Haydon, a friend of Fiona's who's come down from London to pay his respects. This is Ruby St John.'

She winced a small smile and held out her hand. He was of medium height and stocky build, and had prematurely grey hair with black eyebrows, and though there were laughter lines around his eyes when he smiled, she guessed him to be not much older than her. He shook her hand firmly. His fingers were warm; the human contact reminded her how cold the house was, how cold she had been since her mother died. 'Thank you for coming,' she said.

'I'm glad to be here,' he said. 'I'm so sorry for your loss.' His accent was American.

'Thank you. I'm sorry – how did you know Fiona?'

'I found your mother on a family tree I was working on for a client. I'm a historian – I research genealogy for a law firm,' he said. 'Just before she got ill we were exchanging information about her family trees.'

She stepped back. 'It's a really short tree,' she said. 'Did my

mother tell you I am a genealogist, too? It's just me, my mother
Fiona, my grandmother Alice. Our tree is online.'

'I *should* have said, my client is related through your grandmother's partner, Marissa Montpelier.'

'Marissa had a couple of brothers and a sister, but her
daughter, Clara, didn't have any children.'

'Actually, we have found evidence that Clara may have had
a child. A girl, adopted by a family in America.'

The room had fallen quiet – it seemed everyone was
listening now

'I'm afraid you've been misinformed,' she said, keeping her
voice down. 'This is a really small, close family. I'm sure I would
have known.' She felt quite upset that someone could push into
the tight family story she had always loved, of the romance
between Giles and Clara she'd dreamed about, the tragic
heroism of the war.

'I understand. But I have an adoption certificate, for my
client, Mabel Carlson. Her mother was born in 1944 and
adopted into the US in 1945.'

Ruby's thoughts were chaotic. 'There isn't a birth or
baptism record for a child of Clara Montpelier. I would have
found it if there was.'

He pulled out a copy of a piece of paper from an inside
pocket. 'Mabel had this – look along the top.'

Ruby took it, frowning, her fingers shaking a little. It was a
copy of an adoption certificate of a child born in 1944, named
Wilhelmina Carlson. She had been adopted by William Carlson, with a stamp of immigration into the US. In the box for
mother and father, the words 'parents unknown' were written in
ink. Along the top was a single line in faded pencil. *Clara
Marissa Montpelier.*

2

Clara guided the plane towards the rocky Combestone Tor on the moorland, the shadows beneath her falling away as she soared over the summit towards the airfield. Clara turned to line up above the narrow runway. It looked little more than a strip mowed in a rough meadow, even from two hundred feet up.

'Start your descent,' Miles White, her middle-aged instructor, shouted in her ear. Oil from the engine had misted her goggles, and she was struggling to see the red cans lining each side of the strip, but she had landed so many times before that she could visualise what she needed to do. She felt for the movement of wind on the plane, mostly headwind – she would have to control her stall. A little drift slid the tail to starboard. *So funny to use nautical terms to describe the plane.* She had to work harder to steer as she dropped the revs and allowed the plane to start falling. That was what her instructor always called it: he had taught her to call it flying, falling or stopping.

She could see a few mounds in the distance through the oil, and impatiently pushed her goggles up onto her flying cap. The wind started to sting her eyes immediately, but she could see clearly. Two hawthorn shrubs stood just to the side at the end of the runway, by the gate across the moor. The plane was lined up but drifting a little, and she had to work to keep it straight. For once, Miles wasn't shouting at her, although she assumed he would step in if she was likely to crash the plane. Thirty feet, twenty feet... the ground felt like it was sucking the plane down magnetically.

Concentrate. Cutting the power gently, she could feel the judder that preceded the final stall, and she could see the grass racing away underneath her. The wind whistled in the wires between the two wings of the Tiger Moth, and she could feel the plane almost gliding now, lifting a fraction, as she powered it right down at six feet.

She had mistaken the drop to the ground. It was more like ten, and there was quite a bounce as she cut the power and let the plane drop, but then it was level and hit the ground again, the brakes engaging with a squeal.

'Must oil those brakes,' her instructor shouted, although the engine noise had almost gone.

'Have I passed?' she asked, scared to turn around. More lessons would just be so frustrating, and she didn't have much time left to fit them in. She glanced over her shoulder.

He had already unlatched his half-door and started to clamber out. She made sure all the controls were reset for safety, scribbled the time in the plane's logbook for the engineer and added a note about the brakes. Miles was long gone, probably halfway to the clubhouse bar, where she was the only female member.

'Nice landing,' the mechanic said as he passed her. 'For a kangaroo.'

She rolled her eyes, wiped her goggles on a handkerchief that Mrs Goddings would make a huge fuss about laundering, and walked into the single-storey, corrugated iron hangar that contained the bar. She was met by a cheer from half a dozen men that made her jump.

'Well done, Miss Clara.' Miles passed her a glass of wine. 'You have your Class A licence. Goodness knows what you're going to do with it.'

She took a sip, feeling a flush from the cheer, the wine and the sheer pleasure of having passed first time.

'I'm going to fly the Desoutter,' she said, glancing out of the window. It was bright yellow and quite new to the flying club. There was a queue of pilots to fly the monoplane.

'Then what? Join up for the RAF?' Miles said, watching her over the head of a beer. 'They don't take ladies, you know.'

'Maybe they will have to,' she said, toasting him with her glass. 'With war so close.'

Laughter gave way to discussion. Half of the pilots and trainers at the club thought war could still be averted, but Clara's travels in Europe had led her to see the mood in Germany. People there still talked about a peaceful Europe, but their eyes were haunted.

She walked across the sunny yard to the open door to her home, Montpelier House. 'Is anyone home?'

Mr Mercutio, the house cat, stopped to glance at her before he sneaked out through the open back door. He was carrying something rat-sized, probably from one of the stables that flanked the yard. A grey chicken followed her into the hall and she shooed it back out.

Walking through the long hall, she looked out at the back garden through open French doors. Terraced in several strips of lawn, the top garden looked over the house towards Dartmoor, painted in different greens and dotted with bright yellow gorse. Her two mothers sat at a table laid for tea with a white cloth.

Alice was fanning herself with an enormous straw hat, and Marissa was sitting under a parasol.

'Is there any tea?' Clara asked, walking up the last flight of granite steps.

'Darling, just tell us,' Alice drawled. 'Did you pass, or are you going to be driving to the aerodrome every five minutes for three more months?'

'I passed.' There was a little tea in the pot, which she poured into Marissa's empty cup. 'But I want to learn the monoplane next. I'm parched. Is there any cake?'

Marissa leaned a slender hand over the table and rang a handbell. 'Mrs Goddings is bound to have something for you.' She looked over at her. 'You're always hungry. It's not as if we can use the excuse that you're still growing.'

'At twenty-one? Probably not.' She patted her tummy. She and Marissa were tall and boyish, while Alice was curvy and deliciously pretty, with blonde curls and a perfect bow of a mouth, like in a magazine. 'I've worked quite hard today.'

A minute later, Mrs Goddings put a tray down with fresh cups, tea and milk and a few macarons.

'I thought you'd be hungry. That's it, Miss Clara, until dinner time,' she warned. 'Did you pass?'

Clara smiled around a bite of macaron and nodded.

'Well, the staff will all be thrilled for you,' she said, although the housekeeper always said she had palpitations whenever Clara went to the aerodrome.

'So,' Marissa said. 'You've done motoring around Europe, you've learned to fly. What's next? Piloting a submarine?'

Clara remembered the satisfaction of that moment when the plane was just balanced, almost hovering. 'I said, I'm going to learn the monoplane next.'

'To what end?' Marissa's voice, always sharp, was cutting. 'Do you hope to make friends at the club, or go travelling again?'

Clara shook her head. 'I thought it might be useful. If war comes.'

'War *will* come,' Alice said. 'But I don't see why our only child should get involved. Or what use you could be – you can't be a fighter pilot.'

'Maybe they will need pilots to move things around, you know, like medical supplies or people. Or to teach young pilots,' she said. 'Or take reconnaissance pictures.'

'We have trains to transport things, and young pilots won't want to be trained by a girl,' Alice said. Clara could see she was upset.

'And most of the reconnaissance pilots from the last war died,' Marissa snapped. There were a few frown lines across her perfect forehead.

'Well, maybe not, then. But I'd like to fly the new plane and I'm sure I can be helpful somewhere.'

Alice took her hand. 'We worry about you.'

'It's no more dangerous than driving a car, Ma,' she said, squeezing back. 'Anyway, I'm off to have a bath and get rid of this horrid oil. It makes my hair look black.'

She only had to glance at Marissa's head to know what colour it should be: burnished chestnut that looked like it had been moulded into three perfect waves. 'Well, be careful,' Marissa said, looking back.

Clara jumped up and kissed her. 'I will, Mother.' Then she kissed Alice and hugged her, sending the straw hat flying and having to retrieve it. 'Should I ask for some ice? It's baking out here.'

'No, we'll come in.' Alice's fingers looked like they had been dipped in different colours – she must have been painting before it got too hot. 'Mother wanted to get some work done in the darkroom.' Alice made a face. 'Debutante pictures we took in London. But there's a few landscapes I'd like to develop, too, of haymaking over at Duke's farm and the woodland.'

Clara grabbed the last macaron – in her own defence, she had missed lunch. She followed them back to the cool, stone house overlooking the moor. There had to be something useful a qualified pilot could do when war came, and she could feel it building like a distant thunderstorm.

3

PRESENT DAY, MARCH

Having Jake Haydon turn up at her mother's funeral had shaken Ruby. It had also raised a few questions from people about who would inherit the house. She had always *known* it would be her – she'd assumed it, anyway. Her mother had inherited it from Marissa – there was a will, it was all above board. She had a keen interest in genealogy, which came in useful in her job as an archivist; on occasion she'd helped to find heirs for unclaimed fortunes, and knew what a legal minefield it was. If Jake was working for someone who thought they had a claim to the house, it needed to be addressed.

This is my house.

She was due to return to Plymouth that night, and had put down half a dozen live traps for mice, baited with peanut butter. She had caught several of the whiskery rodents, jet eyes glistening in terror, but she was starting to wonder if she needed to take them further away to release them. The numbers weren't going down and she thought she recognised one of them.

Ruby had also wondered if she could get the picture of baby Clara off the wall but the frame was fixed solidly. She did dust it and take a few photographs with her phone; perhaps she could get it appraised anyway. There would have to be some sort of valuation for death duties. She couldn't see a signature, but maybe she didn't need one since it was still in Alice's house.

She had so many happy memories of this room: reading to Grandma Marissa, playing with a biscuit tin of cars in front of the coal fire, singing with her mother on the velvet sofa. That was before Ruby had broken away to go to university, before her mother had been disappointed that she wouldn't come back. But life in an artists' commune didn't suit Ruby. She preferred order and privacy over people living overlapping lives, having individual dramas around the kitchen table.

The breakfront bookcase filling the space opposite the granite fireplace beside the door was full of books that had all faded to anonymous beige. She could see a few woodworm holes in the bottom of the first drawer she opened, filled with old paint tubes. Marissa hadn't been able to bear to throw Alice's things out, down to her hairbrush and moth-eaten jumpers. To love someone that much... It broke Ruby's heart, but she didn't feel like that about Fiona, she felt a painful numbness. She missed her, there was an ache, a feeling that the universe was a little out of balance without her mother but there was relief, too, that the illness was over. Fiona's death had opened up the wounds from her break-up with Oliver.

She drove home to the city in the evening, finding her way almost automatically, the car filled with a few mementoes she decided at the last moment needed to come home with her. A beautiful throw that her mother had woven, just a little moth-eaten, which could be treated by being frozen. A picture of Fiona as a child that had once ended up as a painting, although she couldn't find the picture. Albums of pictures, a few old children's books like *Bambi*, *The Tree That Sat Down* and the Narnia books. A black-and-white picture of Marissa and Alice's hands when they took vows to each other in the thirties, or maybe twenties – the hands were so youthful, just a splash of paint on one of Alice's nails giving her away. There had been no same-sex marriages then – they had exchanged rings and promises in the garden in front of friends.

At home, Ruby opened her laptop and did a search for Jake Haydon. He hadn't been pushy or rude, he just stated what he believed to be a fact, that his client might be Clara's child. He was a historian who specialised in transatlantic family history. A smiling photograph on his company website made her jump a little. He *was* good-looking; she'd been dimly aware of it even when she was being prickly to him back at the house. And she *had* been prickly, as he tried to push into her family legend about the beautiful and heroic Clara and her sad fiancé. Maybe there was more to the story than she'd realised; maybe Clara and Giles had more than just a chaste engagement. But a *baby*? That wasn't so easy to hide in the nineteen forties.

She checked her work emails – a dozen enquiries. And one from him, that had come from her family tree, posted online on a genealogy website.

Hi Ruby,

It was nice to meet you in person, your mother told me so much about you. I'd love you to look into the mystery of why Clara Montpelier's name is on my client's birth certificate. I see you sometimes do private genealogy work...

He'd left contact details. She answered carefully.

Hi Jake,

Thank you for coming to Fiona's funeral. We really have no record of any offspring of Clara Montpelier. I think it's unlikely that she had a child we didn't know about, or that it would go to America if she did. She had the most loving and supportive family, who were so open-minded. Adoptions of that era are unreliable – anyone could have written the name down for some reason. Maybe she was the child of a friend of Clara's? People were so embarrassed about illegitimate babies back then. There are no official records of anything to do with Cara except her birth and death, and her service records, if you can get those. Sorry to be so unhelpful,

Ruby.

The answer took another few minutes.

Thank you for the reply, I wonder if I could have a chat with you some time, pick your brains? I'm coming down to Plymouth next weekend. Could we meet up for a chat? I'll get us a coffee and I'll bring the papers I do have.

Curiosity at what information he might have sparked Ruby's interest. She told herself, as she cautiously agreed, that she wasn't visualising his face as she wrote. Strictly business, she told herself, and he might engage her services as a genealogist on his wild goose chase. She drank coffee at the weekends, and she was in Plymouth. It was no big deal.

Ruby had promised to cover the afternoon shift at The Box, the local archive centre in Plymouth where she worked. She welcomed two new guests to the stacks, checked that they had bought licences to copy documents and photographs, and told a researcher off for putting a water bottle on the desk next to some eighteenth-century maps.

When she got back to the office, her colleague Lissa was

asleep, head on her arms on her desk. She fetched teas for them both and gently woke her up. 'Everything all right this morning?'

Lissa yawned. 'Bunch of students who wanted me to find things for them. I gave them a leaflet and watched them on the monitors. They all gave up by eleven.'

'How are you doing? How's the baby?'

Lissa yawned again, leaned her head on her hand. 'You know. He doesn't sleep. He will never sleep through the night, I know it.'

'He's little, Liss. He'll work it out. You did.'

She stared at Ruby, heavy-eyed. 'His father was four years old before he went through the night, so I'm not expecting any different. It scarred his mother for life, she says.'

'And how old is Arlo?'

'Eighteen and a half weeks.' She groaned. 'If I get back now, I can catch an hour of sleep before my mum brings him back.'

'Go, go,' Ruby said, flapping a paper at her. 'I'll hang around in the archives, see if anyone needs help.'

'You are an absolute star,' Lissa said. 'Are you OK?'

Ruby hesitated for a moment. 'I'm fine. Just sorting things out with the house.'

Lissa sank into her chair. 'I'm so selfish. Your mum's just died and I'm letting you take over for me. How was the funeral?'

Ruby smiled. 'It's not that. I just met a stranger, he turned up at the house. He was talking to Mum about some American family that think they are related to me somehow.'

'What a coincidence. Just when you're about to inherit a famous manor house and everyone's imagining you're a million-aire? It's hardly surprising that new relatives are coming out of the woodwork.'

'Go home. Your tiredness is making you cynical.' Lissa's words had created a kernel of doubt, though. This is exactly what had been bothering Ruby, at the back of her mind. Fiona's obituary had been published, and people could work out that Ruby was the sole heir. She only had Jake's word that he had made contact with Fiona before she died.

'I'm sorry' Lissa said, gathering up her bag. 'See you tomorrow.'

Ruby hugged her and walked down to the large research room, surrounded by files and shelves of books and folders, computers ranged around the room, moveable bookshelf stacks taking up the second half of the room. Someone needed access to a book locked up in the reserved collection, someone else needed help looking something up on the collection index. Once she had sorted them out, she started a new search through the genealogy website for Jake Haydon, looking for the tree he'd posted for his client. Her name was Mabel Carlson and she was the only daughter of Wilhelmina Carlson, known as Billie.

Billie – who was listed as being adopted – was one of seven siblings. Looking down the tree, Ruby immediately saw the anomaly. A dotted line to Clara came out of the blue as if it was fact instead of speculation.

Clara had lived and died in England, spending her childhood at Montpelier House. She had never married. An assumed relationship scrawled in pencil on an adoption certificate didn't prove anything.

Searching for Jake Haydon on the internet brought up some interesting articles. He'd been involved in identifying heirs in a big case in the news recently, and specialised in unclaimed legacies. He lived in London and was listed as having a daughter, Emerald.

Am I making a mistake? It wasn't just about Clara. She had warmed to him and had thought about him rather more than usual. There was something about him, his smile, the way he had looked directly into her eyes, as if he was interested in her.

But part of her was worried he was going to take away the home she had known all her life, and give it to a stranger.

4

NOVEMBER 1939

'I'm here to talk to Wing Commander Levy,' Clara said, standing tall and straight, polished shoes together. 'Clara Montpelier.'

'Take a seat. He'll see you in a minute.' The woman stood up and walked to a tray on a dark wood filing cabinet. A teapot and some cups and saucers sat on top. The woman left the outer office and returned with a small kettle and milk jug. 'Are you here for the telephonist job?' she asked, smiling at Clara.

'Not exactly,' Clara said, and the woman's smile faded a little. 'I'm a pilot.'

'We've had three female pilots ask to see the wing commander already. It's impossible for a woman to take a combatant role.' Her manner was brisk. When a buzzer sounded on her desk, she picked up the tray. 'Would you open the door for me, please?'

Clara did, and saw an airy office beyond it with windows looking over the aerodrome.

'Miss Clara Montpelier, sir.' The door shut behind her with a click.

'Come in, Miss Montpelier,' Wing Commander Levy said. 'Have a seat.'

She sat, pressing her knees and shoes together as they had taught her at school. 'Thank you.'

He looked down at a note on his desk. 'I see from your letter that you have your pilot's licence.'

'Yes, sir. I've experience of both the Tiger Moth and Descutter.' She shut her eyes for a moment and took a deep breath. When she looked up, he was staring at her from under jutting grey eyebrows.

'What do you want to do with that licence?'

'I thought I could teach,' she said, her voice coming out small. She cleared her throat. 'There must be some role for a good flyer in the RAF.'

'I need good flyers who can fight the Luftwaffe, Miss Montpelier. You can't have combat experience.'

She clenched her hands under the edge of the desk. 'I am presently training with young men who intend to enter the RAF,' she said.

'All private pilot training will cease shortly,' he said. He looked again at her letter. Her crested letterhead looked gaudy and ostentatious now. 'Would you mind pouring?' he asked, without looking up. She took a deep breath, then stood to pour – her hand steady, she noticed with satisfaction – and filled the cups with splashes of milk and the strong tea.

She took a cup and saucer, and since she was standing, looked over the aerodrome. There were about twenty old planes, some were battered and one even had smoke marks behind the engine. When she sat down again, he sighed.

'You could probably do a good job teaching, but I have a better idea for you. Although we don't have any women flying in the RAF, we do send pilots to the ATA, the Air Transport Auxiliary.'

She stared at him. 'I haven't heard of it.'

'It's new. We only have a couple of dozen pilots but we're building it up. It's a civilian outfit, you'll need to talk to them. They take women.'

Her heart beat a little faster. 'What do they do?'

He smiled at her, suddenly seeming both kinder and older. 'They fly, my dear. They have flying in their blood. Since lessons will be suspended except for military service, we need to recruit existing pilots until they build their numbers up and can start their own training school. They deliver planes to airbases, from manufacturers or after repairs or modifications.'

Her heart was beating so hard she could feel it pulsing in her ears. 'They are flying as a *job*? Not just as volunteers?'

'I'm warning you, they do nothing *but* fly. A pilot for the ATA might deliver one plane, then pick up a damaged one to fly on for repairs, or he might catch a train back to base. They are mostly men, but they have some women.'

She tried not to stare as a plane, a twin-engine, taxied outside.

He followed her gaze. 'It's an Avro Anson, we use them for training.' It looked sleek and powerful, turning slightly as if to look at her, high in the window. He laughed. 'Would you like to take one for a spin?'

She turned to look at him, her mouth open. 'W-would I like to?' she stammered. 'I should think so!'

'You were looking at it like my wife looks at a new hat,' he said, draining his tea and standing up. 'You're going to have a job climbing into the cockpit in that skirt.'

'I have slacks in my car,' she managed. 'And a cap.'

'It's very comfortable inside,' he said. 'Three seats, and you can squeeze some poor devil in the bomb bay if needed. That's part of the job. We often ferry personnel around as well as planes.' He picked up his phone. 'Let me know if William Carlson is available, please, Stella.'

After a few moments, the phone buzzed and he answered it.

'Excellent. Thank you,' he said, and replaced the receiver. 'We have a young American pilot. He's come over here to volunteer and we're not sure what to do with him. Since the United States is neutral, we can't use him as a combatant. He's been training pilots, but I was thinking he might be better in the ATA, that's why I know a bit about it.'

She stood and followed him to the outer office, just as a young man – not much younger than her, she judged – stopped in the doorway. He had wavy sandy hair, longer than the styles used in the RAF, a curl flopping over his forehead. He was of medium height, barely taller than Clara, with narrow shoulders and slim wrists jutting out of his flight suit. He stared at her with green eyes. His lips curved into a smile, and she could feel herself smiling in response.

'Mr Carlson, thank you. This is Miss Montpelier, who would like to go up in the Anson, if you would be so kind.'

He switched his attention to the wing commander. 'To do what, sir?'

'Just to have a try of the controls. Nothing too taxing. I'll get a phone number for you to make contact with the ATA, Miss Montpelier.'

He held out his hand and she shook it. 'I'm very grateful you could find time to talk to me.'

He smiled. 'I wish I could recruit you straight into the RAF training programme, my dear. Good luck. We might meet again.'

She followed Carlson outside the office building to the aerodrome as she pulled on her driving gloves.

'I'm assuming you have a pilot's licence?'

She gazed around at the crowded airport. 'I have. I've never seen so many different planes, though.'

'We use them for training,' he said, looking her up and down. 'You can't fly in a skirt.'

'Actually, I can, and do,' she said, laughing at him. She was looking forward to proving her mettle. 'But I have better flying clothes in my car. If you could just direct me to somewhere I can change in private?' She led the way to her open-topped car and lifted a bag out.

'There's a storage shed beside the first hangar. I'm happy to stand guard.'

'Thank you.' She started walking with him. 'So, Mr Carlson, what do you do here? Just teaching?'

'The RAF are hopefully finding a place for me. I should have pretended to be Canadian, it would have been easier to join the RAF as a fighter pilot.' He pulled a door open to a long shed. Even in the dark, it only took a few minutes to slip out of her skirt and into the jodhpurs she used for flying. She repacked her bag and joined Carlson outside.

'May I ask why you came here today?' he asked as they walked back.

She managed a dry laugh. 'Believe it or not, I was trying to join the RAF, too.'

He stopped, staring back at her. 'As a combatant?'

'Apparently not. I did think I might be able to teach, but now I'm going to look into the ATA.' She smiled at him and dumped her bag in the car. 'Where do we go?'

'This way.' He kept looking at her, and she could feel her cheeks heat up so she decided to stare back. He was *really* good-looking, she thought. He looked different from the English boys. Perhaps it was the movie star hair. 'The Germans won't train women as pilots but the Russians do.'

He led her to a short ladder up the side of the plane. It was much bigger than the planes she'd been flying: two engines, an all-around cockpit and a gunner's turret sticking out at the top.

'Is this armed?' she asked, a little breathless. It seemed very real, now she was up close, and she was a bit afraid but excited.

'It normally has a machine gun, with a cannon in the turret,' he said. 'But we don't carry ammunition. It's a tidy plane – the

RAF use them for reconnaissance, and they can carry light bombs.'

A few moments were spent fastening the unfamiliar parachute pack to her chest. 'If we do need to bail – and I'm certain we won't – follow my lead,' he said, showing her the seat belt and cable. 'Make sure you're really hooked on. You have a static line, so you won't need to pull anything, the chute will deploy automatically.

She followed his lead and clambered into her seat, and attached the cable. He was impersonal, but she detected a little redness in his cheeks as he squeezed the belt around her waist and over each of her shoulders. She put on the cap he handed her, snugly fitted it over her curls and fastened the chin strap. He ran through the pre-flight checks, then started the engines, an engineer coming to take the ladder and blocks, and they were off, bouncing a little on the rough grass towards the taxiing area at the end of the runway.

The cap had a radio in it, and she listened to Carlson arranging take-off, receiving information about weather conditions and registering a simple flight plan. They would be following training flight path D, around the neighbouring hill and back again. As he throttled the plane forward, she could feel the power vibrating, the G-force pushing her back in her bucket seat.

'Did you learn to fly in one of these?' she shouted to him.

'Nothing like this,' he shouted back, as the plane left the ground and soared into the sky. 'An old crop-dusting stringbag on my parents' farm in Wisconsin. Here, do you want to take the controls?'

She didn't need asking again. 'Yes, please!' She felt for the control stick, and as he let go she could feel the resistance. It pulled to climb higher, and she had to fight to get it to level out.

'We're heading south-south-east,' he said.

The plane didn't feel like it was barely hanging in the sky, unlike her first lessons in underpowered Tiger Moths. It had more than enough power. She had time to check all her instruments, nudge the plane completely level, check the speed. One hundred and fifty-eight miles an hour? It was intoxicating. The plane wasn't straining or pulling, and she guided it to follow Carlson's pointing finger.

'You'll need more altitude, we're going around the hill,' he shouted. 'Make it six thousand feet.'

Just a small pull on the stick and the engines roared obediently, the plane effortlessly climbing. She levelled out at six thousand, watching around her, checking the instruments and making corrections as the wind tugged at the plane.

She took a moment to look at him and grin. 'This is wonderful!' she said, and he grinned back.

'It certainly is,' he said, and for the first time, she wondered if he was talking about her.

5

PRESENT DAY, MARCH

Ruby waited for Jake outside the restaurant. He smiled when he saw her, and she had to remind herself he might be a problem.

'Ruby.' His voice was deep, friendly. 'Thank you for coming. It's lovely to see you again. I hope you don't mind the change of venue?'

'Nice to see you, too. I thought we were just going for coffee to exchange information?' They were directed to a table for two in the window. She sat down and a waiter handed her a napkin – snowy linen – and a tall menu in French.

'The thing is, it's my birthday,' he confided. 'I normally celebrate back in America with my family, and I didn't want to eat alone. It's my treat, I know I'm using up your time and knowledge.'

'Happy birthday! That's very kind, but I should pay my way...' Even as she said it, she thought how strait-laced and silly it sounded. 'What I mean is, thank you.'

'Actually,' he said, leaning in, 'I've treated myself to a whole weekend in town and I thought I would visit the archives.'

'I work there,' she said, before she remembered it was in her signature line of her work email. 'Well, you know that. I'd be interested to see what leads you have.'

'I thought you could recommend some resources to look at.' He smiled at the waiter and looked at the menu. 'Is a starter OK?' he asked, turning to her. He had a really wide, friendly smile. It made her spinsterish heart flutter. *Spinsterish*, what Oliver had called her, while they broke up. The memory still stung. She adjusted her glasses to look at the menu.

'Fine, thank you, I'll have the soup.' He ordered a bottle of wine before she could stop him, and primly asked for a sparkling water.

'Too early for wine?' he asked, looking up at her and smiling again.

'It's a good idea, but I have to drive home. It's your birthday, enjoy it. You could always look up Marissa Montpelier online, there are quite a few resources. She was a really famous photographer. There was a biography, too, full of details of her pictures. I have a copy somewhere.'

He draped his napkin across his lap and his face turned serious. 'I've seen articles about her online. Wasn't she... mentally ill?'

'She had a breakdown after Clara died, and another when my grandmother, Alice St John, died.' She took a deep breath. 'Alice and Marissa were soulmates. Absolutely each other's muse, they were rarely parted. Alice's death nearly killed Marissa; she was always fragile after Clara passed away.'

'And Alice was *your* grandmother?'

'My biological grandmother, yes. And Marissa was Clara's mother.'

'If they were a couple, how did they both have children back then?'

She smiled at the question. 'They were a couple, but back then they didn't worry about labels. A hundred years ago, they were the centre of an artists' community. They each had relationships with a man at least once – they didn't have access to donors or IVF back then. Alice St John was a celebrated young art student when they met, during the First World War. Marissa had got engaged during the war – I don't have any proof but I think her fiancé was likely Clara's father. I haven't managed to find out who he was, though.'

'I should be writing all this down,' he said, as the starters arrived.

'I'll email you the details. Maybe you can make some progress on Clara's father. I haven't been able to find him.' She hesitated. 'I'm finding it hard to see how your client's family could be linked to my family. If her mother was Clara's daughter, how would she end up in America? From what I know of them, I'm sure Clara's mothers would have welcomed a baby into the family, looked after it after she died.'

The soup, a mushroom velouté, was delicious. He ate a bite of seafood ravioli before answering. 'Wilhelmina – they always called her Billie – was born in 1944 and was adopted a year later by Mabel's grandfather, William Carlson. We assumed there was a close connection with the name on the adoption certificate.'

'But not officially, it's just a scribble on the top. You don't know that Clara was actually the baby's mother, and there's no birth certificate. No name for a father, either?'

'No, but...' His spoon paused in mid-air. 'The family story is that William adopted a baby and brought her up with his wife, May. He always told Mabel she was born to a famous lady pilot who lived on Dartmoor.'

'What did Wilhelmina – Billie – say about this?'

'She died a couple of years ago. After she died, her daughter Mabel employed my firm to investigate the story. She was always curious to know if the story was true. Her mother was certain she was born in England.' He looked down into his glass. 'I had some sympathy. My mother died recently, too.'

'I'm sorry,' she said, a knot of her own pain tearing open. 'It's hard, isn't it?'

He looked at her, locking eyes with her. 'It *is* hard.'

'Totally,' she said, sniffing back a tear. 'I'm finding all sorts of things out about Fiona I didn't know. She was an artist, too, like the old ladies. When did you meet her?'

'Three weeks before she was diagnosed. We really hit it off. She told me the news when she had to cancel a phone call we'd arranged. She never told you about me?'

'She didn't tell me much. We've been a bit – distant – over the last few years.'

'I guessed as much, since you call her Fiona. She didn't talk about you very much until she got ill.'

'No.' Ruby shook her head, pushing her empty bowl away. 'I loved her, of course I did. But she wanted me to be more like her, artistic, Bohemian, a free spirit. We weren't on very good terms until the cancer came.' Her attempt at a smile became a wince. 'I was a bit of a disappointment.'

'What she did say about you was very warm and proud. She loved you very much. You do know that, don't you?'

'I know,' she said, brushing dampness from her eyes. 'We got to know each other again when she stayed with me, in the last few weeks before she went into the hospice.'

'I didn't speak to her after that,' he said softly. 'Is your dad still around? Was he at the funeral?'

She shook her head. One of the questions that had made her so interested in genealogy was that she didn't know who her father was. She hoped to find a few clues in her mother's papers, but Fiona had always said she wasn't sure herself. 'I come from a long line of fatherless babies. Brought up by women.'

'Me too,' he said, and finished his ravioli. 'I was brought up by my mom. Her life was one long adventure. She married my dad but was always travelling on projects. They weren't that happy together. She would volunteer on archaeology digs for months at a time. When I was young she would take me along, and I'd miss half a year of schooling but learn Arabic or French or Brazilian. It fuelled my interest in history.'

She smiled at the thought. 'That sounds wonderful.'

'My dad pulled the plug on it once I was old enough for high school. She carried on going off for months at a time and coming back full of stories. Their reunions were difficult, he was annoyed at her, she was less interested in him. They divorced when I was sixteen. He died twenty years ago.'

The waiter cleared their plates and she ordered a grilled seabass, while he asked for a steak.

'Rare but not blue,' he asked, suddenly looking anxious. He looked at her once the man retreated. 'I had a steak in Paris once that looked like it was still twitching.'

She laughed. 'I think the French do steaks *perfectly*.'

He smiled over his wine glass. 'I loved your house, it's full of history and art. I'm just surprised no one ever mentioned it in the family, if Clara had a baby.'

'The house is in chaos after mum's illness, but I'm sure I would have seen something. I'm sure someone in the family would have said *something* if Clara did have a child.' She shrugged. 'There is no birth certificate. I already looked up my family tree when I was trying to work out who my father was. There aren't any photographs of an unidentified baby, as far as I know. You could try to look up Clara's service record, if it still exists. The Air Transport Auxiliary was a unique group of over a thousand pilots, and more than a hundred were women.'

He got a notebook out of his pocket and started jotting down a few notes. 'You looked her up before?'

'I did when I was young, but honestly, I'm so busy tracking down other people's long-lost relatives... and we know all about Clara's life. You've caught my attention, though. I'm going to look into who Clara's *father* might have been. She was born in 1918.'

'I'll carry on checking all the documents into Clara's life, just to rule out the family legend. And you will look into who Marissa's lover might have been—'

'We think he was killed before the end of the First World War. The family story is that they were engaged but it wasn't announced in the society papers. Did you know Marissa was the youngest daughter of an earl? Technically she was Lady Marissa, but she used Montpelier, the family name.'

'The house is called Montpelier Manor?' He glanced up at her.

'Montpelier *House*, yes. It was called Heather House when it was built.'

'When I saw it, it made me think,' he said. 'Clara might have been born there. If she had a baby, would it have been born there, too?'

'There's no record of a birth at all,' she reminded him. 'I grew up in the house with my mum and two grandmothers, and no one ever said anything about a baby. Clara was actually born in St Ives in Cornwall. I don't know why.'

'But if there was a baby, kept secret to avoid scandal, do you think William Carlson might have been able to adopt it?'

'I really think a baby would have remained with her grand-mothers, or maybe be looked after by Giles's family,' she said, a bit snappily. 'I think it's a dead end.'

'Giles?' He looked up from his notes.

'Giles. Clara's fiancé. Squadron Leader Giles Ashton-Wilson, hero of the Battle of Britain. He paid for the memorial in the churchyard.'

'I'd love to see that. Do you think there might be papers, documents, boxed up in the attic of the house? Who do I ask? There were so many people at the funeral. Is there an executor?'

She didn't know if she wanted him to see the house again. Fiona's passing was so raw, so recent...

'My mother left me the house.' Even as she said it, she wondered. Fiona had *meant* her to have the house, but she never wanted to think about death until it was upon her. 'I suppose I'd be the executor, if there was a will. I'm the only heir.'

He started to smile. 'You're the lady of the manor.'

'Honestly? I'm the owner of a crumbling old house.'

'It's a great house. But I can see it needs a bit of work. If it's too soon, too personal, I would understand. But I'd love to look at any papers about Clara.'

She could feel the warmth between them, the empathy in his eyes. 'It's fine. Who knows, maybe it will clarify my claim if you can rule out any other possible heirs.'

He locked eyes with her for a moment. 'I'd really appreciate that.' Before she could answer, he smiled a little, put his head on one side for a moment. 'What do you think about a dessert?'

She smiled back. She would have to guard her emotions with him, he was very charming. He wasn't at all like the kind of men she had spent time with in the past.

'If it had been left to me, I'd have had three desserts,' she confided.

And he laughed. She had made him laugh, which made her smile, too.

Ruby was still dropped into grief from time to time, but sleeping in her own apartment overlooking the sea helped. She could mostly forget that her mother was dead – it felt like it used to when Mum was back at her own house. They hadn't been exactly estranged, but their lives didn't intersect very often.

The last few months, though, Mum had been living with her while she had treatment. It had been awkward at first, as if their differences were all Ruby could see. She was organised, Mum was not, leaving things around the flat, moving things constantly. Books left open on the sofa, spreadeagled like dead birds. Scarves and jumpers were draped everywhere, and bags of embroidery projects followed Fiona around. And the visitors. People Ruby had never met or even heard of came to pay court. Fiona had never disclosed who Ruby's father was, and in the last few weeks, Ruby had pleaded with her mother to tell her. 'If he comes here, you will tell me, won't you?' Ruby asked. Fiona had smiled, exhausted in the final weeks, and pressed her hand. But she hadn't said anything about the half a dozen men who visited singly or with their partners, and Ruby was none the wiser.

Now the flat was empty, and it had been a relief to tidy it up, to pack up Fiona's belongings to return them to the house. Each dropped scarf or piece of medical packaging that had fallen behind the sofa or rolled under the bed was grieved over, rocking her with memories. This was from the syringe driver giving her morphine through the night before she went into the hospice. This was the scarf she bought on a trip to Paris, to see an opera before she got too ill. This was one of her colourful bamboo socks, the only ones she could bear as her body shrank and her feet swelled, towards the end.

Ruby gave in to her tears.

6

'It's happening,' Clara said, walking down to the breakfast table holding a newspaper. 'They are mobilising the RAF to defend against a possible invasion. The Air Transport Auxiliary will be recruiting as many pilots as they can get.'

'Surely not an *invasion*,' Marissa drawled. 'But you do have a letter, maybe they are calling you up.' She pushed a letter, heavily inscribed with words like *On His Majesty's Service* and *Confidential*.

Clara dropped the paper and used the butter knife to slit the top of the envelope. Opening up the crisp, folded sheet, she rapidly scanned it. 'It's inviting me to apply to the ATA, with a recommendation from Wing Commander Levy,' she said, suddenly breathless. She wondered if William Carlson had finally been allowed to join the RAF. Maybe his breakfast had been interrupted by a letter like this, too. 'They are setting up a new unit, and offering training.' At the bottom was a printed line. *The contents of this letter are confidential.* She laughed, covering her mouth with her hand. 'Oh, bother, I've fallen at the first fence.'

'What?' Alice asked, delicately dissecting a kipper swimming in butter.

'I'm supposed to keep this letter secret.'

'Not from your own family, surely, darling?' Alice said, smiling at her. 'Anyway, who would we tell, living way out on the moor?'

'You know everyone for miles around,' Clara said, reading the letter closely as if she could unlock more information. 'On behalf of the Air Transport Auxiliary... we ask if you would be willing to volunteer for service...'

At the bottom was a place and date. 'Oh, rats. It's the day after tomorrow at White Waltham. Wherever that is.'

Marissa held out a hand and after a moment's hesitation, Clara passed her the letter.

'Don't worry,' her mother said kindly. 'I know absolutely *no* Germans.'

'Except Mr Klopf,' Alice helpfully reminded.

Marissa gave her a hard stare over her wire-rimmed glasses. 'He's our butcher,' she said, her voice cool. 'And his family have been here since before either of us was born.'

'He was arrested and imprisoned in the Great War,' Alice said, returning to another sliver of fish. 'Cook sent him food parcels.'

Marissa looked over at Clara and the tiniest twitch of a smile curved her scarlet lips. 'I shall not discuss a word of your letter with the butcher,' she amended. 'White Waltham... I think I've seen a sign to it somewhere. Yes, I do remember. Alice, dear, do you remember going to a wedding in Maidenhead? I think it's nearby.'

'Cissy Marvel,' Alice said, smiling.

'Lady Clarissa *Merville*,' Marissa corrected. 'They had some horrible prawn concoction at dinner. I remember thinking they could have killed half the diners, it probably came up from miles away on the south coast somewhere.'

'It was perfectly fresh,' Alice said. 'I had some and I was fine.' She paused for a moment. 'The fishing ports are probably all being defended now, all barbed wire and landmines.'

'I was wondering how far it is by car,' Clara interrupted.

'Goodness, I'd drive over two days,' Alice said, buttering a slice of toast. 'Is this all the butter?'

'That's a week's worth gone in two days,' Clara said. 'You'll need to send someone down to Duke's farm, see if they have any spare.'

Alice stared at her toast. 'This dreadful war. How else is one expected to eat kippers?'

Clara laughed, leaned over and kissed her cheek. 'You'll be on herrings fried in lard in no time. Mrs Goddings showed me a recipe she got in *Woman's Own*.'

Marissa took a slim pencil from a diary she kept with her all the time, and scribbled something on a page, tearing it out. 'There's the route, as I recall it. Stop at Rushworth Abbey, I'll call ahead. They'd be happy to put you up tonight.' She paused. 'You know Leonard's already joined the RAF.' Leonard Rushworth, whom Clara had a crush on when she was fourteen. Her cousin Isabella had kissed him in the peach greenhouse at his home when she'd gone swimming with the whole family in the lake at Rushworth. The thought of his flying against the Luftwaffe made Clara take a sharp breath. 'He's only a year older than me. He can't have been flying very long, he started after I did.'

'Stop off there, take an evening gown in case they are entertaining, then drive on in the morning.' Marissa turned back to the silver teapot.

'Mother, this is serious work!'

Marissa topped up her cup. 'We need to keep up appearances, darling. Life goes on. Besides, who knows who you will meet there?'

Clara rolled her eyes and looked out over the moorland

beyond the dining room. Farms, moorland, ponies, sheep – it all looked like it had for a hundred years. A buzzard soared on outstretched wings, dipping to look for rabbits. A little snow had drifted down a few nights ago, and splashes of white remained on the north sides of the tors, the rocks breaking through their blanket of browned bracken.

As she thought about her journey to join the ATA, her mind sometimes turned to a young American with sleepy eyes and hair flopping over his face like a movie star.

The drive to Rushworth Abbey was easy, the weather clear with bright spells, and she turned up in time for afternoon tea. Lady Elizabeth exclaimed at how much she looked like Marissa, even though Clara didn't think she did, then told her Leonard and his friends were playing tennis and would join them soon.

They walked in a few minutes later, three energetic young men laughing and joking. Leonard kissed her cheek and introduced her to Freddie and Giles, his friends from the RAF training school. Freddie Harper was young, he looked barely twenty-one, but Pilot Officer Giles Ashton-Wilson looked older, maybe mid-twenties. He was tall and dark, with a large moustache. She selected a piece of delicate angel cake and accepted a cup of tea from her hostess. Giles sat next to her, staring at her with deep brown eyes.

'Leonard says you live on Dartmoor? *Hound of the Baskervilles* and all that. Have you seen the film?'

She nodded, trying to keep her face serious. 'It's all true,' she said. 'Demonic hounds follow people who are destined to die, there's quicksand all over the moor and it's always misty.'

Giles smiled. 'I'm from the New Forest, Lyndhurst. We have Tirel's hound – if you see him you die within a year. It seems like ghostly dogs are all over the place.'

She laughed. 'Well, there was quite a bit of Hollywood

licence in the film, but I liked Basil Rathbone's Sherlock Holmes. I love the books. But the moor isn't really like that. It's huge, it's wild. It makes me feel small.'

'What do you do for entertainment in the middle of Devon?'

She sipped her tea before answering. 'Well, I was learning to fly over the most extraordinary landscape,' she said.

'Learning?'

She shrugged before taking a bite of the cake. It was light and sugary, and she considered her answer before she spoke. 'I passed a few months ago. I've moved on to monoplanes.'

'So *you're* the girl trying to join the Royal Air Force,' Giles said. He had a bit of a drawl in his voice, which made it sound like he was laughing at her.

'I'm planning to join the ATA,' she snapped back, smiling at Leonard over his shoulder. 'I'm driving down to White Waltham for an interview tomorrow morning.'

'The AT what?' Giles asked, but his eyes had sharpened. They were almost black.

'Air Transport Auxiliary,' she answered. 'Moving planes around the country. And you're in training for the RAF?'

'I am. I hope you get in,' he said. 'I have a feeling my lot will need your lot at some point.' And he smiled, which made him disturbingly attractive.

'I hope so, too. There will be a lot of training first.'

'I've finished my training. Just got my wings,' he said slowly. 'Leonard's going into bombers, navigation, all that technical stuff. Freddie's just about to join the bombardier school. I'm hoping to get selected for fighters.'

She nodded, overcome with sadness. All these young men, throwing their hats in the ring against the enemy planes. 'I wish you the best of luck,' she said, suddenly sincere.

7

PRESENT DAY, APRIL

Ruby packed a bag and headed to Montpelier House on Friday evening. It was a lovely drive rising higher onto the moor, the spring skies growing red and purple later as the month went on. The light levels were dropping minute by minute, and she put her lights on as she drove, highlighting daisies among the tufts of yellow grass. The rabbits would decide they were now invisible and come out in force. She often spotted deer in this part of the moor. The red deer stags were enormous now, and even without their antlers they were dangerous. The hinds were frequently seen against the skyline in small groups, or with last year's calves, walking at dusk along the hollows that led down to water. Today wasn't one of those days, but her car surprised a couple of the moor ponies, wandering along the verge with their foals at their side. She slowed to a crawl as she passed the skittish, curious youngsters.

A buzzard wheeled overhead, probably looking for a rabbit, and as she headed off the road and onto a long lane that led to the house, she could hear the first hoot of an owl. A few daffodils had poked their heads through the long grass alongside the drive.

She remembered how much she had loved it here, with a pang that was akin to grief. Throwing off the opinions of everyone who lived at the house, to find herself, had lost her this place. At times there had been a dozen people making art, cooking and eating together, and arguing all over the house, but she loved them all.

She was close to tears by the time the chimneys appeared around the corner, over the remains of the hedge, just a few corkscrewed hawthorn trees.

She parked around the side of the house and carried her bag up to the back door, where she found Maxwell in the kitchen in his large armchair, asleep. He had grown smaller in the last decades; the huge shoulders that had carried her around the gardens as she screamed with laughter seemed like a wooden coat hanger left in his jumper. His white hair was as bushy as ever but his hands looked enormous on his bony wrists. *He's turning into a tree.*

The kitchen was spacious, with a high ceiling. A huge table sat in the middle. A couple of old units sat next to a vast ceramic sink She filled the kettle as quietly as she could from the brass tap, but he still woke up, despite his deafness.

'Ruby Roo?' he called across the room. 'You're back!' His voice was as deep as ever but cracked now.

She switched the kettle on and walked back to kiss his cheek before he struggled to his feet. For as long as she'd known, people had been patching his wing chair. There was a new patch of orange corduroy attached with large stitches.

'Just for the weekend,' she said, holding one of his hands. On impulse, she kissed it, and he gave her a bony, but still strong, hug.

'I'll make some tea,' she said, detaching herself, and wiping an unexpected tear away.

'Coffee,' he added. 'Not that instant nonsense Pony likes. Are you coming to sort out your mum's things?'

She got his favourite cafetière out from the drainer, stained and crusted with grounds. She washed it before she scooped in the coffee. 'I was going to look through her documents, see if I can find a will.'

'She burned most of her personal papers when she was diagnosed,' he said, leaning back.

Ruby twisted around. 'Why would she do that?'

He shrugged. 'I don't know. A woman of many secrets.'

She turned back to the cleanest of the mugs, rinsed it out and dropped a teabag in it. 'What kind of secrets?'

He smiled as she put the cafetière and a cup in front of him, knowing he'd want it black. 'You know. She had a lot of friends,' he said, winking at her. 'Men friends.'

'Maxwell, she was nearly eighty. I doubt if she was out dancing the can-can.' Her memory flew back to those last visitors Fiona had received while staying at Ruby's apartment, before the ambulance took her away to the hospice for her final weeks.

He tapped the side of his nose. 'I'm not going to tell all her secrets, lassie. But she had a lot of men, all her life. But she did like to keep them all – separate.'

In her early life, before she'd begged Fiona to let her go to school to make local friends instead of being home educated, mother and daughter had spent every summer on the road in a converted delivery van. They travelled from one ragtag festival to another, all through spring and summer. Music, ecology, Buddhism, art – the festivals varied in flavour. But it meant living in their old, hand-painted van for a week or two at a time. Fiona had worked as a steward and ran workshops, from glass painting to tarot reading, while Ruby had been given simple tasks and played with the other children. On sunny weeks when the festivals were in full swing, it was idyllic, with lots of children to play with and food from all around the world. But when it was raining and muddy, or before the festivalgoers arrived, it was bleak and miserable. But her mother loved it. She had always said these transient communities were her tribe.

'I'm showing a friend around the house tomorrow,' Ruby said, sitting next to Maxwell and holding her mug. 'Well, a friend of Fiona's. He came to the funeral.'

He looked up and his mouth drooped at the corners. 'Estate agent?'

'No! I'd give you plenty of warning if we have to do that. Probate hasn't even gone through because we don't have a will. No, it's someone looking into a family tree that mentions Clara.' When Max looked blank, she added, 'He's American. He's an heir hunter.'

He looked at her from under white eyebrows that almost obscured his eyes completely. 'He's trying to find some relative we don't know of, of your mother's?'

'Not quite. His client is a woman who might have some kind of claim if she is related through Clara.'

'Who never married nor had children,' he answered. 'Why is he coming here?'

'He's interested in the house, and his client wants more information.' Ruby said, looking around the kitchen. 'I can't think it will do any harm, just to let him look around again, and he asked really nicely,' she added.

She ran her hand over the table. This kitchen had played such an important part in her life – the sagging spice rack crammed with jars, the table with small holes from woodworm and big holes from deathwatch beetles, the legs chewed all around by a teething puppy. It had once been painted a bright yellow, but the paint was peeling back to the blue that she recalled from childhood. It smelled of bacon and baking.

'Marissa had siblings, didn't she? Could they have a claim?'

'Marissa left the house to Mum. She and Alice were as good as married, and the will wasn't contested.' Uncertainty was creeping in. 'Do you think – if he could prove this lady was related biologically to Marissa – she might have a claim over the house?'

'Maybe. Is there any chance Clara *did* have a baby?' he asked. 'That would make this woman Marissa's great-grand-daughter.'

She slid her fingers over the biggest insect holes in the top of the pine table, long unwaxed or cared for. A sketch of a dragon was incised into the surface in blue biro, she remembered doing it. 'I don't know. There isn't a record of a child, and we've never heard about one.'

Because she'd never thought to look for one. She'd only searched *Clara Montpelier* and had found birth and death certificates and a few newspaper stories about her heroic career. Now, Jake had paperwork that intrigued her as much as worried her. A cynical whisper reminded her that the pencil note could have been added at any time, even after the death notice in the local newspapers, by someone with opportunistic intentions.

'They probably wouldn't have advertised that she was having an illegitimate baby back then,' he said, tapping his mug. 'They shifted them out to childless couples.'

'They weren't worried about the reputation of the family,' she said. 'They were two lesbians raising their family out in the open. They weren't hiding Clara, and Marissa was single when she had her.'

'No, but everyone knew Marissa had *nearly* been married. Her fiancé died during the First World War – they made allowances.'

She was curious. 'Do you know who Clara's father was, then?'

'No one ever said.' He slurped his hot coffee loudly. 'I thought the engagement was announced in the papers some-where, that's what rich people did. They would have been worried about Marissa's reputation. It was a different time.'

'I never found any announcement when I was doing the

family tree. But if Clara did have a baby, surely Alice and Marissa would have wanted to bring up a baby themselves after Clara died?'

He leaned back in the chair, which creaked. 'Marissa took Clara's death really badly, so they say. You know the people around here say she went completely mad, ended up in an asylum.'

Ruby could take that with a pinch of salt. 'I know she was terribly upset...'

'Upset? She took a car and drove it off a cliff,' he said. 'I'm sure I saw a newspaper clipping of it somewhere. She had to be rescued.'

Ruby knew family histories often compounded stories until they left the facts far behind, but maybe there was a paper trail. 'So, you think they just gave the baby away, if there was one? Alice was still here – she could have looked after a child.'

Alice was probably busy looking after Marissa.' He managed a lopsided smile. 'Maybe I heard some vague story when I first came here. But that was in the sixties, before Pony came. Marissa was very remote and distant by then, you couldn't ask her personal questions. Alice was still around too, and she'd had your mother, Fiona, who was a teenager. Don't you think it's odd that no one acknowledged the fathers in this house? They both doted on Fiona.'

Fiona had given Alice and Marissa someone to love. She had grown up in a multigenerational household at Montpelier House surrounded by her mothers' friends.

Well, Marissa left the house to Fiona in her will,' Ruby said firmly. 'Even if Clara did have a baby, and even if she had a daughter, they are a long way out of the line of succession.'

He shrugged, but she had worked enough cases investigating wills to know that the biological line would always give someone an original claim, even if it could be later superseded.

Until now, the weight of the old house and the hippy,

artistic community she had fled as a teenager had pressed down on her, but the thought of losing it reminded her of how much she had loved it. The attic bedroom she'd had as a child, so cold she often crept into her mother's bed when it was icy or snowing outside. The hall hung with generations of coats, some belonging to long-dead artists and writers. *Who knows? We might have a Virginia Woolf gardening jacket or a Patrick Heron raincoat.*

The idea of someone else taking the house was unbearable.

8

MARCH 1940

Clara pulled her car into the gravelled parking area, next to a hand-painted sign: *ATA Headquarters, White Waltham.*

It was a large grass airfield, with just one runway visible, and on the far side, a run-down hangar. She turned to a low hut that had a wall of windows facing on to the car park. A couple of chairs sat outside it, their paint peeling away.

She banged on the door, and a woman opened it. She was tall and angular, with jerky movements, probably in her late thirties.

'Ah, Miss Montpelier, I presume?' Her voice was rich and cultured, almost as deep as Marissa's.

'Clara Montpelier, yes.'

The woman extended her hand. 'Roberta Darwin, late of the London Flying Club. Call me Bobby, Clara. You'll find a few of us around here, just joined. You started flying on Dartmoor?'

'A local flying club attached to the Roborough aerodrome. It's been commandeered by the Air Ministry now.'

'They all have. Come in,' Bobby said, shutting the door behind Clara. It looked like a scout hut with a few benches and a long desk. 'It's a bit primitive at the moment,' she said. 'They're building us a better place behind this one. We haven't got an official base yet but we do have a group organising ferry pools in Bristol – operational hubs with airstrips.'

Clara looked around. It was raining outside again, and she was glad she hadn't put the roof down on the car. Spiderwebs hung from each corner of the windows, weighted down with dew. 'How many pilots do you need?'

'Easily a thousand,' Bobby said, and Clara swung around to look at her. 'We have a few hundred men, mostly experienced pilots who aren't fit enough or are too old for the RAF. And we have twenty-one female pilots so far, and a few joining us from overseas. We even have a few Polish girls being sent over from the Polish Air Force. Three of them flew here straight from Poland, hopping over Europe ahead of the tanks, refuelling a horrible little three-seater monoplane.'

Clara sat on a chair next to an unlit coal stove that had a little spirit burner on top. 'How do I qualify? If the ATA would want me.'

'Oh, you're the right sort, they'll want you.' Looking at Clara's face – which had lost its smile – she added, 'I don't mean the debutante type, I mean the loves-flying-and-chose-to-learn type. We're all keen flyers. One of our best girls was a wing walker in a circus, learned to fly in her spare time. We have a couple of long-distance women, too, who have raced intercontinentally, and an American group is being formed to join us.' She lit the burner under a tiny metal kettle with a match. 'Tea? It's all I can offer, I'm afraid. It's colder in here than outside.'

'Yes, thank you. What do I need to do?'

Bobby searched among a handful of papers on the desk. 'Here you are. This is the address and number of a Service Flying Training School in Gloucestershire, called RAF South Cerney. Take your certificates and your logbook. They will probably let you have a couple of lessons in one of their

Airspeed Oxfords or a Hawker Hart before the official test. You might have to wait a day or two for someone to get around to your tests, but there's a very good pub nearby called the Black Queen that has rooms.'

Clara was shivering, maybe as much from excitement as the cold. 'I'll visit on the way home to Devon.'

'I'll ring ahead for you.' She reached for the telephone on the desk. 'No, it's not working yet, I'll call from the base. If we say you'll be there for eleven tomorrow? There's another one of our pilots going down, you might meet up and have a chat.'

'Another lady?'

Bobby laughed. 'I don't think any of us fall into the category of "ladies" for the ATA. No, it's a man, an American, another stray non-combatant.'

Clara stood and looked out over the hangar, words painted along the doors faded to grey. 'Does that say... de Havilland?'

'They started the airfield as a flying school. We will be able to use the old shed once we get organised, and we'll have ferry pools all over the country as well.' Bobby concentrated on pouring water hissing with steam into a tiny teapot. 'We've flown over a thousand missions already, delivering new planes,' she said, dusting off a couple of chipped cups. 'No saucer, I'm afraid. No milk, either, but the tea's good Pekoe China.'

'Who do I contact for more information? When I pass the test.'

Bobby glanced over at her. 'You're very confident.'

'The only woman in a flying club has to be confident,' Clara said, grinning and lifting her cup to clink against Bobby's. 'She has to be twice as good as the men, too.'

Clara had arrived quite late at the Black Queen pub, and they had managed to find her a good room overlooking the village green. After a hearty breakfast the next morning, despite rationing, she booked her room for a second night and dressed in a smart trouser suit to go to the airbase. Although cloudy, it wasn't raining, and the visibility looked good for flying.

She walked up to the main gate, somewhat officiously guarded by two older soldiers with handguns on holsters. 'I am here to see Wing Commander McMurdoch. I believe I am expected? My name is Montpelier.'

One of the men consulted a clipboard. 'I thought that said *Clive*. Doesn't that look like *Clive*?' he said, showing his colleague.

'*Clara* Montpelier,' she said. 'Here to flight-test for the Air Transport Auxiliary.'

They looked up and stood a little taller. 'If you go to the building on the left and take the second door from the right, you'll find him there. In the mess.'

As Clara approached the mess she heard a wave of raucous laughter. She just caught the booming voice of someone inside. '...They'll have to put flying on the curriculum at Roedean, next!'

She hadn't been at the prestigious girls' school. But it wasn't the first time she'd dealt with prejudice against female pilots.

She took a deep breath, pushed open the door and walked in.

A large number of men sat at long tables, drinking tea and smoking cigarettes. As her eyes adjusted to the smoke, she could see some were staring, many grinning, not kindly. A whistle cut across the laughter from the back of the room.

'Well, at least this one's a looker!' someone else said.

She lifted her chin a little and said, 'I'm looking for Wing Commander McMurdoch.'

One of the younger men pointed to the roof. 'He's just taking a Yank up, putting him through his paces.'

'Excellent,' she snapped, and stepped back out of the mess to look around. She could hear a heavy hum in the far distance, and managed to locate the tiny plane high in the sky. *He's going to make him do a spin.* The idea that she might be asked to do the same made her heart beat faster. Her instructor had always told her to practise spins, because if her plane went into one spontaneously, she needed to be able to recover it. The buzzing stopped as the engine cut out and the sound of birds singing intruded as she shaded her eyes and watched.

The plane's nose was high, enough to induce a stall, but low enough to avoid a tail slide. The pilot turned the rudder neatly until the wing dipped into a spinning roll. One, two perfect twists then the plane eased out of the dive and the engine started again It circled the airfield then came in for a smooth, easy landing.

She shielded her eyes to see who was climbing out, and her stomach gave a lurch as she recognised the pilot's slim shoulders, and sandy hair flopping over his forehead. *Carlson.*

She walked a few steps forward as he and an older man with stripes on his shoulders approached each wearing a flying suit and parachute.

'Miss Montpelier? McMurdoch.'

'Wing Commander,' she answered, shaking his hand. She nodded to William Carlson, who smiled back. She still found him good-looking, with his slightly crooked nose and broad forehead.

'I understand you want to try out for the ATA, too?'

'Yes, sir,' she said, gazing back at him. She didn't feel nervous any more; there was a challenge in his eyes which brought out the fighter in her.

'Do you think you could do a few spins?' he asked, which turned her stomach hollow for a moment. She knew how to do one, and she'd pulled out of a spin several times, but hadn't deliberately gone into one. 'Or do you fancy a loop? What speed would you aim to be going at the top of a loop?'

'About fifty-five,' she answered quickly, grateful for her

almost obsessive rereading of her favourite flying textbook. 'Depending on the weight of the plane, and horsepower, obviously.'

'Well, we have Sutton harnesses installed. Let's give it a go, shall we?'

She glanced at Carlson, who mouthed *Good luck* at her. 'Certainly, sir.'

William handed her his parachute and she followed McMurdoch to the plane. After a couple of steps, she turned to William and said, 'Wait for me?'

A small chorus of laughter and comments came from the half a dozen people who had followed her out. But he nodded and smiled.

She had passed easily. Even her loop was textbook.

'Lovely landing,' William said, grinning at her. 'Are you in?'

'The ATA? Definitely. I'm off home tonight to tell my family, then I report to White Waltham for training on Monday.'

'I'm in too,' he said. 'They won't take me in the RAF, not unless America joins the war. I wanted to have a combatant role.'

'We all did,' she said. 'But this is important war work, too.' He looked a little shy and it made her smile. 'Would you join me back at the pub for a little lunch before I drive back? I have been offered a tour around the base first.'

'Me too,' he said, deflating as if with relief. 'And I would love lunch. You'll have to give me a lift, though. I don't have a car here and I've been bunking in at the base. I'm taking another plane up tomorrow, to get some hours towards my Class 2 licence.'

'Well done. We'll have to compare notes at the pub. I'd like to get mine, too.' She laughed at him and he grinned at her.

He looked down at her clothes. 'I hope I won't have to dress up too much. I only have spare overalls and one clean shirt.'

She shrugged. 'It's a pub. No one will mind.'

His smile slipped a little. 'I wouldn't want people to think you're dining with your chauffeur. I'm down to my last few dollars.'

She was puzzled. 'Who cares what other people think?'

'Says someone who has never had to worry?' he asked, gently. 'I'm surprised at how much class matters here.'

'Doesn't class matter back in America?' she asked a little sharply.

'*Money* matters, and I don't have any until I start getting paid,' he said, then stood up straight as the wing commander brought an older man forward.

'This is Pilot Officer Cranford. He'll show you around our current stock and our new Spitfires.'

She followed them, feeling like she'd been told off a little by William. By the time she got to the hangar and was shown one of the brand-new Spitfires, the thought had evaporated.

They were sleek foxes, and looked agile and fast and aggressive. Some of the planes she had been learning in appeared heavy and slow next to them. The paint was so new they smelled of solvents.

'Where are these going to be deployed?' she asked Cranford.

'These beauties are off to Norfolk, delivered by some of your chaps. They have been tested and checked, and are ready to fight the Germans.'

'If they come,' William murmured behind her.

'They'll come,' she said, running a hand over the edge of the wing so gently it prickled like static electricity. 'I was in Germany two years ago. They are spoiling for a fight.'

Cranford nodded. 'Intelligence has already told us they are amassing planes close to the channel. An invasion support

fleet in case our chaps in France have to make a strategic
retreat.'

'How many planes are being delivered each day?' she asked.

Cranford laughed. 'Worried you won't get enough work?
We estimate that we need to fly two to three thousand missions
to start with.'

'A year?' she asked, turning to see William staring at the
plane with the same greedy admiration that she was feeling.

'A month,' Cranford corrected. 'And when planes start
getting worn, or damaged, the ATA – you and I – will be flying
them back to be repaired or scrapped for parts.' He touched the
engine housing. 'This is a Rolls-Royce engine. Most of the parts
can be reused even if the engine is burned out or crashed. The
planes cost over six thousand pounds each, and the engine is a
third of that. You'll be flying everything.' He nodded to her and
walked off.

'So, we just need to get our relevant licences?' she said,
turning to William.

'Class 2 for a Spitfire or a Hurricane.' His eyes were
glowing as he looked up at the machine. 'I'd like to keep in
touch,' he said. 'Until I get into the RAF we'll be colleagues.'

The idea of William flying against the powerful German
fighters made her feel sick.

9

PRESENT DAY, MAY

Ruby woke up in her childhood bedroom the next day, the sun flooding the attic room with light from the dormer window. There were several cracks that had been repaired with tape, the yellowed strips casting shadows on the sloping ceiling. It was cool – it must still be early. She pulled on a black and silver dressing gown, from her Goth era. *I must look like a wrestler about to fight.*

No one was up on her side of the house. Max had moved his bed down to the long-abandoned library off the dining room, no longer feeling safe on the stairs. Pony still creaked her way upstairs each night, and rarely came down until midday. Ruby smiled at the thought, as she let herself into the yard at the back of the house, catching a glimpse of a cat in the ferns behind the terrace.

The damp slates were achingly cold against her feet. Shallow steps made out of granite led up to the first grass terrace, overgrown now with leggy laurels and hydrangeas with dried flower heads the size of her fist. She let the chickens into their run, scooping their food into a tray. She walked up to the next terrace, just touched with the early light. The shadow of the three chimney stacks, each with four mismatched pots, made the edge of the grass look castellated. There was an ancient bench on the edge of the terrace, where the patio had almost disappeared under moss and lichens silvered with dew. She arranged the dressing gown around her and sat down.

The moorland stretched away in front of her, painted yellow and red and green with old leaves, and dotted with hints of purple from the emerging heather flowers. Small clouds caused shadows to deepen the hues. In the east, a haziness suggested low cloud would cover the house within the hour.

She breathed in. The smell of the moor was like nothing else, somewhere between a herb garden and old books. Behind her, the wall separating the vegetable garden was swamped with old raspberry plants and blackberries that overspilled onto the patio. For a moment, she couldn't bear the idea of never coming here again, never being able to sit here, drawing energy from the very stones and soil she was born from. And then she noticed how the back wall had lost great chunks of render, how several slates had slipped towards the guttering, which no longer clung neatly to the wall. It would cost hundreds of thousands to save the building and restore it. Money she didn't have.

Fiona's personal funds, when they came to her, would be a few thousand and a lot of her half-finished textiles. Maybe the contents of the house would help with a restoration fund, but it wouldn't be the place she loved without the great tapestry over the stairs, Leda in front of the dining room windows, the baby on the hay bale in the living room.

It was too cold to sit for long until the sun rose higher. On her way back down to the house, she found a chicken pushing through a large hole in the wire, so she blocked it with a watering can she filled with water from the tap, and collected the eggs. There were three from half a dozen hens – they looked fat and content but were probably pretty old. Another problem she would have to solve, rehoming six elderly chickens.

She found Max wheezing back from the studio bathroom. She scribbled the date on the eggs in pencil and put them in the enamel bowl on the windowsill. She knew he would wash in the kitchen sink, so left him to his ablutions and went upstairs to get dressed.

Jake was coming to visit later in the morning and the idea made her feel light, a little breathless. In which case, she might as well give him a house tour, so she'd better make her bed and tidy up. Her mother had made her a quilt as a baby and it was still draped over the double bed in her attic bedroom. She folded it up and put it on the wicker chair she had painted white long ago.

Downstairs, she walked into the drawing room, where Marissa had spent the last couple of years of her life. When Ruby was little, she was taken to see her grandmother once or twice a week. A hospital bed had once been placed behind the sofa, and a commode had been tucked behind a screen. Nanny Prince had looked after Marissa, but as time went on it was too much work for her alone, and a nurse had been hired. Ruby had watched the proud, beautifully groomed lady shrink and twist in on herself, watched her hair turn white, except for a yellow fringe from her cigarettes, still smoked with a silver holder. She was always cool and reserved, but Ruby never doubted that she loved her. Only Ruby was allowed to disturb her peace by playing with the other children on the front lawn, reading books from school or wrapping her swollen feet in bandages to play doctor. Now the room was as dilapidated as she remembered her grandmother, a shadow of its past self.

She had warned Jake that the long driveway was so overgrown it felt like you were pushing your car through a scruffy hedge. His Range Rover had clearly made light work of it, but there were leaves stuck in one of his side mirrors. Ruby plucked them out and dropped them on the drive as he got out and stared up at the house, his mouth open. The sun lit up the grand wall at the front, but the sides and back weren't rendered. Each granite stone looked like it had been placed by a craftsman, and the light softened the cracked windows and peeling paint on the frames.

'It's beautiful. It's *huge*,' he said. 'I didn't get a good look last time. To be honest, I was a bit overwhelmed.'

'It's not as big as it looks,' she said. 'It's only two rooms deep, built in the eighteen hundreds by a sea captain. And it's in poor repair, it would cost a fortune to restore. You probably saw the best rooms.'

He followed her up the stone steps to the front door, turning to look back down the hill. 'Where are we? I mean, on Dartmoor? I lost track of where the big towns are.'

'There aren't any large towns. We're near the middle, a bit north,' she said, pointing at a distant tor perched on a hill. 'That's Fox Tor, to the south-west. That tor there is Combestone, and that little church spire is Hartford village, three or four miles away.'

He took a deep breath. 'That's wonderful. And you own all this?'

'Just the house and a couple of acres of scrubland that used to be garden.' She ran her fingers over the paint peeling away from the large wooden front door. The captain had had a sailing ship carved into it, below a diamond-shaped window that illuminated the hall inside. She could see at least three generations of paint. 'This financial liability will be all mine once probate goes through.'

'I rent a flat near my office,' he said, as he turned to look at the hall. 'Four hundred square feet. My wife got the house in Connecticut in the divorce. I can't imagine owning something like this.'

The word 'wife' jolted Ruby. She hadn't given much

thought to the forty-odd years he'd lived before she met him. Maybe he had a new partner – she knew nothing about him, he was a stranger. The idea wasn't a pleasant one.

She led the way through the front door. 'This is my favourite part of the house,' she confided, waving at the hall. 'We're all represented here. Marissa's walking sticks, a pair of my boots under the dresser, Alice's paints in the drawers.'

He laughed. 'You could almost fit my apartment just in here,' he said. The flagstone hall was twelve feet wide and the full depth of the house, with French doors out into the yard, the paved area at the back leading up to the garden terraces extending across the whole width of the house. A huge dresser sat along the right-hand wall, between the door to the dining room and the kitchen. A hall stand was draped with old coats and jackets, and a handmade umbrella stand was filled with walking sticks and brollies. On the other side, double doors, carved and ornamented but painted with hideous fawn paint, led to the drawing room. She flung them open and he walked in, eyes immediately drawn to the ceiling and the ugly hole. At least she had pulled the sofa back before she had left after the funeral and it wasn't getting splashed any more.

He looked up at the collapsed ring of plaster, blackened and trailing horsehair. 'What happened here?'

'Just a leak, that didn't get looked at.' For years. Fiona rarely came in here and just hadn't noticed. She had stuck an old plastic bin underneath it, to collect the water, but it became too heavy at the end for her to empty it. The Persian rug underneath had gone black and rotted, over the parquet. 'The whole roof needs doing. We patched it last year but my mother couldn't afford to fix the ceiling.' A plaster cornice decorated the edges, the fruits and leaves cracked in a few places. 'We'd need a conservation expert to mend it. This was all the captain's and his wife's design, when it was Heather House.'

'He had quite a vision. Did you get a quote for the roof?' He turned around to survey the whole space.

'Once. It was many thousands, so we sort of switched off.' She sighed. 'It seems such a shame.'

'It must have been a grand house in its time.'

She watched him walk around the room, his fingers brushing furniture, making marks in the dust. It wasn't until he turned to the back wall that he stopped and stared at the picture of the baby.

'It's one of Alice's best paintings,' Ruby said, standing next to him. 'It's probably valuable, maybe enough to help restore the house, but it's not signed. We had a lot of artists coming and going over the years – it could even be by one of them but I'm sure it's one of Alice's.'

'Who is – who sat for it?'

'It's Clara, as a baby,' she said, smiling back at the picture involuntarily. 'The big dog is one of my grandmother Marissa's.'

He moved closer, leaned on the back of the sofa and stared up at it. 'It's remarkable,' he murmured. 'The baby is so animated. Are you sure it's not anyone else?'

'We had a really small family,' she said. 'Just women, really. Marissa and Alice, each having one child. Then me, the only grandchild. How about you?' She sat down next to him.

'My mother was one of eight children,' he said. 'I think there were three sons.'

'Good grief. Do you keep in contact with any of them?'

He glanced down at her. 'My mother and I kept in touch, but we didn't meet up too often. We only met up for Thanksgiving from year to year as a family, she was always away on projects. My grandmother was such a lovely person, very welcoming.' He looked back at the picture. 'Oh my goodness,' he breathed and his face fell. 'She reminds me of a picture that Mabel showed me. Of her mother, when she was about three.'

I think babies all look a bit alike.' Ruby couldn't read his expression.

I suppose so, but... if Clara did have a baby, could this be *her?*'

She swallowed hard. 'No. It's really Clara,' she said, looking up. 'I've known this picture all my life, don't you think someone would have mentioned if it *wasn't* her? Anyway, if Clara had had a baby, why on earth would it have gone to America? She had two loving mothers and a fiancé who could have brought her up.' Ruby stood next to him and stared up at the picture. 'Giles was a war hero, too – I'm sure he would have had a say if he and Clara had had a baby together. If it isn't Clara, it's just an infant, it could even be a boy. Or one of the farmer's children. Alice painted a lot of the local people.'

He squinted at the picture. 'The baby's wearing very lacy clothes for a farmer's child.'

It was true, it was an expensive-looking dress with the impression of embroidery across the chest. Her blonde curls were wild, falling around her ears, not yet long enough to reach her shoulders. 'They adored Clara. That's why they kept the picture in pride of place, she was the centre of their world.'

Does it say who painted it on the back of the picture?' he asked, squinting up at it. 'I can't see a signature.'

It's very like other oils by Alice,' she said, 'and it's never left the house, as far as we know. We can't get it down,' she admitted. 'At some point, someone screwed the frame to the panelling.'

I'd love to know more,' he said, his dark green eyes luminous in the sunlit room.

If we get it down, I'll let you know,' she found herself promising.

10

FEBRUARY 1940

After their aerobatics and the successful flying examinations, Clara and William retired to the Black Queen pub. They were able to order sandwiches in the lounge bar, and to the landlord's horror, they both ordered a half of the local ale.

William laughed when she ordered it.

'What did you expect me to ask for? Champagne?' She folded her arms. 'You and I will fall out if you keep thinking of me as *posh*.'

'But you are, aren't you?' His voice was teasing. 'How many silver spoons were you born with?'

She half smiled. 'None, actually. I don't even know for sure who my father is. I'm illegitimate. That was a big problem for my mother's family. They wanted to cover it up, get me adopted. She was only eighteen when she became pregnant by her fiancé. He died in 1918, she never told me his name. So, no debutantes' ball for me, or for her, either.'

His smile had faded. 'I'm sorry, I didn't think...' he stammered, and she laughed back at him.

'I'm perfectly happy, and my mothers are amazing. Extraordinary. One's an artist, you know, the other's a famous photographer.' She thanked the waiter bringing their glasses. 'And you're mostly right,' she conceded. 'Mother is rather well-off. Her father is an earl, she's really *Lady* Marissa, and Ma is the Honourable Alice St John.'

'Two mothers?' His brow was wrinkled.

'That's what I've always called them,' she said. 'It's a romantic story, really. They set themselves up with me in this beautiful house on Dartmoor, they changed the name to Montpelier House and formed their own artistic salon.' She smiled at his surprise. 'It feels like a haunted house, it never feels empty. The previous owner married an American lady and their daughters sold it to us, so there have only been two families there.'

'How did they feel about you joining up?'

She thought about it as she sipped. The dark beer was rather bitter, she had to concede. 'They let me do whatever I want to do, what I feel I need to do. I learned to drive and went travelling around Europe. I learned to fly. They weren't keen about my working for the ATA but they don't complain.'

The sandwiches were ham, with generous portions of meat. 'The landlord has his own pigs,' the waiter told them, putting a pot of hot English mustard on the table. 'Let me know if you need anything.'

'Thank you,' she said, adding mustard and smiling up at him. She turned back to William. 'What about your parents?' she said, and took a large bite.

'Much more conventional. I'm the eldest, my mother would have preferred me to stay home but my dad understands. He fought in the first war, the Third Battle of the Aisne, with the American Expeditionary Force. He was injured, but came home and got back to health. They run a dairy farm and grow wheat back home in northern Wisconsin.' He looked down at the plate. 'How's the mustard?'

'Hot,' she mumbled.

'Maybe I'll skip it,' he said, and smiled. 'I just want to get more experience of flying, keep my hand in. They'll let me fly fighters when America enters the war.'

'If America does,' she said.

'We did last time. I think we need to. The Germans aren't going to negotiate a peace.'

Clara ate her food and drank her beer. She signalled to the waiter and called for two coffees.

'Is that all right? I have a long drive ahead,' she explained. 'Where are you going next?'

'I'm off for training in Gloucestershire.' He took the coffee, looked around. 'Is there cream?'

'There's a dribble of milk,' she said, pushing a tiny jug over. 'And sugar. I think I'll be joining White Waltham at first.'

'They do advanced training there,' he said. 'How many hours in the air do you have?'

She calculated the few hours she'd had over the last couple of days and told him. 'Just Class 1. I'm hoping to train for Class 2 to fly the more powerful fighter planes.'

'Still light,' he said. He had three times as many hours but in only two types of plane. 'I'd like to write to you,' he said. 'Just to compare notes,' he added, hastily. 'I'm seeing someone back home.'

Something inside her tensed. 'What does she think about your joining the ATA?'

'Proud, I think,' he said, adding in a rush. 'She won't agree to a formal engagement until the war is over. Once America joins in, it shouldn't be long.'

Thinking about the sleek and deadly machine in the hangar, she hoped not.

Three weeks later, Clara was well into her training at White Waltham, and more pilots were starting to arrive. Most were men, but the women stood out, and tended to work together. Clara was one of the least experienced pilots, and was required to do more flying hours and in a wide variety of higher-powered single-engine planes before she could progress to twin-engine planes. There was a lot of classroom work, too, about everything from geography to the use of hydraulic landing gear and advanced equipment. Slowly she began to understand the scope of the work.

Using only a handbook for each plane, the pilots would be required to take off in most weather conditions, including cloud cover that the RAF would avoid. The pilots would have no radio contact with the ground, no help from radar. Every lesson took her further and further, to learn every geographical feature in the south-east of England and the Channel. She would have to fly on instruments and maps, on whatever weather came up.

While she was in training, White Waltham had their first fatality. Arnold Cavanaugh, a fine pilot but with a severe limp, overshot the runway with a damaged plane when his brakes failed at Poole. It turned out that a German bullet was wedged in one of the brakes. The cold, hard facts were recited to them at roll call one morning, then no more was said. Several of Clara's friends knew him well and went to the funeral. Clara had to stay to fly missions but contributed to the flowers.

A more pleasant surprise was a letter from William.

I've flown a Hurricane! Just a few times around the airbase, but what a plane! I cannot wait to finish my Class 2 training and start flying missions. I will be based at Aston Down next month, they are just setting up operations there. I don't know how far that is from White Waltham, quite a way but maybe only a couple of trains. We could meet up in London and compare notes, if you like.

He carried on extolling the virtues of the Hurricane, but she was reluctant to reply. She had been very pleased to hear from him, and felt quite giddy. But she reminded herself he was sort of *engaged*, and resolved not to write back until she could go to sleep without thinking about him.

She sent him a quick, casual note a few days later, hoping he would get the message. The answer came by return.

I'm so pleased to hear from you. I wondered if I'd offended you by writing. I didn't want to presume on our very brief acquaintance, but it's quite OK for girls in the US to have male friends. I hope you don't think I was being pushy or forward. I don't have many friends yet in England, and I would like to count you as one.

She *had* to write back after that, because she had just flown her very first Spitfire. She babbled in a scrawled letter back to him.

It's like wearing a plane, it's so responsive. I don't know how those hulking great pilots are going to fly them, they are so snug and perfectly made for the female form. Four of us took it up over the day, we are all in love. I've passed Class 2 so I shall get my first orders on Tuesday. I'm still not qualified to fly twin-engines yet but we have several smaller planes to deliver to have guns fitted. I'm staying here at White Waltham for the moment, there are several girls here, and we've got a couple of Poles joining us soon. We'll be operational! Maybe we'll end up delivering planes to the same airfield one day. Thank you for writing to me, I think of you as a friend, too.

After six weeks of flying almost every day, passing examinations in navigation and basic engineering, she was finally given four days' leave. For a moment, she considered trying to meet up with William but knew that would confuse her even more. He wasn't like anyone she'd ever met before. Sometimes he wrote about his grandfather's farm in Wisconsin, the little town he grew up in, the hikes and camping trips he had enjoyed as a boy. England seemed crowded and somehow exotic to him.

She found herself thinking about him; he crept into her dreams, and she read and reread his letters. He was curious about Devon because his father's grandfather had been born there. In one of his letters he revealed that his ancestor had been born a few miles from where Clara lived, and she then wrote saying she would get a picture of the village where his family had emigrated from.

Writing about home decided her. To get away from work, and to avoid endlessly checking the schedules in case their paths overlapped, she packed up and caught the train home. She couldn't wait to breathe the fresh air of Dartmoor and lose herself in the vast landscape.

11

PRESENT DAY, MAY

As Jake was visiting for the day, Ruby had arranged a little lunch. He was struggling to use their limited Wi-Fi to contact his client for more information. He had opened the scanned certificate for them both to pore over but it didn't tell them any more. A baby had been adopted, Wilhelmina Carlson, and a name was informally scribbled along the top – Clara Montpelier. There was no evidence of any connection between them but it remained a puzzle for Ruby.

She took out an embroidered cloth from the huge airing cupboard in the main bathroom, and laid it on the table up in the garden. It was an excuse to get some of the mismatched china off the dusty dresser in the hall, judiciously washed and dried, and to set out a few sandwiches and a bowl of fruit. The weather was very mild, and sunshine was reaching over the house to the top terrace.

'Someone's watching us out of that window,' he said, squinting back at the kitchen.

'It's OK, I put food out for them too, in the kitchen. They're our feral artists,' she explained. 'Pony – Penelope – is an abstract painter, and Max is a sculptor. We used to have up to half a dozen staying at a time, from the time Marissa and Alice took over the house. Lots of them were quite famous.'

He sat in one of the cast-iron chairs, now rusty. 'Did Max do that huge sculpture out the front?'

'Leda and the swan, yes.'

'That must be worth a bit, too,' he said, nodding as she held up a Crown Derby teapot with a Royal Doulton lid. 'Although I doubt if you d be able to get a crane up here to move it.'

He seemed very focused on the financial value of things, which annoyed her, though she didn't know why. 'Well, it would be valuable, if *he* chooses to sell it, it's not mine. His last piece went for about forty thousand pounds. Easily enough to pay for it to be moved.' That was eight years ago, and he hadn't sold anything since. He was just giving her a hundred pounds a week now, towards all the bills. He was costing her money, really. 'But it's his sculpture.'

'And you have the house. That must be worth a packet.'

She wasn't sure whether Americans were just more comfortable talking about money, or if he had another agenda.

'There's no guarantee I can keep the house,' she reminded him. 'By the time we've taken off a fortune for renovations, and paid agent's fees and death duties, I'll be lucky if I can pay off my mortgage on my flat in town.'

He nodded, sipped his tea, made a face. 'Do you have any sugar?'

'Oh... would you prefer coffee?'

He made another face but smiled. 'English coffee isn't exactly – to my taste. I've acclimatised to tea, my office runs on it. One sugar is fine.'

She stood. 'What does your job entail? What is an heir hunter, exactly?'

'I help draw up family trees and find missing connections,' he said. 'I work with a firm of lawyers, but my degrees are in history.'

'I'll get the sugar.' She walked down and glanced back at
him as she approached the back door. Another chicken had got
out, there must be another hole in the run, so she shooed it away
from the hall.

Pony and Maxwell turned to stare at her when she got to
the kitchen. They hadn't touched their lunch.

'Is he going to cheat you out of your inheritance? If he's
working for this American who thinks she's Clara's granddaughter?' Pony hissed.

'It's not that simple.' Ruby took the sugar bowl off the table
and collected a clean spoon. 'If Clara had a baby, she was
adopted and would inherit from her new family, not Clara's.
Anyway, Marissa's will left it all to Mum, and then it comes
to me.'

'Does that still work if she was adopted in America?' Pony
asked, her eyes roaming back to the window. Ruby looked out at
the garden to see Jake trying to defend her chair from several
chickens by throwing them crumbs. She gathered up a handful
of grain from the biscuit tin on the windowsill.

'I don't know,' she said, feeling her shoulders tense.

As she walked towards the kitchen door, Pony raised her
voice. 'When was this supposed baby adopted?'

'About a year after she was born,' she said. That could fit
with the picture. But she still couldn't imagine there was a baby
no one had ever talked about, and couldn't believe Alice and
Marissa would ever have given her away.

She walked back up the garden, throwing the grain on the
grass to lead the hens away from the table. 'I'll get them in in a
minute,' she said, putting the sugar bowl down for him. He
helped himself to a spoonful, looking up at her as she sat down.

'The grey one grabbed one of your sandwiches,' he said
apologetically. 'It flew up onto your chair.'

'That's OK,' she said. She looked over at him. 'Can I ask you
something?'

'You think I'm helping Mabel get your house,' he answered. 'She's more likely to try to buy it off you.'

'You don't think she's entitled to it?' she asked bluntly. 'If she is Clara's baby's daughter, she's a descendant of Marissa, which I am not.'

'Was the house Marissa's rather than Alice's, then?'

'Well, she's the Montpelier,' she answered. She had lost her appetite. She watched him nibble the corner of a sandwich. 'And when Marissa died, she left everything to my mother. The will was accepted by the courts and nobody contested it.'

He shook his head. 'I think you're right, but I need to dot all the *I*s for my client.'

'I'm still sure Clara didn't have a baby.'

'Despite her name being on an American adoption certificate?' He sipped some tea.

'Scribbled in pencil.' She looked up at him. He seemed earnest, his gaze unwavering. 'I don't know why. I don't think she can have a claim. Anyone could have written that.'

'I don't even know if she's hoping to inherit your house,' he said, but he sounded less certain. 'I think she's just concerned that all that family history will be wiped out if you decide to sell.'

'*My* family history.' She could see his point, though. She ate a triangle of ham sandwich and threw the crust into a pile of leaves to distract the chickens. 'I'll look through any papers that are left. Mum must have left some bits and pieces from the past. I've never found a birth certificate in the records, though, or any photographs. Was that your client's mother's only name, Wilhelmina? Was there a birth surname noted somewhere? How about immigration records?'

'I don't know. I assumed they changed her name after her parents adopted her. I could ask my client to rummage around, see if there's an earlier name. Are there any other records I could check?'

'I've *really* looked at the official records,' she said. 'I was always interested in Clara's story, she was a bit of a heroine to me.'

'I'm not surprised. Do you still have anything of Clara's?'

'A few bits and pieces. More of Alice's and Marissa's, to be honest.'

She fished a tiny moth out of her tea before taking a sip. The dust from its wings had left a film she imagined she could taste.

'What about pictures of any babies you can't identify?' he added. 'Surely, they would have taken some – Marissa was a photographer. I'd love to find pictures for Mabel, even if the baby wasn't Clara's. Could her mother have been a friend of hers?'

'Maybe,' Ruby said. 'Perhaps they wanted contact with the birth family after the adoption, and someone knew her name and put it on the paperwork. But what about the baby's father?'

'Do we know anything about Clara's circle of friends, colleagues?'

'There might be something in the local papers or service records. They really knew how to bury a secret back then,' Ruby said. 'Personally, I'd like to find out who Clara's father was, too, look up this war hero father who died in 1918. No one ever said who he was, and Grandma Marissa wasn't the kind of person you asked impertinent questions of.'

'If Clara *did* have a baby, it would probably be more important to find out who could have been her lover. He could be Mabel's grandfather.'

'Well, she was close to Giles Ashton-Wilson, I know that.' She looked back at the kitchen windows. 'Maybe she's just trying to connect to her mother, now she's died. Maybe there's something in her belongings?'

That was a natural impulse she could feel in herself.

'You may be right.' Jake looked down at his tea. 'Sometimes,

I think there might be something personal in my mother's books, or in her pockets.'

She teared up immediately, feeling the tug of grief in her chest. 'I've done that, looking for anything. Shopping lists, bus tickets, a last note to me.' She tried to smile. 'Shall we go in?'

He nodded and gave a little wave to the two old faces pressed against the kitchen window. They disappeared, quite slowly. 'Are they your guard dogs?'

She laughed. 'Absolutely.'

She brought Jake through the hall to meet her bristling defenders. Maxwell sat defiantly in the patched chair in the kitchen, half blocking the way around the table. It forced Jake to sidle past him, then be offered an uncomfortable stool at the end of the table. She introduced them formally but neither offered a smile or a handshake.

'We have cake,' Ruby said, flapping her hands at Max to move his chair back. 'Pony?' The old lady crept around the kitchen, leaning on the table.

'I suppose we might have had,' she said. 'But I expect it's all gone.'

'No, we definitely do,' Ruby said, lifting a colourful tin down from a high shelf. 'I put it here, out of your reach.'

Max spluttered something that might have been a laugh. 'That was sneaky.'

'I just wanted to make sure we all had some.' It was studded with golden sultanas and halved cherries, sprinkled with baked sugar.

'So,' Pony said in a biting tone. 'What do you think of the house? Ruby's house.'

'It's a wonderful piece of history,' he answered meekly, as Ruby cut him a slice of fruit cake.

'This is Pony's recipe,' Ruby explained. 'She calls it Granny's cake. It's an old recipe.'

'We just thought you might be having a look around. In case you wondered who owns it,' Max said, mumbling through a mouthful of crumbs.

Jake took the plate from Ruby. 'I know exactly who owns it. Fiona inherited from Marissa, and she's left it to Ruby. Did Fiona leave any mementoes to anyone else?'

Pony waved away the idea. 'She didn't write a will. It should all go to Ruby, we all knew it was what she wanted.'

Ruby put her slice neatly on a cracked plate. 'Jake is employed by a client who is working on her family tree. He'd still like to have a look around.' Her mouth had gone dry. 'She might like a few pictures, if she is a relative of the family.'

'I thought you said she wasn't,' Max said, belligerently. 'We are fairly sure Clara never had a baby.'

'She's not intending to make any claim on the house,' Jake said in his rich baritone, sounding more American. 'Which would be useless anyway, if Marissa Montpelier left it to Ruby's mother. But she would like to know more, like why Clara's name was written on the birth certificate of a baby adopted in the US. Her whole family would be interested.'

'Scribbled,' Pony grunted. 'It could mean anything.'

'Ruby's been through enough,' Maxwell said, glaring at Jake over smeared glasses. 'With her mother's death.'

'Jake understands that – his mother died last year,' Ruby said, holding out her hands for his spectacles. 'Let me clean those for you.'

Pony leaned forward. 'We all heard stories about Clara. What was this supposed daughter like?'

'Wilhelmina – Billie – was tall and blonde. She ran a charity in her retirement and was a professional singer.' He pulled out his phone and pulled up a picture. 'Opera.'

Maxwell squinted at it after Ruby handed his glasses back.

'She looks a bit like the pictures in the darkroom,' he said slowly. 'I mean, there's a slight resemblance to pictures of Clara.'

'The darkroom?' Jake looked across to the kitchen door, where Ruby pointed.

'It's just a study at the back of the house, behind the parlour. Marissa painted out the window and used it as a studio for her photography.'

'Can we see in there?'

Ruby shrugged. 'OK. But it stinks of chemicals.' She finished her cake and led the way.

The room was in bad shape. Water had been getting in around the rotted window frame, and dark paint was peeling off the glass. A table sat in the middle of the room, stained black in places, bleached in others. Old rope criss-crossed the ceiling with clothes pegs holding hundreds of prints of different sizes, all curled up. A huge enlarger sat in the middle of the table, rusted and dusty. Chemicals stood in large bottles around the floor, among stacks of boxes.

Jake pulled down the corners of a few of the hanging prints and squinted at them. 'They're pretty faded in places,' he said.

Pony had followed them in. 'Marissa didn't allow many people in when she was alive,' she warned. 'I don't think the ceiling is very safe, be careful.'

Ruby lifted a fragile box onto the table. Inside was a jumble of photographs, some folded in half, some stuck together with mouse droppings. 'We could look through these, at some point. They're original Marissa Montpeliers,' she said. 'I suppose these are her reference prints.' She lifted one up, of a tall woman in an evening dress next to an enormous vase of lilies. 'Look, this is from 1951.'

She looked around at the boxes, some tied with string, others taped up. Damp had crept up them, making a black tideline. One of them was marked in pencil. She bent over it. 'This is from 1925, this one 1922.' She looked up at him, her face hot from bending over. 'Maybe there are pictures of Clara here as a baby, she was born in 1918!'

He grinned back at her, looking as excited as she felt. 'There must be some family shots. Can we look through them?'

She glanced back. There were over twenty boxes. 'We could make a start.'

'It looks like she marked some of these with names and dates,' he said. 'Maybe we'll find a picture of Clara, and who knows, maybe a mysterious baby.'

12

APRIL 1940

Pilot Third Officer Clara Montpelier returned from training and reported for her first day of duty at White Waltham. The other pilots were sat around doing puzzles, playing cards, and a couple were doing exercises at the back of the office. Bobby Darwin, now Captain Darwin, was just as casual and welcoming. She gave Clara her first chit from Ferry Pool 1, a multiplane mission to Nottingham.

'You'll be flying a pilot as a passenger to Northolt – he's just been released from hospital. Then you need to fly on to Cheltenham with parts. There, you should be able to pick up a Hurricane to deliver to the training school in RAF 12, north of Nottingham – make sure you have enough fuel. Betty will fly your Anson back from Cheltenham, she's dropping off a Spitfire. You can catch a train back south; we don't need you for two days, and you have your service pass for all rail travel.' She handed over the shiny new card. 'You have to pay for pleasure trips, though.'

The journeys were listed in scruffy handwriting on a single sheet of paper. A round trip of more than two hundred and fifty miles, and a lot of it in the Hurricane she had heard about but not yet flown. 'Thank you,' she said, with real gratitude but some nerves. 'Quite a first trip for my Class 3.'

'We'd have liked to ease you in with a local delivery,' Bobby said. 'But honestly, the speed at which you acquired your test suggests you're ready for anything. You can start your Class 4 training for the more powerful planes when we get a chance – that will make you really useful. The Germans are starting a big offensive, so we're going to have a lot of damaged planes to retrieve and get mended.'

Clara nodded seriously. The casualty figures were starting to build up over the Channel as the troops were pushed back to the coast.

'Oh,' Bobby said, turning back to her from the newly refurbished office desk. 'Could you drop the mail over at the barracks when you go to pack? We're getting quite a bit now, and most pilots are out already.'

Clara took the bag, which was heavy with packages and letters, and slung it over her shoulder. 'Any advice? For the mission?'

Bobby grimaced. 'Treat it like three training flights. And make sure you fill in your logbook. We'll both be hauled over the coals if you don't.' She paused and leaned forward. 'Honestly, you'll understand a lot more when you've done it. We can't really prepare you in advance.'

'And what happens if I run into some Germans?'

'Altitude is your friend. If you have good visibility, stay close to the ground. They will be looking for the RAF boys.'

'But I can't call it in?'

Bobby shook her head. 'Absolutely no radio, even for weather reports. You'll soon get the hang of it.'

'If I don't crash on a foggy runway somewhere, I'll treat myself to a couple of drinks before I head back.'

Bobby laughed. 'That's the spirit.'

. . .

In the mailbag were three pieces of mail for Clara. One was a heavy fruit cake from Mrs Goddings and her mothers, which she left out for people to share when they got back to barracks. Holding a generous slice in one hand, she read the two letters addressed to her. One was a telephoned note from Giles – a huge surprise, as while they had enjoyed a few dances at Rushworth Abbey, they mostly talked about planes, and she had thought no more about it.

If you're in my neck of the woods, which I happen to know you will be because I have contacts in the ATA, do you want to try the new club that's just opened in Nottingham? They have illegal amounts of gin and a fantastic band. I recall you had quite nimble feet for a tall girl... he had written. Contacts in the ATA? She was puzzled before she recalled that one of his cousins had been looking for a way to help the war effort through flying despite having lost some fingers. He might have access to information about the jobs coming up.

She studied the map on the wall, covered with pins marking their missions. She could stop at Nottingham for the night, and then head back south in the morning by train.

She shivered a little in anticipation. Giles seemed dangerous, his attitude was adventurous and opinionated and she was drawn to him. But she wasn't sure she even liked him.

The other letter was from someone much more likeable. William had made a forced but tidy landing at RAF Chelveston on the grass runway there. The plane was undamaged, so he'd been bought a number of rounds at the base bar and now had a hangover. He would be on leave in two weeks' time, perhaps they could meet up?

She took another bite of cake. She liked William. She could share any of her work-related fears with him, as well as the funny incidents that came with the job, like the day she set off on a training flight – with an open cockpit – and found the base cat sitting on her shoulder. She'd managed to land both safely, whereupon Humphrey stalked off looking for mice and she went back to the office to her colleagues' laughter.

Giles was different. He had treated her rather as she imagined he would a friend of his sister, rather dismissive and teasing, but there had been a dark look in his eyes that suggested he was interested in more. She would have to smarten up her flying suit and pack something suitable for a club. She thought about her sparse wardrobe, mostly hung with uniform skirts and jackets, and flying suits which swamped her. He had already seen her one evening dress and he moved in the kind of circles that cared about fashion.

'Well, there's a war on,' she mumbled to herself. Maybe she could smarten the gown up with her crystal necklace, because they weren't allowed to have expensive jewellery on the base in case of theft. Her hair would be flattened by her flying helmet, she would probably be covered in dust and oil...

She walked over to the base phone with a handful of change. 'Operator, please.' As she waited, one of the other girls walked in, covered with oil. 'Help yourself to cake,' she hissed to her, pointing at the tin. 'Yes, operator? Can you suggest a hotel in Nottingham that has rooms with baths? For tomorrow night, yes.'

By the time she had booked a suite in a hotel which knew all about the club – new, good music, plenty of gin – she was more confident about the mission. Three flights, three planes, and Giles's company at the end of it. He had given a number at his base, and she left a message that she would meet him at the club by ten tomorrow night, and finished her slice of cake.

She sat down with her writing supplies to pen something to William.

Dear William,

Well done on your landing, I hear it's a tricky, short runway. One of the girls landed there and ended up in a sheep field but undamaged, just lost a tyre. Hope you're well and not too homesick for Wisconsin. It would be nice to catch up in Oxford or London too when our schedules align.

Kind regards,

Clara.

13

PRESENT DAY, MAY

After meeting Pony and Max, Jake had booked a night in a local bed and breakfast, so he could come back on Sunday morning to help sort through the pictures and any papers. He turned up in time to help Ruby arrange all the boxes of photographs on the dining table. She was disheartened to find that most didn't have a surviving date on them.

The large room wasn't used much – it had been dirty and damp when they had people back from the funeral, when she had thrown a couple of old cloths over the mess. She had to squeak back folding shutters to let the low sunlight in, followed by ten minutes with cloth and sprays to get years of dust off the mahogany table. When she put the lights on, half the bulbs in the chandelier were blown.

'This is a gorgeous room,' he said, looking up at a ceiling rose in better shape than the one in the drawing room. 'And huge.'

'I used to love Christmas in here,' she said. 'There are leaves for this, you can easily get twenty people round it, all our friends and neighbours, visitors.' She pointed at the far end of the table. 'And Grandma used to order a huge tree for the window. The tree lights reflected in each side of the bay – it made it look as if there were thousands of them.' The thought that she might never see them again thumped her in the heart. She switched on a couple of tall lamps in the corners while he walked to the window.

He stared out at the view. 'Wow.' When she stepped beside him, she could see what he was enraptured by.

The tips of the long grasses and dark gorse bushes were touched with light from the sun. The tor opposite was glowing, and there was a golden shadow over the ground. Framing the view were twisted trees, twenty feet high.

'The front garden is a bit wild now, but the house is about six feet higher so we look over the moor. It's exactly south-facing – the builders knew what they were doing.' A few shrubs were trying to grow but were already bending from the relentless winds from the west.

'You sound like an estate agent,' he said, looking around the room. 'What's that door?'

'That's Maxwell's room.' A low half-glazed door was set in the wall but a curtain covered the glass. 'It's the old library.'

'There are a lot of books in every room so far.'

'Even in the bedrooms. There are thousands of them. And pictures everywhere,' she said, running her fingers over a large photograph in a frame. She brushed the glass with a cloth. 'This was Marissa.' She was posed, very stylised, her long nose turned in profile, her hair ordered in perfect waves. Ropes of pearls decorated a tailored suit, one hand thrust into a pocket. 'This must have been from before Alice died. She stopped dressing up when she lost her.'

'Were they very close?'

'Completely. Marissa had a breakdown after Clara died, but she fell apart again after she lost Alice. She never really recovered. I remember her wandering around like a ghost, her hair in a bun, wearing a long black dress.'

'Was she strict?'

Ruby tried to remember. 'She was stern, but she could be very kind. She taught me to read, and showed me how to take a good photograph. But she hated noise of any kind, so I had to be quiet.' Her strongest memory of her was after she died, and was laid out on her bed, while they waited for the undertaker to come. She had passed away alone, sometime during the night. The thing Ruby recalled the most was how white she was, her snowy hair brushed back from her forehead. Her eyes weren't quite shut, and it looked like she was peeking out at Ruby to see if she was crying. But she didn't, because Grandma Marissa hated anyone making a fuss.

'What other rooms are there?'

'There are six main bedrooms and two in the attic, two big bathrooms upstairs and a small one in the loft. Behind the scullery and off the library there's a wing that houses the studios, and a garden cloakroom. Alice had the biggest studio, it has double doors leading on to the garden, where the fruit garden was. There are two smaller spaces, and on the other side the drive used to lead up to a big garage, full of Maxwell's stuff. It used to be a stable for four horses. Max used to do all his welding in there but brambles have mostly taken over the drive.'

'So, what other artists came here?'

She stepped back into the hall. 'Let me show you the studios, off the kitchen. Many modern artists and writers used to come for a month or two, before my time. One of them was my mother's father, but we don't know who he was. He stayed with Alice after Marissa went into a hospital. She was ill for three years, and Alice must have been terribly lonely. She filled the house with friends. She got pregnant at some point. I know the baby was a huge surprise to both of them, but it inspired Marissa to help look after baby Fiona.'

'Don't you want to find out who *he* was? It was your grandfather.'

Ruby smiled. 'Alice didn't want to talk about it; she would only say that the baby was born out of kindness and comfort and love. No one in this house talks about fathers. After both my grandmothers died, my mother opened the house up again to artists and students to come and rent a room and some studio space, to help pay the bills.'

'No one knew who the fathers were? No one even guessed?'

'Well, I expect Alice and Marissa knew, but they didn't tell anyone. Lots of the visiting artists were married, any one of them could have been my grandfather, but that would have caused such a scandal. When Marissa came home from the hospital, she took Fiona on, she adored the baby. They both did, she was spoiled rotten.' Her voice wobbled. 'Honestly, they were so close, it was hard to remember we all weren't just born out of their love.'

'When did Alice die?'

She shrugged off the cold feeling around her neck. 'I was three. It was sudden, she was about eighty years old, younger than Marissa. She died when I was ten.' She stepped into the yard from the kitchen and turned right to open the first of the studio doors. 'This was originally a washhouse. There's a chimney in the corner where they used to boil up laundry in a big copper. It's around somewhere in the garden.'

'And your own father?'

'Mum never wanted to discuss it. All I know is that he named me, and went off travelling. She always expected him to walk back in, but he never did. His name isn't on my birth certificate either.'

'Was it difficult, growing up without a dad?' He sounded so sympathetic she looked up.

'We were happy. It's hard to know what you're missing when you've never had it. Fiona grew up here, she loved the artistic commune, the house she created after Marissa died. She had all her friends living with her, when she wasn't off travelling. She took me with her a lot of the time.'

His eyes met hers. 'She never told you who your father was? She didn't leave a note or anything?'

She tried to look like she didn't care. 'Nope. But it's OK. Whoever it was, she said, was nice. Gentle, kind.'

'I think I'd rather know,' he said, and she looked away. It was an old wound.

'I thought I might find something in her papers but Max said she burned a lot of them when she received the diagnosis.'

'Why wouldn't she want you to know?'

Ruby shrugged. 'Maybe he died, maybe she didn't know for sure who it was. You've got to understand, it was a really hippy place, free love, art is king, all of that.'

She pushed open the door at the end of the low room to a larger one with a skylight, the glass cracked and mended with tape and partly insulated with bubble wrap. 'This is where Adam used to paint. He was a graffiti artist. He lived with us for a few years, I had such a crush on him when I was twelve. Then he moved his girlfriend in, she did mosaics. After that I lost track of who was in and who was out.' The last door led to the biggest studio, lit by a range of north-facing windows and a glass roof. It was filled with canvases piled against one wall, many of them painted over to reuse. 'This was Alice's painting space. I ought to look through these. None of them are finished.'

'You sound like you struggled growing up here, sometimes?'

'Sometimes.' She winced. 'Is it that obvious? I loved the people, Marissa, Fiona, Pony, Max, but I didn't like living like that. I preferred structure, I wanted to get good grades to go to university, and get a job. It didn't help that I hadn't got an artistic bone in my body,' she tried to joke. 'I loved history, I loved the timelines and the changing societies. Much of my work is saving and cataloguing resources like letters, journals and pictures, for future generations.'

'What you do is important. You look after the past, help people connect with it, conserve heritage.'

She turned away to brush a tear from her cheek. 'The last time I stayed up here, a year ago, Mum tried to get me to move back home. She must have already known she wasn't going to beat the illness. But I'd just bought my flat.' *And Oliver had really, really gone for good.*

'Then she got sick? That must have been around the time that she and I started emailing each other.'

'We spoke on the phone intermittently, and she didn't mention the cancer for months. Not once,' she said, her hands shaking. 'Until she called to say it was terminal.'

'That must have been terrible.'

'So, she moved in with me, and the district nurses came out and helped. Until the very end, when she went into the hospice.' The tears gathered on her eyelids and she let them roll down her cheeks. The empty hospital bed in her living room had been an agonising reminder until it was taken away. In the last few weeks of her life, they had spoken about so many things, but Fiona wouldn't answer the questions Ruby wanted answered, like who her father was. She had fantasised that he would just turn up at the funeral. Instead, Jake appeared, who may or may not be building a stranger's claim to the house.

Shafts of light came in through the skylight, catching the dust and picking up spatters of oil paint on the concrete floor, splashes on the walls around voids where Alice had hung her canvases.

'You love this house,' he said, starkly.

Her heart hurt at the thought of losing it. 'I do. I did, but it's so much in the past.' She wiped her eyes with her sleeve. 'Soon Max and Peny will be gone and it will just weather away to a ruin. Even if I could save it, how would I live here? There are eight bedrooms, for goodness' sake, I can't even afford to heat it. Mum died and it's painful, just going through everything of hers, clearing up.' She smiled at him through watery eyes. 'This is cathartic, really. I'll sort through all the junk and papers and keep a few mementoes.'

'Like the painting of the baby.'

'I'd love to keep it.' She shook her head. 'But I'm not sure where I would put it in my flat. It's huge, but it's always been part of my life.' The back wall of her apartment jumped into her mind, opposite the windows overlooking the restless sea.

'It's such a beautiful picture. Do you think you'll end up selling it? I'm just thinking of my client, Mabel. If she believes it might be her grandmother Clara, or even her own mother, she might make you an offer.'

She closed her eyes for a moment, took a deep breath. When she opened them he had clamped his hands together as if he was unconsciously begging. She managed a smile.

'We could talk about it. Let's find out who the baby in the picture *is* first.'

14

APRIL 1940

The following day, Clara was excited for her first flight as a third officer, with a smart new uniform fitted with a shiny stripe and the wings sewn on over the breast pocket of the tailored suit from Austin Reed. The actual flying was easy. But locating each airfield and relying on hand signals to arrange the landing was trickier. Sitting for the first time in the Hurricane was a delight, although she had limited hours in an aircraft with a retractable undercarriage. The plane was bullish and powerful, obedient to every slight movement, and apart from clunking loudly when she brought up the wheels, uneventful to fly. She had been working on her landings, and touched down with barely a bounce in the improved undercarriage, taxiing to the grass in front of a hangar where more planes were waiting.

A couple of RAF boys came out to greet her. They seemed surprised to see a woman step out as she removed her cap to reveal a head of chestnut curls.

'Good flight?' one asked.

'Good. Weather's coming in, though,' she replied.

By the time she had completed her paperwork, dusk was beginning to fall, so she called for a taxi to take her into the city.

She waited outside as darkness drew in, and other than a couple of guards silhouetted by the gate, it was quiet and she felt very isolated in the blackout. *In an hour, I'll be in a bath, getting ready for some dancing.*

'Waiting for someone?'

She jumped at the sound of a man's voice. 'Just a taxi,' she said.

'I could give you a lift, if you like.' There was an unpleasant note in his voice, as if he was drunk.

'I'm meeting a friend,' she said, using her preprepared excuse. 'It won't be long now, but thank you.'

He moved along the wire fence and she could see how he blocked out the limited light. 'I think you and I could find a better way to spend the evening,' he drawled, his voice rough.

'Maybe if I wasn't already seeing someone,' she lied, moving away from the stench of stale smoke and beer on his breath. Not just beer, something stronger, too. 'But not today.'

'I might not be here next week,' he said, a match flaring to show his face for a moment, the yellow light reflecting in his eyes. They looked hungry, flickers of something dark. 'I'm a pilot.'

'I'm a pilot, too. It's a dangerous job,' she snapped. 'We lost one of our flyers last week. A Hurricane being moved for repair came down in a forest. I'm not interested.'

For a moment she stared him down through the darkness, not sure how much he could see but filled with anger. Who did he think he was? Would he treat a man in service to his country this way?

'Your loss,' he said, turning away.

She could hear something else in his words, a sadness, defeat. 'Take care up there,' she suddenly blurted out.

He didn't answer and she could already see the dim lights of the blacked-out taxi trundling onto the road that ran along the airfield.

. . .

The encounter left her filled with sadness, even as she checked in, filled the bath and sank into the complimentary bath salts that smelled like lavender. The room was costing her a week's wages, and a tip would have to come out of her allowance, but it was worth it. The maid took her clothes away to launder, and she dried herself in luxurious towels wondering if she could shake off the melancholy and go dancing. But Giles was expecting her, that tipped the balance.

By the time she had dried her hair, slipped into a precious pair of silk stockings, one of her last pairs from before the war, and into her satin evening gown, she felt better. And looked better, too, although the dress was hanging off her a little. Constant work and rationing had taken any softness from her body.

'I look like a boy,' she told herself, turning this way and that in the first full-length mirror she had looked in for weeks.

She repeated the observation to Giles after she'd been escorted by a waiter to a small table by the dance floor.

'You look like a fashion model,' he said, looking her up and down approvingly. 'I'm making all the other chaps jealous. I ordered champagne, is that acceptable? The gin's actually a bit rough.'

His dark curls were severely cropped, his brown eyes gleaming with hazel highlights under the chandelier. High cheekbones and square chin jutted from his face, with its wide moustache. Like her, he looked like he'd been tested back to a thinner frame, too, his broad shoulders appeared to be wearing someone heavier's jacket.

'Lovely,' she answered, staring at him. 'It's so good to see you. I hardly see anyone outside of the ATA. I haven't even been home very much.'

'The "attagirls",' he said, smiling. 'You're all over the news-

papers at the moment. The glamorous life of a transport pilot.'
They sat down in spindly, gilded chairs and watched people in
chiffon, silk and satin slide past as if there wasn't a war going on.
Hems were higher this year, she noticed, wondering why she
had ever cared about fashion. They looked elegant.

She took a sip from the cold, bubbly wine. 'Lovely,' she
breathed, taking some more.

He smiled back over the rim of his glass, staring at her.
'Careful. Have you eaten?'

'Not for a few hours,' she said, noticing a clock sparkling
from one of the decorated walls. 'But I don't care. Can we
dance?' She tipped back the rest of the glass, enjoying the
warmth that was spreading through her.

They had danced together at Rushworth Abbey so she
knew he was a good partner. But now he seemed to fit perfectly
against her as he guided her effortlessly around the room. The
music was muted but pretty, and the opposite of the war.

'How long has it been since you went home?' she asked, his
hand warm in the small of her back.

'A couple of months. You know. The Phoney War is over,
but it seems like the war's just being fought in the air. Mostly
they try and engage us over the south coast.' He guided her
away from a couple that were arguing. Both seemed a little
inebriated, but her own head was spinning too.

'We've lost a couple of pilots already,' she said, in a low
voice.

'Us too,' he said, and he pulled her closer. 'It's a bloody business. We've been waiting for a group of Polish pilots to join us.
They can't come fast enough for me.' She let him sweep her
back towards their table. 'Do you mind if we sit down? I need
some food even if you don't.'

'Please,' she said. 'My feet aren't used to these heels.' After
her bath she had slathered them in hand cream to try and
conceal the blisters and corns her flying boots had given her.

He smiled as he sat down. 'They look all right to me.'

'So, are you flying Spitfires yet?'

He topped up their glasses and lit a cigarette, after offering her one. She waved it away. 'We have been for the last few months. They are improving them. How about you?'

'I've tried a couple. I might be moving to Hamble soon, so I'll be delivering them straight from the factory. How do you find them to fly?'

He blew smoke away from her. 'They are nose-heavy and they can buck like a racehorse. And they are so small it takes a few minutes to squeeze in. But they are powerful, I prefer them, even if I get cramped.'

'I've always thought they were meant for a female pilot.' She sipped some more of the wine. 'Look, we need to eat something or we'll get squiffy.'

He turned to wave to a waiter. 'Is the kitchen still open?'

'For biscuits and snacks, sir,' he replied.

'We'll have a plate of each,' Giles said, smiling back at Clara. 'I want you squiffy, not drunk.'

She knew what he meant, she knew what he wanted. In that moment, maybe she wanted it too, privacy and contact that didn't mean anything. Just going with their human nature.

'You're assuming a lot,' she said, reaching over for his cigarette, letting the smoke curl around her face. 'You're assuming I'm *that* sort of girl.'

'I know you weren't *that* sort of girl, not before. But things are different now. We could both be dead in a week.'

She put the cigarette back in its ashtray. The acrid taste made her wish she hadn't taken it, and she washed it down with a sip of wine. 'I'm sorry,' she said, nodding at the waiter who put down two plates. 'I think dancing is as close as I can get right now.'

He nodded, taking a nameless piece of fish balanced on a cracker and consuming it in one bite. 'Is there a chap?'

'Goodness, no!' she said, but as she did, William's face popped into her head. 'Not really. Most of the men I meet are engaged or married,' she explained. 'Or on airfields I might never visit again. How about you?'

He leaned back, looking tired. 'Oh, you know. Mother's always trying to set me up with suitable girls. And there are a few hangers-on at the airbase. But then I saw you in Rushworth...'

She laughed. 'Where you teased me, called me names and danced with everyone but me until you'd had a few drinks.'

'You counted?' His lip curled up and his eyes twinkled. 'You were watching me.'

'Well, you were the tallest man there. You have no idea how hard it is being the tallest girl in the room.' She took a short-bread. It tasted more of flour than butter or sugar, but she realised how hungry she was. 'All the other men were younger than me, too.'

'Before the war they'd have started calling you an old maid,' he said, watching her closely. 'What were you doing when you should have been going to debutante balls and getting married, like my sisters?'

'Didn't your mother tell you?' she asked, risking a slice of the fish delicacy. 'I wasn't presented at court at all. I learned to drive, bought a car and went around Europe.'

'That must have been interesting. Did you fall in love?'

She smiled, turning away the probing enquiry. 'Oh, in every country,' she said, sighing. 'But I did art classes – I'm hopeless, by the way – and scaled mountains. That took up most of my time.'

'I somehow missed you in those years.'

She half smiled. 'Well, I think your mother would think I wasn't very suitable. I don't have a father, you know. And my mothers – well, I have two mothers.'

'Quite a Bohemian set,' he said. 'I don't see why that should reflect on you.'

'Well, it does. Anyway, I preferred my adventures.' Clara sat back and looked around the room. Its white walls looked as if some previous staining was creeping back in, and the paint on the gilded chairs looked a little flaky. 'I wonder what this fish was?' she said, wiping her fingers on a napkin.

'My guess is smoked eel or something else inedible,' he said, picking one up and staring at it. 'Not exactly London fare.'

'Well,' she added, 'it is the middle of a war.'

'So, I can't persuade you to come back to my hotel and open a second bottle?' he said, inspecting the label.

'Probably not.' She reached over and took his hand. 'You could kiss me, though,' she dared.

He looked taken aback, and in that moment she saw he was a little less confident than she had first thought. He leaned forward, his face serious. His lips were warm, and she clung to him for a moment because the club was cold. His moustache tickled a bit and when she pulled back, he sighed. 'I wish you would change your mind. I have a nice room.'

'So do I. And we both need our sleep,' she said, letting go of his hand. The kiss was sweet, and for a moment she'd forgotten where they were. But as she pulled away, the face, eyes still closed, wasn't William's.

15

PRESENT DAY, MAY

Ruby had brought as many of the boxes of photographs home as she could fit in her car. The old cases were mildewed and fragile. She had wrapped them in plastic and they were now producing an odour of their own, like bad mushrooms, in the corner of her living room. She had offered Jake a couple of boxes to look through, but he had demurred, as he said he didn't know any of the people and places, and would just be looking for pictures of Clara. Instead, she gave him a few names and dates to research himself, on the ace pilot who Clara had dated during the war. If Clara *had* had a baby, she guessed it was most likely to have been his.

Having created so many family trees for other people, she couldn't work out why she hadn't dived into more detail about her own family. To some extent, Clara was the heroine of her childhood, the beautiful pilot who travelled with a toolkit, overalls and a ballgown in her duffel bag. Her death had been shocking. Ruby had spent a whole summer trying to get her mother to explain exactly what happened. Having been born two years after Clara's death, and with Marissa so fragile, Fiona hadn't been told much. 'No one talked about death back then,' she had said, then confirmed it by not talking about her own illness until her treatment failed. Ruby still felt bruised. If only she had known her mother was battling cancer, she would have spent more time with her, but things were unravelling with Oliver and she hadn't seen the signs…

She looked out of the window over to the Hoe, the stretch of green in front of the sea. It was dark, and she could see her own reflection duplicated by the double glazing. She was unsettled by going home, meeting up with Jake, looking around her mother's belongings. On impulse she called up her closest friend in town.

She left a message. 'Inaya, are you around this evening? I'm just back from Dartmoor. Oh, and I met someone.' Even as she put the phone down, she was shocked at herself. Met someone? No, she hadn't, she was just talking to someone who might be a sort of heir hunter, who probably wasn't even single and might be after her inheritance.

Inaya didn't waste any time getting back to her. 'OK, girl, have you eaten?'

Ruby smiled at her reflection in the mirror. 'I haven't. Can we go somewhere within walking distance? I think I need wine.'

Inaya texted her the name of a great Italian restaurant on the quay, and they agreed to meet in fifteen minutes. On impulse, Ruby changed her shirt to a silk one Fiona had gifted her and she had hardly worn. It was like taking her mother along for dinner. She paired it with a jacket, and stepped down the stairs to the ground floor. She had avoided checking her mailbox in the building's lobby – so much of her mail was forms and letters to do with probate. But one in her cubby was addressed by hand and covered in American stamps. She almost opened it, but instead, tucked it into her handbag to sort out later.

. . .

Inaya met her outside the restaurant with a huge hug. Ruby wasn't tall, but Inaya was tiny, slight, with brown skin and expressive dark eyes. She had dyed the front of her hair pink, which went with her top.

'I'm so glad to see you!' She held Ruby at arm's length. 'Are you OK?' she put her head on one side. '*Really* OK?'

'*Mostly* all right,' Ruby said, smiling.

Inaya tucked her arm into Ruby's and they walked into the brightly lit restaurant which, fortunately, had a couple of tables left. 'We could always have eaten at the bar,' she said, as a tall young man seated them, smiling and chatting in fluent Italian. 'We might meet some handsome young single men...' she murmured in an aside.

'Neither of us has got the energy for all that.' Ruby managed to speak enough Italian to get water for the table, and the menus.

'He probably speaks perfect English,' Inaya said, reading the wine menu. 'I know what I want already.'

Ruby followed her finger to a bold – and expensive – choice. 'Go on, then,' she said, throwing caution to the universe. 'Since I might be an heiress.'

'You said you didn't think the house would be worth much,' Inaya said, looking at her over the food menu. 'What do you mean, might be?'

'There might be a rival heir, in America.' It sounded cold, snapped out like that. 'I mean, someone who thinks she's actually related to Marissa, unlike me. Her investigator came to the funeral, he'd been in contact with Fiona.'

'I've never been to the house,' Inaya said. 'What's it like?'

'Big, falling down. I suppose it must be worth quite a bit as a site – just a fraction of what it would be if it was renovated. And there are a few nice things inside. We found boxes of Marissa's old negatives and photographs. They might be worth something to someone.' She sighed. 'It's my entire history. I've never realised how attached I am to the place. He – the investigator – has made me wonder how many secrets and ghosts the place holds.' She looked at the menu. 'I'm starting with *bruschetta al pomodoro e basilica*, that's bread with tomatoes and basil to you, and some chicken in cream sauce.'

Inaya squinted at the menu. 'I'm having the wild salmon.'

By the time the waiter had returned and they had ordered food, the wine was opened and poured into two enormous glasses.

'So, tell me about this person you met?' Inaya said, leaning forward. 'Is it the investigator?'

'Yes. He's representing the possible heir I mentioned who thinks she's related through my grandmother Marissa.'

'Can't you distract him from helping his client?' Inaya laughed, then her smile faded as she looked at Ruby. 'Did I say something wrong?'

'No!' Ruby sipped the rich, delicious wine. 'I've met him a few times now. He's sort of nice. I felt – I don't know. We had dinner on his birthday. I invited him to look around the house.'

'*Sort of nice?*' Inaya put her own glass down. 'Tell me. Is he good-looking?'

Ruby smiled then. 'I think he is. Jake's a silver fox. He's a bit older than me, and he's tall. I guess he's about forty, he works for a genealogy firm in London. He's doing the family tree for his client and thinks her mother was born to my aunt Clara. I was never told about a baby, not ever, and there's no birth record. Her mother *was* adopted in America but there is no record of her birth parents.'

'So he has no proof?'

'Not really. Just a handwritten note on an adoption certificate.'

Inaya frowned. 'Didn't they record the birth parents properly when there was an adoption?'

'Not in that era, apparently. This man just arrived in the

US with a motherless baby and applied to adopt her. I can't find any record here of a birth to Clara Montpelier at all, let alone an adoption.'

'Could he have been the baby's dad?' Inaya asked.

'I don't know. Maybe.'

Their food arrived and the waiter topped their glasses up.

'What was Clara like?'

'She was a proper heroine. She flew planes – all sorts of bombers and fighter planes – back in the war, delivering them to the RAF. She was super stylish, too, living at the big house, swanning around in cars and planes and riding horses. When she died, Grandma Marissa never really got over her loss. I only knew her as wearing black and struggling with her mental health. Grandma Alice was lovely, apparently, but she was nearly eighty when I was born so I didn't know her for long.'

'I thought my family was strange,' Inaya said. 'I'm the only one of four children who isn't gay, and I'm the only one who isn't married.'

Ruby smiled and tipped her glass to Inaya's. 'To old maids.'

Inaya grinned back. 'To young, sexy spinsters. And silver foxes. Tell me more.'

'Not much to tell. Oh, I have a letter to read,' she said, fishing out the thick envelope. She spread it open to the side of her plate and read down the single sheet. 'It's from Jake's client, Mabel! She wonders if we had ever thought about doing a DNA test to prove, or disprove, a link between *our* Clara and *their* Clara. Apparently she sent her own DNA for testing a few years ago but didn't get any matches.' She thought about it. 'Well, there would be no use me doing it, I'm not related to Marissa or Clara, I'm Alice's granddaughter. Clara's has been dead for eighty years, but there might be things in the house we could use.' Ruby turned the letter over, scanning the brief lines again. The idea was intriguing. 'She probably has items from her mother with hair or skin on too that we could match to Clara, if we could find a hairbrush or something.'

'Ugh. Very forensic. Why would you do it? Are you sure you want to find a load more heirs to contest your inheritance?' Inaya's words were kind but a little incredulous. 'You don't even have probate yet.'

'I'm sure it will be fine,' Ruby said, sipping her wine. But a little doubt still lingered at Mabel and her family's possible interest in her house, which felt more precious as she uncovered every memory. 'But they've got me questioning now.' She wondered if something – maybe Clara – was compelling her to help find the truth.

Later that evening she unpacked the first box of photographs, labelled 1943. If Clara did have a baby, it must have been born before she died. From a stack of society photographs of beautifully posed young women and men probably taken for magazines or family collections, a single picture, just a snap, slid out.

It was lightly touched with white powdery mould. Ruby brushed off the mildew with her sleeve, staring at the slightly fuzzy image. The leggy girl sitting on the grass, her head thrown back as she laughed, was definitely Clara. Behind her, another figure was sitting with his hand on her arm. He was also laughing, a handsome man, the flash of white teeth under a dark moustache. Squadron Leader Giles?

She was so curious now, about this other daughter of the house, this other fascinating life. She could feel the pull towards talking to Jake about it, about meeting up again to compare notes on Clara.

16

MAY 1940

The following month, Clara was asked into Captain Bobby Darwin's office late one evening, having delivered two Tiger Moth trainers and a Hurricane with a coughing engine for urgent repairs during the day. She had flown an Anson back to base.

'Clara, excellent. No problems?' Bobby looked older, tired.

'No trouble. Looking forward to a few days off, to be honest.' It suddenly struck her that Bobby might be cancelling her leave. Clara felt an urgent need to see William that whisked her breath away.

'Yes, of course. But I'm giving you advance warning that we're moving you to Hamble next week.' She turned over a piece of paper. 'We've had to move so many people around. We lost two pilots this week, one early this morning. Katherine Barker hit a barrage balloon cable near Maidstone, she was killed outright.'

'Oh, no!' She knew Katherine was newly married. 'I'll send a note to her family, if you can give me their address.'

'There's more. A Lossiemouth pilot crashed in low fog, hit a hillside yesterday and is in hospital. We need you to join the all-women's group at Hamble. There are some very experienced pilots there, and they are flying a lot of Spits. Are you happy with that?' She looked up at Clara.

'I love flying Spitfires.'

'Good. It's been a bad few days, we need to consolidate. The Germans look like they are about to push into France. Pack up your things and get on a train to Hampshire as soon as the weekend is over. I'll organise some accommodation.' She lit a cigarette and took a long drag. 'Have you got something nice planned for your days off?'

'Just meeting a friend,' Clara said, wondering where the fluttery feeling came from in her chest. 'One of ours.'

'Well, stay in touch.' Bobby smiled, but she looked a decade older than she had when Clara had joined just a few months ago. 'We'll probably see you again when you come back for bomber training in a couple of months. We can only send two pilots at a time – it's getting busier every week.'

'Yes, ma'am.' Clara stood up and held out her hand. 'Thank you for giving me a chance.'

Bobby stood and clasped her hand firmly. 'Well, you've been a tremendous asset. Let's hope your luck holds.'

It took three hours for the train to get to Oxford; it was held up twice by air raid warnings and then a herd of cows wandered onto the line.

She got out at the station, scrabbling around in her pocket for the piece of paper with the name of William's lodgings.

'Clara!'

And there he was, striding towards her, arms out. Within a moment she was in them, being kissed, lost in the moment. She pulled back, suddenly breathless.

'Will – I don't know...'

'I'm sorry,' he said, grinning, his uniform cap pushed back on his head. 'I'm just glad to see you. Can't I kiss you?'

She could feel a blush warming her face. 'I thought you were an engaged man.'

His grin faded, and he gave her a more chaste peck on the cheek. 'We had just got engaged when war broke out, but she didn't want to hold me to it. We write – as friends – when we can, but not as much post gets through, it's reserved for US military personnel. Which I am not. Let's walk to the park, there's a café. I'll take that bag.'

She let him, because he had already swung it out of her grasp. 'So, what are you doing now?'

'I'm at Ferry Pool 5, Thame,' he said cheerfully. 'But I'm applying for the RAF again.'

'Can you do that?' She knew his US citizenship had held up his applications before.

'America will be in the war soon enough,' he said, leading the way across a street. 'But in case they still argue, I've applied for Canadian citizenship.'

She stopped and grabbed his arm, laughing. 'You can do that?'

'My great-grandfather Samuel emigrated to the US in 1835 from North Devon, with his brother Isaac heading for Canada. I'm making a spirited case that that makes me a bit Canadian.'

She laughed at the idea, having to skip to catch up with him. 'Will it work?'

'If it doesn't, I'll keep practising on Hurricanes and Spitfires until America comes into the war.' He slowed down as they reached the entrance to a small park. 'I love flying for the ATA, but I want to do more. I want to fight back.'

Clara had a horrible feeling that she didn't want him up there, being shot at by the enemy pilots. 'I've got a friend who's joined the RAF. He's been up there most days. He's lost a lot of colleagues, it's brutal.'

'Is he an old friend?' William looked up at her through his sandy lashes. 'Boyfriend?'

'Gosh, no.' She couldn't explain what Giles was to her. 'I don't know. I met him through someone I knew in childhood. I just care about him, up there every day, being shot at.'

'He's lucky.' He smiled widely, and this time, she let him kiss her until a couple of passing soldiers in uniform started whistling. His arms were warm, and he smelled of fresh soap and toothpaste.

He pulled back, stared at her, and she couldn't help laughing. 'What's wrong? Don't you want to kiss me?'

He took her hand. 'I think about you all the time,' he confessed. 'I never thought I'd be allowed to kiss someone like you. So beautiful, so classy. Out of my league.'

She took a moment to think about it. 'Maybe we wouldn't have met before the war, but we're equals, aren't we? Just two ATA pilots enjoying ourselves when we're not risking our lives up there. We can just keep it light.'

'I'm not a "keep it light" sort of guy.'

'That's all I have right now,' she said. 'And I expect you'll go back to America and your very understanding former fiancée.'

'If we survive,' he said, his eyes glowing.

'We have to survive,' she said, and let him take her hand.

17

PRESENT DAY, JUNE

After mulling over Mabel's letter for a few days, Ruby had finally made contact with her by email to arrange a phone call. She answered on the first ring, but the voice at the other end still made her jump.

'Ruby, is that you?'

'It is. Hello, Mrs Player.'

'Oh, you *must* call me Mabel!' the voice rang back. 'After all, I might be a cousin of sorts, and it is the twenty-twenties. So, you've been talking to Jake. Did you get the pictures we sent you, of my mother, Billie?'

Ruby opened the folder on her laptop and flipped through to the photo that resonated the most. Billie, two or three years old, sat in a flouncy checked dress, with a newborn baby on her own lap. 'I was very drawn to the one taken in 1947, the one with the baby.'

'Oh, that one is with my aunt Joan, she was just a couple months old. Then there were four brothers, another sister who passed away as a baby and me. By then, Billie was married to my father. I was born in 1967.' Her voice was filled with warmth.

'Was it nice, having so many aunts and uncles?' She could hear the longing in her own voice. 'I was an only child, so was my mother.'

Mabel laughed, a high-pitched giggle. 'Well, I was an only child, too, but I grew up close to all my cousins.' She paused for a moment. 'We were treated exactly the same by everyone, no one cared that she was adopted. She was quite a forceful lady, but so kind – all her siblings loved her. I miss her terribly. What was it about the picture that you liked?'

Ruby brushed a tear away with a finger. 'Jake wanted me to compare the pictures to a painting we have at home. And some of the pictures of Clara which I scanned for you.'

'Well, your Clara was a beauty, that's for sure. Billie was a plain, gawky thing but she was striking as she grew older. Tall, very tall, like your Clara, but I don't see much similarity otherwise.'

'Jake described her as beautiful,' Ruby said before she could stop herself.

'Well, I think she grew into her looks as she aged, but she was clumsy with a snub nose and a wide mouth as a young woman. Men liked her, though, but she didn't want to settle down too early. Remember, she was young in the sixties and seventies, times were different then. She ran away to college in New York as young as she could, with my grandfather mumblin' and moanin' about it every day. But he was proud of her, deep down.'

'What was her relationship with her adoptive parents like?' Ruby asked.

'Well, William came home from his service in England with a baby – that must have been difficult for his mother. He told how his closest friend had had a baby out of wedlock, and no one else could take the child. So he brought her home, and after a week of thinking and talking, he and May agreed to get married, and take the baby. She had a different name at birth, but they called her Wilhelmina, after William.'

'Taking on a stranger's baby is unbelievably kind, even if they were friends,' Ruby said.

'Well, that's what I thought. Quite unusual, really, but I remember something my mother told me before she passed. She'd been told her mother was born to a female pilot, and she'd always suspected that my grandfather had had compassionate feelings for her. He wanted to help a close colleague, and was such a kind man.'

'Kind – like romantic?'

'Goodness, no, he was a very moral, upstanding man. He broke off his engagement to May while he was away at the war, but they were still friends, they wrote letters regularly. They married as soon as he returned.'

Ruby's pencil stalled over her notes. 'So – you think this pilot could have been Clara Montpelier?'

'Well, her name was written on the adoption certificate, wasn't it?' asked Mabel.

'Just in pencil, added later. Anyone could have written that, at any time,' Ruby said, her analytical head whirring. 'The actual certificate only holds Wilhelmina's name, not her old one. Perhaps they added it so she could track down the birth parents after the war, and maybe Clara was a friend or relative of the parents.'

'I don't think they ever did. And how did my grandfather get permission to bring a baby from Britain to the US?'

Ruby had been wrestling with that one. 'I haven't been able to find any records of a baby emigrating from the UK with the name Montpelier *or* Carlson. But the armed forces had their own rules during the war.'

Mabel's voice was excited. 'Well, I'm just *so* intrigued, I would love to come over and help in the search myself,' she said. 'I could stay in London and come down to meet you, if that would be OK. Maybe find some of that DNA we need to see if my mother was Clara's baby. If that's acceptable to you – I'm not after your inheritance. I just want to know where my mother came from. Where I came from.'

Ruby found herself agreeing, although the idea of comparing DNA made Ruby nervous about what they would uncover. 'We would have to find something to test, there's not much left from Clara's time. We'd have to use a forensic laboratory – it would be expensive.'

'It sure would. Jake explained all that. But I've got things of my mother's. And I'm happy to pay,' Mabel said, her voice soothing. 'And I would love to see the house, the one Billie *might* have been born in. I'd like to stay nearby for a night or two. Can you recommend a nice hotel?'

'Jake stayed at Foxglove Cottage, that's very good.' Ruby felt a little bulldozed. 'I could show you around,' she said, dubiously. 'But I'm working all week in Plymouth and would only be able to see you at the weekend. I have tenants in the house, too.'

Mabel went quiet for a moment. 'How about I fly over to London and meet with Jake, then we could both drive down to Devon, if he s available. We could stay the whole weekend. I'd welcome his help.'

Ruby couldn't argue with that, and anyway, she did want to see Jake. Which left four days to find more photographs to help their search, as well as track down anything that might have DNA on it from Marissa, or even more unlikely, from Clara.

In person, Mabel Player was a stout, grey-haired woman with an energetic handshake. She arrived at Montpelier House on Saturday morning with Jake.

While she stared up at the ceiling of the hall, some twelve

feet overhead, Jake smiled at Ruby and said in a low voice, 'This is very kind of you.'

'I'm really curious myself, now,' she admitted. 'I've never doubted the stories I was told, but it's a puzzle.'

Mabel turned right round, looking down the hall. 'This is a fantastic house. It's got so much character… It's so tall – it must have wonderful views.'

Ruby smiled, and looked down the hall with a more critical eye. The French doors were shut but rattling against the brisk breeze, there was mud on the tiles and she was acutely aware of the dust on the assorted items on the dresser. Gardening gloves bundled in pairs, a sheep's skull Ruby had picked out of a river on Exmoor as a child, old post, stacks of film canisters and packets of photographic prints from decades ago, a selection of collars and leads from dogs Ruby could barely remember.

'My. It's like an upmarket thrift store,' Mabel said, walking over and picking up one of the walking sticks leaning against the oak dresser. 'And this – bureau?'

'It's a Welsh dresser,' Ruby said, glancing back to catch Jake's eye. He smiled back, and it put a lightness in her step as she pushed the door open to the drawing room. 'The picture's in here.'

She could hear a gasp as Mabel walked in ahead of her. 'Oh, my goodness. What a shame.'

As Ruby followed her, she could see she was looking at the blackened parquet below the hole in the ceiling. 'It's cosmetic,' Ruby said. 'The ceiling can be restored once the roof is mended properly. It has a temporary fix for now.' She had got a local builder to patch it with tarps and buckets, but it wouldn't survive a moorland downpour or a storm.

Mabel slowly rotated, staring out of the bay window. 'Oh, my. That's the most beautiful view.'

Jake walked up behind her. 'Isn't it? This area is where the Carlson family comes from, from this part of Devon.'

'So this is Dartmoor?' She turned to Ruby, her dark eyes wide. Her round face and small mouth looked nothing like Clara, but Ruby noticed a similarity around the eyes.

'We're right in the middle of the moor,' Ruby explained, pointing out of the window. 'Down there are the streams and rivers that make up the river, the East Dart and the West Dart. They join up at Dartmeet, near the bed and breakfast.'

'We can't book in there until two o'clock,' Mabel said, before swinging around to look at the enormous fireplace, with its more modern wood burner. Turning again, she caught sight of the painting of the child on the hay bale. 'And this is the picture.'

A sound at the door made Ruby swing round. Pony was standing there, looking even more shaky and wild-haired than usual. 'Max says he's not having any breakfast,' she said, in a hoarse stage whisper. 'And he's not getting up for *anyone*, even Americans.'

Ruby turned to Mabel. 'Max is very much part of the old house. One of the last artists.'

'Well, I'm sure we don't want to disturb him,' Mabel said, looking back at the picture. 'I've seen pictures of Clara online. The baby in your painting doesn't look too much like her.'

Ruby stood next to her. 'I think babies all look a bit alike.'

'They do, dear. But there's a look of my mother around that large chin. And those wild curls; Billie stayed blonde her whole life.'

Ruby couldn't see it; she still thought it was Clara. 'The picture needs cleaning. But I can't work out how to get it down.'

Pony piped up from the end of one of the sofas. 'Last time it was taken down, they screwed the frame to the oak panelling.'

Ruby turned to Mabel. 'It's probably the reason Fiona – my mother – didn't sell it.' She stared up at the sky behind the figure, visible through the open end of what had been the stables. 'I've always loved the birds flying over the barn,' she said, walking closer. 'I always thought they were summer swallows. When was Billie born?'

'She was adopted in 1945,' Jake said, standing in a row with the three women. 'We don't know exactly when or where she was born.'

'If she's a British baby, how did she get to the US?' Ruby asked. 'She was just a baby, how did she travel? It was in the middle of the war.'

Mabel stared up at the painting. 'My grandfather was wounded in the February, and shipped back to the states in March. He inhaled smoke from an engine fire, he had a weak chest the rest of his life. I assumed he brought the baby back with him then, and adopted her, you can see the date on the certificate.'

'And who gave permission for her to be adopted?' Ruby said, looking at them. 'I wonder why she didn't remain with her surviving family, or why she wasn't adopted by another family here.'

'But suppose she didn't have a family?' Mabel asked. 'Think about it. Clara dead, her lover dead, his – or her – best friend takes the baby back to the US for a wonderful life.'

'But Clara's two mothers would have welcomed and loved any child of Clara's. Which is why I'm really struggling to believe that Billie could have been Clara's baby. I'm sorry...' She sighed, and feeling she had to offer something, said, 'I supposed I could reach out to Giles's family, her fiancé...'

Jake's voice softened. 'If he *was* the baby's father.'

Ruby's frustration boiled over and her voice came out with a snap. 'And if *Clara* was the mother. All of this is relying on one line of pencil at the top of this adoption certificate. It's all just a theory. We don't know when Clara's name was written.'

'Well, we know my mother was adopted a year after Clara died.' Mabel said. 'It just makes such a romantic story. Listen to me, making a fairy tale out of what was probably a tragedy. Where was Clara buried?'

'In Hartford churchyard, a couple of miles away,' Ruby said. 'I'm happy to take you down there. There's a gravestone and the original builder of the house and his family are buried there, too. We could walk down tomorrow, if you like. It's near Foxglove Cottage.'

'I would love that,' Mabel said, pressing her hand. 'Even if Clara isn't Billie's mother, she was a heroine.'

Mabel wanted a complete house tour, and since she hadn't shown Jake the whole house on his previous visit, Ruby took them around the bedrooms.

'I didn't show you this before because I'm not certain it's safe,' she said, pushing open the door to the largest bedroom. The middle of the room was empty, the furniture pushed to the sides. The main bed frame, a rococo-style antique bed that Ruby had always associated with Marissa's body lying in state, was dismantled and piled against the marble fireplace. Rolled-up rugs were fraying beside it, probably full of moths, and a large chest of drawers had been hand-painted with flower motifs.

Jake walked in, followed by Mabel, and he took hold of her arm. 'We'd better stay around the edge,' he said, looking at the blackened boards in the middle of the room. Above, the ceiling had suffered the same fate as the one downstairs, the remnants of the plaster hanging from horsehairs. 'Where's the leak? In the attics?'

'One of the old servants' bedrooms, yes. It has a skylight that's been letting water in.' Ruby followed them around the edge, but they were both staring out at the view. She hadn't been in here for a couple of years and had forgotten how good the view was, twenty feet above the garden. Looking over the cars and the scrappy hedge, she could see across to several of the moorland peaks, Huccaby and Laughter Tors, and far beyond she could just see the church on top of Brent Tor.

'Was this your grandmother's room?' Mabel asked, turning to her.

'This was Alice and Marissa's room,' she answered. 'They had their own dressing room behind, it's a bedroom now, above the darkroom. When Marissa got older, her maid slept in there, in case she needed anything in the night.' She couldn't imagine Marissa asking for help, but she didn't know what she was like behind her closed door. Fiona had once told her that she needed injections at night, that Jenny was as much a nurse as a maid. It was the room that had the loudest whispers. A shiver ran down her back as a draught found the bare skin of her neck. 'Let me show you the other front bedrooms.'

The one on the other side of the landing was equally grand and with as good a view, and was in much better condition. It had been Fiona's and there were still a few bits of the larger furniture in there, including a sofa and television along with scatterings of her clothes. 'This was your mother's?' Jake asked.

She nodded and walked through to open the adjoining door to the room over the library. 'And this was my room when I was little,' she said. The room was filled with cardboard boxes now. 'It's probably got all my swimming certificates and school pictures in here somewhere.' The idea brought prickles to her eyes.

The windows had the same gorgeous view, warmed by light streaming in from the round side window that had been put in when she started school. Life at the house was like that: she went off one morning and when she got back there was a hole in the wall, ready to have a porthole installed. Another day she'd come home to a stained-glass picture of moorland hares hanging in the round window, which she'd adored. A couple of pieces had dropped out over the years, but it still lit the room with all sorts of colours.

'What is the picture of?' Mabel asked. 'It doesn't look religious.'

'It was three hares in a circle,' Ruby said, lifting up the two missing pieces. 'They share three ears. It's supposed to be lucky.'

'That's lovely,' Mabel said. 'What a wonderful place to grow up.'

'It was,' Ruby said, tapping the cast-iron radiator. 'Freezing in the winter, though, and boiling in the summer. The front of the house is directly south-facing. I moved up to the attic when I got older.'

'Would you mind if we see there, too?' Mabel said.

Jake intervened. 'We don't need to.'

'I don't mind. The room behind Fiona's, it's Pony's – Penelope's – so we won't go in there. The bathroom is in between.'

The bathroom was long and thin, with a window on the end, and Ruby had loved having a bath as a child, looking out over the hedges and rock ridge that protected the house from the east wind. The slipper bath was copper, and Mabel was fascinated by the old sink, in crazed blue and white porcelain, with matching WC and an overhead flush.

'It's amazing it all still works,' she said, running her hands over a towel left drying on the radiator. 'Don't you have a shower here?'

'In the attic,' Ruby said, but honestly, she preferred a bath. Showers were for getting ready for work, at the flat. 'There's a loo and sink in the attic, too. Very modern for the era.'

She showed them both attic bedrooms, one impassable with sodden lumber, buckets and tarpaulins directly under the leak, and the other one was hers. The brass-framed bed clanked when Mabel sat on it. 'How lovely,' she said, before standing on tiptoes to look out of the skylight. 'More views,' she said, and Jake walked over too, but he kept his eyes on Ruby.

'Are you really ready to let all this go?' he asked, his voice soft.

'Actually,' she said, surprising herself, 'I might be. I've been going through the boxes of pictures but they are all studies for portraits, her work. There's nothing personal. I only found that one I showed you, of Clara and Giles. I'm sorry.'

'That's all right,' he said, holding her gaze. 'Maybe we'll find something in the archives.'

'Oh, that reminds me,' Mabel said. 'I logged on to a genealogy site before I came over, once Jake had given me his last name. I found quite a few pictures of this Giles.'

She swiped a few times on her phone, but the lack of service defeated her. Ruby smiled. 'Come downstairs, I'll get you on the house Wi-Fi in the kitchen,' she promised.

'I don't want to disturb your housemates,' Mabel said, looking awkward for the first time.

'You won't. Pony is so nosy, she'll probably want to join in.'

In the kitchen, over a large pot of tea and a pot of coffee for Mabel, she logged on using Ruby's laptop. 'It was this picture I was curious about.'

Ruby had seen it before, the broadly smiling hero of the Battle of Britain, thick dark hair, flying suit, helmet swinging from one hand. But this was a wider image than the cropped one she had seen in the *Dartmoor Observer* of the 1940s. Two other pilots stood to one side, allowing him to take up the spotlight. One of them had a dark, curly fringe...

'That's Clara!'

'I thought it was,' Mabel said, with some satisfaction. 'I must have searched through hundreds of images to get this one.'

'I never thought to look up Giles before,' Ruby said, gazing at his strong jaw and high cheekbones, prominent dark eyebrows and that preposterous moustache. She involuntarily glanced at Mabel. 'Wait here...' She lifted down the photograph from the hall and dusted it off before putting it on the table.

Mabel studied it. 'Good grief, he was handsome, wasn't he? He could be my grandfather – I suppose I could resemble him. It's funny, I just thought I would look a bit like Clara.'

'Well, it wouldn't be impossible that you might take after Giles. But I can't see anything obvious.'

'After Clara's accident, wouldn't *his* family have taken the baby? If it was his. I mean, they were engaged, weren't they?' Jake said.

'I don't know. They wouldn't have any formal rights. And the engagement wasn't announced officially. They wouldn't want to advertise an illegitimate baby.'

Jake glanced at his watch. 'We know he survived the war. After our drinks, I'm going to take Mabel off to the hotel.'

'It's just a bed and breakfast,' Ruby added, looking to Mabel. 'They rent two rooms out to visitors. It's not the Ritz.'

'It's charming,' Jake said, as she remembered he had stayed there before. 'And Hazel and Zosia couldn't have been more welcoming.' He turned to Mabel. 'But we'll eat at the pub in the village.'

He looked as if he would have liked to ask her to join them. She almost suggested it, but thought he'd probably had enough of her by now. She smiled instead. 'And we'll all go to the churchyard tomorrow. I'll pick you up, around ten?'

18

MAY 1940

There was an innocence – and honourableness – about William, Clara decided, as she leaned her head against the train window. They had gone to the cinema and laughed through the cartoons like children. They'd had dinner in a dirty café that opened late and served sausages and mash. He talked about the beautiful landscape near his home town until she had to counter with the grandeur and wildness of Dartmoor. He had grown up near lakes so wide you couldn't see the opposite shore – she countered with the vistas over the English Channel, viewed from the high points of Hay Tor. He had a deep love for his family, talking about their emigration from places she knew in Devon, to set up a new life where they were able to thrive and be successful. William's father had over a thousand acres on his farm, and also ran several businesses, including a car salesroom. They exchanged favourite cars and finally planes.

'And you've piloted a Spitfire, now,' she said.

'A Mark II, yes. I guess you'll be flying the new ones all the time, if you're moving to Hamble.'

'I hope so.'

'I've been down there a few times,' he had said, putting a few shillings on the table. 'This is how you tip, isn't it?'

They walked hand in hand to the station, him carrying her bag, her carrying both their coats. The walk in the dark had seemed to last forever, and it was a shock to be greeted by a blast of steam as a train came to a halt at the platform.

'I'll write,' she had said, turning to him. 'And send my new address when I get to Hamble.'

'What about this other fella?' he said, his voice a little strained.

'I'll write to him, too, although he rarely writes to me.' She took her bag. 'We have to keep this light, remember? Just friends, who care about each other.'

'Friends?' he replied. She could just make him out in the red lights at the entrance of the station. 'I don't kiss my *friends* like that.'

'Please, Will,' she had begged. 'I don't have room in my life for anything else right now.'

He had looked away, the low light catching his jawline. 'As long as I'm the only one you are kissing,' he said, finally.

That had sparked a little anger. 'I don't expect you not to write to your ex-fiancée,' she had said. 'I can kiss who I like.'

'That's not fair,' he said, when the whistle had already blown. 'May and I have been friends since we were children.'

The train pulled away, and tears prickled at the corners of her eyes as she leaned against the shaded window alone.

She had to change trains to get to Hamble, and the night train rolled in just before dawn to collect milk churns, boxes of produce and sacks of potatoes and post.

She got off and stretched, tired out. She had barely slept the previous night in her single room in a women's hostel, and had only dozed on the train. The stationmaster came over to greet her.

'Miss Montpelier?' he said, handing her an envelope. 'The

girls have left you a bicycle, it's in my office. And instructions on how to find the house.'

'Laburnum Cottage,' she read out. 'Turn left, ride for about half a mile, then take the right turn at the fork. House is third on the right.'

'That's about it,' he agreed. 'I've got a parcel for them, if you don't mind taking it as well.'

She balanced it in the basket on the front, slung her bag over her shoulder and took off down the lane.

It was a soft landscape, she decided, clouds of hawthorn blossom in hedges either side of the narrow road, flowers bursting into bloom along the soft verges, and none of the tumbled stones of the moor. Fields had oak gates leading into well-grown crops, in what looked like rich soil. Trees grew straight and tall out of ancient hedges, bursting into leaf, the landscape crowded in a way her home vista never was.

She found the fork, took the right turn down a small lane, and counted off the houses. Laburnum Cottage was a long, low house, with whitewashed walls and thatch almost to the tops of the ground-floor windows, with three tiny dormers tucked into the roof.

She checked her watch – barely seven. But before she could wonder whether it was too early to knock, a woman almost as broad as she was tall bustled out of the doorway.

'You must be Clara Montpelier,' she said with a broad accent and a huge smile. 'I'm Lizzie, the cook and housekeeper. We've made up a bed for you already. The girls will be down for breakfast any minute. And Mrs Landscombe is already at the church. She does the flowers there,' she confided. 'She's your landlady. We've got some of our own bacon for breakfast today.'

'That sounds lovely. Do you – does Mrs Landscombe – have a farm?'

'Bless you, no. Just a few hens and pigs, in the stable where we used to keep the horses. The hunters went at the beginning of the war.'

Walking up the stone steps to the house, Clara was pounced on by two pilots she had met at White Waltham, Faith Brackley and the Honourable Marjory Edwards, both promoted to second officers.

'You'll love it here,' Faith said in her northern accent, tucking her arm into Clara's as Marjory took her bag and the parcel. 'Who's the parcel for, Marj?'

'You, by the looks of it. But the censor's been through it.' They walked into the kitchen, Clara salivating at the smell of bacon.

The parcel was taped up and covered in officious print. 'It's just some old clothes from home. I haven't anything new to wear, so I'm doing some old things over.' Faith drew out what looked like a summer dress with flounces and pockets. 'There must be enough there for a blouse and some decent shorts. Look at that skirt, it's enormous! Fashions have changed.'

Marjory, who was inches taller even than Clara and had short, dark hair, pulled out a chair for her. 'You must be exhausted.'

'I really am,' she admitted. 'I can never sleep on a night train and it was packed.'

When the housekeeper returned, the girls immediately jumped up. 'Lizzie! Clara is almost perished, haven't you got anything for her?'

'I'm sure she'll live another five minutes. Clear off that table and I'll see what I can do.'

Marjory took her arm and led her to a long sunroom looking over the garden. 'They've given us this room for our own parlour. Darling Mr Landscombe even set us up a drinks trolley. He sneaks the odd bottle in here for us.' She directed Clara to a wicker chair full of cushions, next to a huge aspidistra plant. 'Just don't water the plant, it's on a strict diet.' She sat opposite and smoothed back her hair. 'You haven't been made up to second officer yet?'

'I've passed the exams, I just need a few more hours in the air.'

Faith came in trailing the pile of pretty fabrics. 'Well, it's lovely to have you. We've lost a couple of pilots to other teams. We're trying to stay all girls here, it helps with the billeting arrangements.'

Clara watched the two stretch out the fabric and hold it up against the shorter, blonde Faith. 'It suits you,' she said, a little sleepily. 'That print reminds me of the summers before the war.'

'Wimbledon and Pimm's, dancing at parties with champagne,' Marjory said. 'Young men playing cricket on the village green.'

Faith laughed. 'I lived in the middle of Manchester,' she said, nudging her. 'Much less champagne and Pimm's for me.'

'Well, young men played cricket everywhere,' Marjory said. 'And we played lawn tennis at the club, and went on holidays to Brighton.'

It was as if a cloud had come over the sun, although nothing had changed. So many of those young men were gone forever. The three girls sat quietly with their thoughts in the early sunshine, which slanted through bamboo blinds, until Lizzie called them for breakfast.

19

PRESENT DAY, JUNE

Ruby led the way across the small churchyard. 'Clara's over here,' she said, turning to take Mabel's outstretched hand. 'Careful, it's a bit uneven.'

'I noticed,' Mabel said, and took Jake's hand, too. Ruby suspected she wanted the reassuring contact in the wet grave-yard, the long grasses dripping with dew. Snails were everywhere, sliding up the mossy stones, over the paths.

Ruby stopped in front of a simple, tall stone in white marble. In profile was a carved face, eyes shut, like an angel. Spring flowers rambled over the surface of the stone, blossoming in pimpernel orange and speedwell blue. 'They based the carving on the real Clara,' Ruby said, her voice quiet. 'Alice designed the whole thing, and wrote the words.'

'Clara A. St John-Montpelier, born 11 November 1918, died 16 November 1944,' Jake read out in a subdued voice. 'They double-barrelled her name.'

'She's just Montpelier on her birth certificate,' Ruby said, brushing away a tear. 'I suppose Alice wanted to claim her as a daughter, too. She loved her, she looked after her as well.'

Underneath, in italics, were the words *Daughter of the moor*.

'She really was,' Ruby said. 'She went to primary school here, and then she had governesses and tutors before a few years at boarding school. She rode, drove and flew all over the moor. Even when she went to Europe, before the war, she wrote home every week. My grandmother kept the letters, I read some of them when I was a child. Marissa hated her going away, I suppose they both did. One of her tutors was a local First World War hero. He taught her to drive when she was a teenager.'

'I wonder if she used both names on her daughter's birth certificate?' Mabel asked, her expression lightening.

'*If* she had a daughter. But no, I searched for it.' Another idea seeded in her brain. 'I never tried Clara St John by itself, though.'

She brought out her phone, tapped the screen a few times. 'There are a few birth certificates with Clara or Clare St John listed as the mother. We could look into it when we get back to the house, if you like.' One stood out. Early in 1944, a baby girl *had* been born in London. 'I suppose the family might have tried to conceal the birth of a baby,' Ruby said. 'But if this was Clara, that would mean she worked pretty well right through her pregnancy and went back very soon after the baby was born. Then she died.'

The thought that Clara might have died knowing that she would never see her baby again brought tears to Ruby's eyes.

She glanced across to see Jake, hands folded in front of him, eyes shut. She waited for a few moments until he looked back up.

'It's sad, isn't it?' he said. 'So young to die. Do we know how?'

'Yes, I know it was a wartime plane crash. My family never wanted to talk about it. The ATA probably has records, but I don't know if they've been released yet.'

'Oh.' He looked away and sniffed.

Mabel was openly teary-eyed. 'How dreadful. And so young.'

'Clara was such a heroine to me.'

'She sounds like a remarkable person,' Mabel said, squeezing her hand. 'A powerful woman.'

'There's more family records inside the church, if it's open,' Ruby said, guiding Mabel over the tufted grass. 'I know there's a scholarship Marissa set up for local children.'

The church was less than two hundred years old. Ruby could remember when the roof was corrugated iron, rusty and with peeling paint, but it had neat slate tiles now.

Jake looked around. 'Is this – Hartford Chapel?'

'It used to be,' Ruby said, leading him around to the side of the church. 'It's called St Mary's now.'

Mabel looked up at a foundation stone. 'This used to be a Bible Christian chapel.'

She stood beside him. 'Until 1938, yes, it says so inside.'

'We – my family – emigrated to set up Bible Christian communities in North America,' Mabel said. 'My great-great-great-grandfather settled in Wisconsin. My ancestors settled near Madison. We are at the top, by lots of lakes. Maybe our ancestors came from this area.' Her voice had gone higher. 'Maybe right here!'

Ruby smiled at her while Jake tried the door. It swung open easily. A very tall, heavy-set man was standing on the other side wearing a bright shirt over a clerical collar. 'Ruby! Nice to see you.'

'This is Leon, our vicar,' she explained to the other two. 'We were hoping to see the burial record for Clara Montpelier, if we can.'

'Of course. Come in, it's a bit wet outside,' he said, ushering them in. 'Sorry, I've got a bit of child labour going on. Young Krystof is helping me dust before the service tomorrow.'

A boy popped his head over the pews and ducked back down again.

'This isn't Bible Christian any more?' Mabel asked, after Ruby introduced them by name.

'No,' he answered. 'Many of the chapels became Methodist over time, but the Church of England bought this one for the locals. There are quite a few over the whole of Devon. Ruby could take you to the most famous one on Brentor, if you're here long enough.'

Mabel walked over to the boy. 'It's good to make the church nice, isn't it? I'm looking for someone, she's called Clara and she used to fly airplanes.'

Krys gave a gap-toothed grin. 'She used to fly planes called Spitfires and Mosquitoes, a long time ago,' he said. 'We learned about her in Sunday School.'

'We like to read all our gravestones through the year,' Leon explained. 'Some of the burials go back to the early eighteen hundreds. We have a world-renowned naturalist's grave, and a famous seafarer.'

'Captain Marshall?' Ruby said, smiling. 'He built our house. He was the first inhabitant. He had lots of children,' she told Krys. 'They must have had a lot of bunk beds up at Montpelier House, because they also had six servants. It was called Heather House back then.'

Mabel tucked her hand into Ruby's arm. 'This is sad, isn't it? Morbid. Her family was left to grieve,' Mabel said softly. 'Her poor mothers. It occurs to me that we've all recently lost our mothers. I can't imagine how difficult it would have been to lose a child.'

Ruby looked around at Leon carrying a large leatherbound book. 'I think the whole family was affected by it. Marissa never really got over it, and Alice – well, Alice decided to go wild and have a late baby. Fiona, my mum.'

Jake smiled. 'I'm glad she did.'

Leon put the book on the donations table behind the pews. 'Here. 1931... 34... it's the church accounts so it's painfully detailed.' He turned over another half-inch of papers. 'This was when it was still a Bible Christian chapel. They kept better records than we do. Here... 1944. Oh.'

It was laid out in perfect copperplate, barely faded with time. '*Funeral Miss Clara. Thirty-eight pounds, six shillings and fourpence,*' Ruby read.

Jake leaned over her shoulder to see. 'That's several thousands in today's money. Why did it cost the church so much? Presumably there would be a funeral director involved, too.'

'Look here,' Leon said, running a finger lightly over the detailed account. 'The sexton prepared an extra-large site to allow for her to be buried between her two mothers over time.'

'She is,' Ruby said. 'Their names are on small stones either side. That site would have to have been hacked out of the granite – graves are hard to dig here.'

'Most of my parishioners are cremated and their ashes interred instead,' Leon said.

Ruby stared at the accounts of everything from repair of a cracked window to the giving of alms to a poor widow. 'Leon – does this book include christenings? Is there anything for 1943 or 1944 involving Clara?'

He turned the pages back carefully. Although the paper was thick, it was looking a little ragged at the edges and was starting to yellow. 'Matthew Duke, born second of March, 1941. Thomas Crannock... oh, and a burial for poor Thomas too. Poor little scrap.' He turned the page again. 'Alissa St John. Born thirteenth March 1944. No father named.'

Ruby leaned forward. 'Oh, my goodness. There *was* a baby.'

Mabel grasped her arm in a hug. 'You found her!' she said in a whisper.

Leon tapped the entry gently. 'Do you know, there were a lot of these illegitimate births during the war, but they usually have something judgemental added to the record. Like this one: *George Baxter, unfortunate, born to Mary Baxter*. This Alissa is recorded very respectfully, daughter of Miss C. St John, no mention of a father.'

'That's amazing.' Ruby took out her phone and snapped a picture of the page. 'So, Billie was Clara's baby all along?' She stared at a tearful Mabel, who was drying her eyes. 'You and I are cousins. I'm so pleased.'

'Me too.' Mabel reached her arms out for a tight hug. 'So we are.'

Ruby sniffed back a couple of tears and smiled hazily at Jake. 'I never thought to ask in my own church,' she said. 'I feel daft – some family history researcher, this was right under my nose.'

'The records are all digitised in the archives,' Leon said. 'But it's unusual that no one put the mother's full name in. I'm not even sure that's allowed. We wouldn't do that now.'

Ruby looked at Mabel. 'You were right. Your Clara is my Clara. Your mother was probably Clara's baby.'

Mabel touched the record reverently. 'I was beginning to think I was wrong, that my grandfather had just written the name down for some other reason. Like she was a friend of the baby's mother or something, or godparent.'

Jake put his hand on her shoulder. 'We'd like to find out as much as we can about Clara. It's become a bit of a personal quest for me, now.'

'And we'll look for the baby's father, too,' Mabel added.

'We'll order that birth certificate,' Ruby said, staring into Jake's bright eyes. 'We'll find her official record.'

20

AUGUST 1940

After the disaster of Dunkirk, Clara was finally given a few days' leave. The tors touched the blue sky at the top of every hill, purple loosestrife and acid-yellow gorse spiking from the grass. The taxi dropped Clara on the winding moorland road below Montpelier House, and she had to lug her bags up the drive, past the shrubbery nodding with flowers, to the front terrace of the house, bleached by the sun. She was so tired her joints ached, her eyes were heavy and the warmth made her sleepy. When she pushed the door open, she was surprised to see her old schoolfriend, Sukey Rushworth, in the hall.

'We hoped you would arrive in style, in a Spitfire!' she said, hugging Clara hard. 'Goodness, you're so thin. We'll have to fatten you up a bit.'

Clara returned the hug. 'It's lovely to see you, Sukey. I didn't realise we had guests.'

'I think Marissa wanted to have a house party for you, like we used to do, before the war. She invited a few of our friends.'

After dropping her bags by the coat stand and hanging her jacket up, Clara allowed herself to be steered into the front parlour.

'Surprise!' everyone shouted. Ma and Mother were standing next to Leonard Rushworth, who had the blank, tight face of someone who had been in combat. Cousin Isabella and another of Marissa's nieces were there – she couldn't recall the name. And Giles, standing towards the corner of the room, taller than the other men, darkly handsome, raising a tea cup to her in a toast.

Marissa came forward and kissed her cheek. 'Darling, welcome. We thought we would have a break from this dreadful war, hear a little laughter again.'

'Then she invited *us*,' the unnamed cousin said. 'All working for the war effort, all exhausted.'

Alice hugged Clara warmly, the top of her head fitting beneath Clara's chin. 'But they got here yesterday, so they're all rested and fed. Marina came down from Cambridge with Leonard and Isabella, and Giles came on the train.'

Marina. Clara could remember her bellowing when she got stuck on the home-made and very steep slide that used to live at the back of the house, shooting the children down two terraces into a heap on the lowest lawn.

'I'm afraid I'm very tired – and very dirty. I'll go and change. Ma, could you come with me?'

Alice and Clara walked up the broad stairs together. Mrs Goddings had washed and aired Clara's pre-war wardrobe out for her, and she bustled about Clara's bedroom, running some water into the sink and topping it up from a jug.

'There you go, lovey,' she said, testing the water. 'The boiler's off in the bathroom.'

Clara was so tired, tears filled her eyes. 'Thank you.'

Between them, the older women undid her buttons, helped her undress and then Alice pulled back the bedcovers. They smelled like the moorland wind, the gorse flowers and fresh, wild thyme. 'You need to sleep,' Mrs Goddings said. 'I'll come up before dinner, you can go down then.'

'Can I have some tea, first?' Clara said, lying in her underwear on the sheet, while Alice pulled up the blankets. 'I'm so thirsty and hot, it's the train...'

'Here's a glass of water,' she said. 'You'll be asleep by the time Mrs Goddings comes back with the tray.'

Clara drank the smoky peated water from their own spring. Then closed her eyes.

Clara felt her face warm before she pushed open the door to the front parlour, three hours later. 'Sorry, everyone, Mrs Goddings put me to bed like a five-year-old.'

Isabella came forward to kiss her cheek. 'We all felt like that yesterday. We don't get much time off these days.'

She drew Clara into the room, where she smiled and nodded to everyone and Leonard held her hand for a moment. 'How's the flying?' he asked.

'You know. Tiring. It's the constant changes I find difficult, and I can't always fly back to my digs. But I'm not complaining, it's helping the RAF. How about you?'

His mouth tightened into a thin line. 'Do you remember my friend Freddie? Too young to join up when you met him at Rushworth.'

'I remember,' she said. The gentle, slight young man who had been trying and failing to grow a moustache.

'He was shot down six weeks after getting his wings.' His face was haunted, his jaw clenched. He looked ten years older.

'I'm so sorry.'

Giles stepped closer. 'But we're not going to talk about all that, old chap,' he said gently. 'Let's have a few days away from the ghastly business.'

'No. Sorry.' Leonard attempted a smile, though he looked like he was in pain. 'Did Sukey tell you her news?'

Clara turned to look at her. 'I've been promoted to top-secret work for the government,' Sukey said. 'Listening to phone calls, mostly, and transcribing them. It's terribly dull work but I enjoy living with the girls I work with. Nothing like the exciting work you get to do.'

Clara quickly reviewed the latest deliveries she had made, trying to find a more light-hearted memory. 'I enjoy delivering new planes,' she finally said. 'Shiny and smelling of new paint.'

Giles laughed. 'As someone who flies those shiny new planes, I wish the Germans would treat them better.'

Clara joined Isabella and Mother on the long sofa. 'No, Giles is right. Let's talk about fun things. We're still young, after all.'

Isabella smiled at her. 'I'm about to get engaged,' she confessed. 'We haven't announced it or anything, but he's asked me and I've said yes. We're just waiting for some time when we're both off.'

'Oh, that's wonderful!' Clara said. 'Lovely news. Do we know him?'

'Well, he's a friend from my college days.' She smiled around the room. 'He's at the War Office at the moment – at least he's away from the front. But he says his landlady's cooking will carry him off if he doesn't get into married quarters.'

Over the general laughter, Marina sat on the arm of the sofa. 'How about you, Clara? Any young men?'

'I don't really have time,' Clara said, smiling generally and avoiding Giles's gaze. 'No one serious, anyway. Let's get the war out of the way first.'

'We managed to meet up at a club for a few dances,' Giles added, his deep voice resonating around the room. 'And quite a lot of wine.'

'Yes, one trip took me to Nottingham,' Clara stammered. 'It was nice to meet up with a friend for a couple of hours.'

Marissa rose to her feet. 'I think Mrs Goddings and Beth

would like us to go in to dinner,' she said. 'After all the trouble she's gone to, despite the rationing, I think we should go through.'

The dining room was lit by candles, and although the sun hadn't gone down, it was far in the west, and the curtains were left open to the red sky, which seemed very strange to someone used to the blackout.

'A few more minutes, before we draw the drapes,' Marissa murmured as she walked behind Clara to look over the moor.

'Have you even seen an enemy plane here?' she asked, as people found their places. Giles made a space next to himself for Clara.

'A few, heading for Plymouth,' her mother answered, patting her shoulder before walking to the head of the table. Alice was sat at Marissa's right hand, as she always had. 'But nothing for weeks, they tend to fly along the coast, if our boys don't catch them.'

Mrs Goddings had done them proud, with thick vegetable soup followed by venison, harvested in the forest behind the house. Vegetables were from the garden, the sauce rich and gamey, and discussion faded away. After rationing and the poor-quality food brought in by ship or on dusty trains from the countryside, they savoured these tastes of the moor. Mrs Goddings and the maid had crammed local herbs in with the meat, slathered it in butter from a local farm and roasted it. Clara thought it tasted like the wild moor at night, when the deer ranged freely and stood on the ridge against the purple sky.

'I missed this,' she said, leaning back from her empty plate. 'We're so lucky in the New Forest, we eat like kings, but everywhere else rationing is harsh. Home food's the best, though.'

Giles sipped from a glass of wine, shutting his eyes. 'All we get to drink now is watery tea or pale ale. This is lovely.'

'We're getting to the end of the good wine in the cellar,' Alice said, smiling down the table. 'But we can't complain, so many people have it worse.'

Conversation wandered around the table as plates were removed and two puddings were brought out: one was a summer pudding made from strawberries and raspberries, the other a chocolate steamed pudding with clotted cream.

Marina was an organiser for the land army, and had stories to tell of the pressures being put on local agriculture and the ingenious ways people were getting around them. Isabella was locked in an office most of the time, and living in barracks at her top-secret base for the rest. Sukey worked as a stenographer for the War Office, and her fiancé was working for the organisation of the Home Guard. Clara could see the strain on them all. Before the war, they would all be talking about the next party or race meeting or shopping trip to Paris. Now they weren't even certain they would survive the year.

Marissa clinked her fork against a glass. 'I would like to have offered champagne,' she said, 'but instead, we have some delicious cider Alice decanted into old champagne bottles with a spoonful of sugar in each.'

'Only one exploded,' Alice said, with glee. 'Fortunately, it was on its own, on the floor of the scullery, or it would have set them all off.'

'The cat didn't come in for a week,' Marissa said, slightly smiling. 'More importantly, no one was hurt by Alice's ingenious experiment.' She lifted Alice's hand to her lips for a moment. 'And she's made a batch of ginger ale, too.'

Alice smiled back at Marissa. 'Not so explosive, but they do blow their caps off from time to time. You will all have to help me drink them before they become even more alcoholic.'

The drinks were delicious, and more potent than Clara had expected.

Clara could feel Giles moving in the chair beside her to look at her, and when she turned he was disturbingly close. 'Perhaps we should have had ginger ale,' he said, looking at her lips. She looked at his dark eyes.

'Maybe we should take a walk, burn off some of that potent cider first,' she said, smiling. 'Anyone else?'

No one seemed to want to move but Giles stood up. 'I'll get your jacket,' he said. He returned with her velvet coat – the housekeeper must have fetched it down. It smelled of cedarwood and faintly of mothballs and had a fur collar.

'As if we were going to a theatre,' she said, and laughed, wrapping it around her. It was warm and comforting, but from another age, when she wouldn't step into boots to walk around the garden but don silk stockings and elegant heels for London pavements. He looked smart, too, with his uniform coat and turned-up collar, cap at a rakish angle. 'It's not even cold.'

'We'll impress the sheep,' he said, catching her under the elbow with a warm hand and guiding her towards the front door, 'and it's cooling down already.'

'Don't go far,' Mrs Goddings warned. 'And here's a torch, Miss Clara, you know what those steps are like.'

'We'll be visible to the deer,' she said, standing in the doorway. 'They might want revenge for their fallen comrade.' A black and white mask retreated into the shrubbery, a badger waiting for them to go.

Giles took her hand as they walked past the parked cars on the drive, down through the formal gardens that led to the road. They could see for miles over the moor, the grass almost black now, a single car with dipped headlights progressing slowly over a road miles away. The moon, filling up, hung overhead, touching the tors with silver light, a few stars coming to life. 'I missed this,' she breathed before Giles's head blocked the view of the sky. His kiss was warm, his moustache tickled – she pulled back, laughing. His arms pulled her closer.

'I want you, Clara,' he said, and she let him kiss her again.

He was so warm and familiar and alive, she couldn't help but respond to him.

She caught her breath, and pushed him a little away. 'That's very flattering, but...'

'I don't just mean I want you. I want to marry you.'

She froze, confused. 'Now is not the time...' she said. 'Giles, we're in the middle of a war.'

'Tell me why this isn't the *best* time to get married?' he asked. 'I could be dead next week, you the week after. Can't we take what happiness we can?'

His arms tightened but she held him off. 'Giles, I don't know. There... there's someone else.'

He caught a breath, loud in the silence. 'Someone serious?'

'No. I mean, he's a friend. A close friend. A colleague.'

He let go and looked over the moor. She caught a flash of his vulnerability, the softness beneath his facade. He was so vibrant, so alive, and he made her feel weak. The thought that he could die at any time was terrifying.

'We're alike, you and I,' he said, eventually. 'Adventurers. Travellers. We're doers, not quiet people. I know my father would love me to marry one of our neighbours' daughters. They would chair local charities, help manage the estate, have half a dozen children.'

'You'd be bored to death,' she said, without thinking.

He turned to her, and she leaned towards him. His kiss was intense this time. She forgot the moustache, their bantering, and hugged him close.

'You wouldn't bore me,' he said, fiercely.

'No, I'd argue with you. I'd drive you mad,' she said, smiling in the darkness.

'Sleep with me,' he asked, shaking her a little by the shoulders.

'Where?' she said, laughing a little. 'In my childhood bedroom, or in the guest room you're sharing with Leonard?'

He huffed out a little vapour. 'Another time. A hotel.'

She caught the lapel of his coat and he placed his warm hand over her chilly fingers. 'Despite all evidence to the contrary, I'm not that sort of girl.'

'I know you're not. But surely, nowadays, you could spend the night with your fiancé?'

She could feel the pull to him, the simplicity of the equation. But if she got engaged – or married – to Giles, every question with William would remain unanswered.

'I'm not ready,' she answered. 'I'm not being demurely missish, I'm just not sure. I'm fighting in this war, too.'

His eyes glittered as he looked at her. 'If we were engaged, I'd have a say in that, too.'

'You'd try and ground me,' she said, letting him kiss her once more. 'And I'd try and ground you, too.'

That made him pull back, at the thought that she might have a say over his service. 'I have to fly,' he said, sighing a little. 'But this war can't last forever.' He swept a hand over the curls that were flopping into her eyes. 'If we both survive – would you marry me then?'

She thought about the simplicity of it. A man of her class, her upbringing, her experience and with her passion for flying. 'I might,' she said.

'I'm asking if you love me,' he said.

She looked at his profile against the jagged outline of the moors ahead, and for that moment, she did. 'Maybe. Give me more time,' she breathed, before he kissed her again.

21

PRESENT DAY, JUNE

Ruby had loved meeting Mabel, who was kind and enthusiastic. She and Jake found they had a lot in common, as they chatted while wandering around the churchyard. Dogs not cats; Italian food over burgers; they had both studied history at university. Driving back to the city late on Sunday, she felt a pull towards Montpelier House and its people. Jake had already taken Mabel back to London, and the house had felt dark and empty with just Pony and Max in it. She hadn't realised how much their lights were starting to dim. They seemed shadowy when she had left, at one with the whispering ghosts.

She had an appointment with the solicitor, Mr Salcombe, on Monday morning at his office in the city.

'Miss St John. I'm so sorry again for your loss.'

'Mum – my mother mentioned speaking to you a few months ago.'

'I was trying to get her to write a proper will and testament,' he said, making a face. 'I couldn't persuade her to, but she said her intentions were noted down in one of those internet wills. I was hoping you had found it?'

'No,' Ruby said, surprised. 'I was hoping you had found a copy, and that's why you wanted to see me.'

'I wish I did,' he said, pressing his fingertips together. 'At the moment we have notified our intention to apply for probate. As her only child, you would be Fiona's natural heir, but there are a few things we need to ascertain before applying.'

Ruby frowned. 'I am her only heir, aren't I?'

'That's not the issue,' he said. 'The problem comes from further back. Marissa left her entire estate to your mother, who was the only child of her unofficial partner, Alice. At the time, there were no other claimants or possible heirs excluded, but I can tell you, the will was drawn up very inexactly. Not by a solicitor.'

'What do you mean?'

'It all goes to you unless someone challenges Marissa's will. If Clara had a biological heir we didn't know about' – he looked away – 'theoretical heirs should have been explicitly debarred, but Marissa just willed the estate to Fiona. It was accepted because no one else came forward. But now... there seems to be an heir.'

Ruby felt sick with anger, clenching her fists in her lap. 'Someone has come forward? I understood they weren't going to make a claim.'

'When we notified our intent to apply for probate on your behalf, you were given a case number. Any enquiries are automatically attached to your claim, and I was told straight away that someone had been noted as a *possible* claimant, attached to the file by Jake Haydon.' He looked down at his notes. 'Are you aware of this?'

Ruby was shaking, looking down at her hands. 'I have met Mr Haydon. He came to the funeral, he'd been talking to my mother, apparently. He thinks Mabel Player is Marissa's great-granddaughter.'

'Is she? We ought to know, if we're going to protect your inheritance.'

She shook her head, more in denial, as she answered. 'She might be. We found a Miss C. St John who gave birth to a baby girl in March 1944. I've ordered the birth certificate – we think the baby might have been my aunt.'

'Well, I have the copy of Marissa's will – which was granted probate at the time – so we can start with that. It's unlikely to be overturned – the authorities hate to declare they made a mistake. But there is one other issue.'

She looked up, aware that her eyes were welling up. 'Go on.'

He pulled a couple of tissues out of a box on his desk. 'We do need to talk about death duties, inheritance tax, especially if you are the only heir.'

Ruby nodded, but had to dry her cheeks, still staggered that Jake hadn't warned her he had applied to challenge the will with Mabel. Mr Salcombe carried on talking, but she couldn't concentrate. She interrupted him.

'Can you just give me the bottom line?' she begged. 'This is all difficult.'

'Of course.' He grimaced. 'I'm afraid the government will tax your inheritance quite heavily.'

She knew there would be some tax, but his tone was terrifying. 'Is there any money at all? I know Mum paid death duties when she inherited from Marissa.'

'Fiona was left a good sum which mostly covered the tax, although she had to sell a few other assets for help pay for it. Unfortunately, your mother hasn't left *you* very much money. It did worry her once she realised she was going to' – he cleared his throat – 'pass away. But the house, contents and grounds are worth a considerable sum, and that should leave you a decent sum of money when the estate is settled.'

'But I *have* to sell the house? How much is this tax bill going to be?'

He managed a sad smile. 'We don't know, and I don't like to just guess before the house and contents are valued, but I suspect it will be something between four and six hundred thousand pounds.'

Ruby's breath caught in her dry throat. 'Half a million pounds in *tax*?'

'Maybe. It could even be more, depending on the contents, but I don't think it could be much less. It's a large estate, even if the house is in poor condition.'

'Lose it?' The tears came quickly, scalding down her face. She helped herself to a few more tissues and buried her face in them. Distantly, she heard him walk to the door and call his secretary for tea. She was shivering with shock; she had spoken about selling but had never really believed that she would have to. Even with a damaged roof, the house must be valuable and it sat on several acres of gardens. It would probably end up as a hotel, or a wedding venue. The idea made her cry even more.

'It's too early to say,' he said soothingly, patting her shoulder as he passed her on the way back. 'Your mother thought that it might be possible to raise enough money from specialist auctions, of paintings and photographs, to at least pay some of the tax. You will be allowed some time to pay, if you wanted to keep the building. But it sounds like it needs a lot of repairs.'

'There's nothing of any real value,' she said, mopping her eyes and blowing her nose. 'I'm sorry, it was just – a shock.'

'Of course. When she was told there was no more treatment available, we talked it all over. I couldn't persuade her that she needed a properly drawn-up will, although she did get a few valuations done.'

'Valuations?'

'There are some sketches in the family rooms, a few antique pieces and especially the painting in the drawing room of the baby. It would be useful to know more about it, especially the sitter.'

'The baby...' It was the one thing she couldn't imagine selling. She had always been there, smiling serenely from her hay bale seat in the doorway of the stable, with the birds flying in the blue sky above. 'I always thought that was Clara... Marissa's daughter. But there's some doubt now.'

'If it is,' he said, 'it might give it added value.'

'Jake – Mr Haydon – thinks it might be of her child, Mabel's mother.'

Mr Salcombe looked interested. 'Adoption might negate her claim.'

'We think she was adopted in America. Does that make any difference?'

He was scribbling notes. 'Possibly. I can find out. If this baby is Clara's child, who was her father?'

'I think she was engaged – informally anyway – to Giles Ashton-Wilson, RAF hero.'

He made another note in his florid handwriting. 'But illegitimate? Is it possible for you to contact his family? It might be easier for them to talk to you than through a lawyer's letter. Sometimes these issues are quite delicate, but I'm happy to write if you prefer.'

She tucked the tissues up her sleeve and looked straight across the desk. 'No, I'd like to do it. You know I'm a genealogist?'

'Your mother did say. I assume you might be able to make contact discreetly, as he was a friend of Clara's. He might even have acknowledged a child at some point.'

'Doesn't that make you wonder why he didn't take the baby? Or his family?'

He shrugged. 'Nothing families do surprises me any more. It sounds like an intriguing story. While Mr Ashton-Wilson may not have acknowledged a child, he may still have known about one, and the identity of her mother. That would give us more context.' He smiled at her, a little sad. 'Who knows? He may have made financial provision for the child himself. We'll keep in touch, if that's all right? I have your email address. It's quite a mystery.'

'What else do I have to do?'

His secretary brought in a tea tray. 'I will send a surveyor to see you, who will value the house and possessions. He's an auctioneer, too – he has a good sense of what something would be worth at auction, rather than what it might make on the open market. It's best if the valuation is as low as possible for the tax. He might be able to advise you if there is any chance of saving the house, should you want to try.'

As she took the cup, she could feel tears bubbling up again. Ruby had never felt so connected to the house, now she was almost certainly going to lose it.

22

The war became relentless. Month after month of missions, trying to get back to her quarters, trying to get back home for a few snatched days. Christmases were missed, birthdays overlooked. Going on a training course to fly larger planes was a welcome change.

Clara leaned her head on her hands and looked at the jumble of numbers in front of her. *One hundred and sixty-five gallons of fuel,* she jotted down again, *at top speed of three hundred and sixty miles per hour...*

'Still working on that last question?' a voice came in her ear. She jumped.

'Will!' She looked around and smiled. Everyone else had finished and gone for lunch. 'What are you doing here?'

'Same as you,' he said, as she stood up and hugged him. 'Practising to pass my exams first time so I can move on to four-engine planes.'

'I'm still on Spitfires,' she said, moodily. Suddenly, she saw the answer to the question and sat down to scribble the workings on the corner of the sheet. 'Sixteen minutes of direct flight in combat,' she said, triumphantly.

'The calculation formula is exactly the same on the next paper, just different planes.' He sat on the corner of her desk, holding an unlit cigarette in his hand. 'Come and get some lunch.'

'If you tell me what you aren't telling me.'

'I'm finishing up my ATA training, the same as you,' he said, grinning, his top button undone. 'Because I'm joining the air force.'

'The RAF finally believed you were two per cent Canadian?'

'No,' he said, his smile slipping. 'The US Air Force is on its way. I'm joining the advance guard of the Eighth Air Force at RAF Grafton Underwood.'

'Because of Pearl Harbor,' she said, looking up at his tense face. She remembered seeing the photographs of burning and sinking ships in the harbour. The headlines had screamed: OVER TWO THOUSAND DEAD, BRITAIN DECLARES WAR ON JAPAN. It felt like the war would never be able to end now. 'I read about it. It was dreadful.'

'Well, we needed to come into the war sooner or later,' he said, tapping the cigarette on the desk and putting it between his lips. 'How else are you going to win?'

She stood, batted him with her bag, and followed him out into the sunlight. 'I don't like the idea of you being shot at.'

'My job looks like it will be flight training and teaching map-reading,' he said. 'England's a lot more crowded than most of America. And it's covered with airbases, with more to come. We're building our own so we don't get in the way of the RAF.'

'Will you fly joint missions?'

He offered the cigarette to Clara, and when she shook her head, lit it for himself. 'If we're going to dominate Germany the way it's hitting Britain with the Blitz, we have to,' he said, his voice sober. 'Those civilians won't know what's hit them.'

'Like Londoners are suffering with the bombing,' she reminded him.

'I know two wrongs don't make a right,' he said, and they walked together towards the dining hall. 'But we have to keep Germany on the back foot. Anyway, I'll be training them. But I might also go up as fighter support for bombing missions.'

She thought of Giles, who was up there every day, flying the powerful but temperamental Spitfires alongside other fighters. 'I don't want you fighting,' she said, the words coming out involuntarily. 'I have too many friends up there already.'

'It's a war. Wouldn't you fight, if they would allow you to?'

Shoot down the Luftwaffe planes shrieking over the countryside? The thought was terrifying. 'If I had to. But we have pilots already trained to do that.'

'Not enough,' he said, his eyes shining. 'The RAF has already lost thousands of air crew.'

'I couldn't bear it if you were shot down,' she said, catching his free hand. 'Will, you'd be a brilliant tutor. You've got so many flying hours, in so many planes.'

He turned to look at her. He was standing so close she could have kissed him, but she held back. He put out the cigarette. 'If I had someone to stay on the ground for...' he said, in a low voice.

She looked away. 'You have someone to *live* for back in Wisconsin. Not to mention your family, your friends.'

He put his hands on her shoulders and turned her towards him. 'I told you. We called it off until after the war, and then, maybe I'll want to marry someone else. You, for example.'

'Does she know about me? Does she know you're thinking like that?'

He smiled. 'Of course she does. I've always told May everything. And she's off nursing, who knows if she'll be interested in me once she's been working with all those handsome doctors.'

'*Would* you stay out of combat – for me? If I asked?'

His expression changed. 'Would you give up flying for the ATA? Stop delivering shot-up, broken planes halfway across the country for repairs or scrap?'

'It's different. They aren't likely to invade America,' she said. 'This is my country, this is all I can do to save it.'

'Fight to the end,' he said, 'like Mr Churchill promised.'

She stepped closer. 'Please, Will. I couldn't bear to lose—' *Both of you. Either of you.*

He touched his lips to hers gently, and she closed her eyes.

'I couldn't bear to lose you, either,' he said, 'but you keep picking the damaged planes that say "one landing only" or "keep speed under two hundred".'

'I'm still here,' she joked, opening her eyes. 'It turns out I can land most things.'

'Until the one you can't,' he said, looking deep into her eyes. 'Clara, if we did get married, would you give up flying for me? Do something else useful?'

'If we married, would *you*?' she asked.

'It's not the same,' he said, pulling away.

She stared at him. 'It's *exactly* the same.'

23

Ruby had settled into a new normal. Work four long days in the city, then go back to the house for long weekends to look after Pony and Max, and focus on sorting out the house. Every room was packed with stuff, that had all meant something to someone but now was just damp and dusty. It was a relief to come back to her job after the summer.

Ruby sat opposite her colleague Lissa at the coffee shop in the corner of the building. It had been a long shift but exciting, with a new collection of poetry papers being donated to the archive. It was time-consuming to start cataloguing while the collection room was full of people researching everything from the history of tea strainers to a famous unsolved murder.

'I thought you'd be in a rush to get home to Arlo and Jono,' she said, placing a large latte next to Lissa.

'No. I want to enjoy the quiet, and tank up on caffeine for the evening,' Lissa said, reaching for her cup. Ruby smiled, looking around at the crowded café.

'I thought Arlo didn't cry much,' she said.

'No, he hardly ever cries, but it's so much work making sure he doesn't,' Lissa said, resting her head on one hand. 'And now he shouts, and laughs at everything. It's lovely but it's all the time.' She took a sip of the coffee. 'He's adorable, don't think I'm complaining. He's the best thing in the world, but it's so full-on.'

Ruby felt a tug of something in her stomach. 'It sounds amazing,' she said, her voice coming out soft. She and Oliver had just started planning their future, a future in which he would move into her flat, and maybe they would get a puppy, and then think about having a baby... It felt as if her whole future had disappeared when she ended it with him. Then she had been hit by her mother's illness.

'How's things going with your American?'

'He's not *my* American. He might be trying to steal my house for his client, Mabel.'

That made Lissa sit up. 'Wow. Really?'

'She might be able to challenge the will. Not Mum's, she didn't leave one, but my grandmother's.'

Lissa grasped her wrist and squeezed it for a moment. 'I'm sorry. It sounded like he was a nice guy.'

Ruby bit the head off the complementary gingerbread man she had been served. 'He is a nice guy,' she mumbled through the spicy crumbs. 'I haven't seen him for a while.'

'Was he right about your pilot lady ancestor?'

'I think he is. Clara might be Mabel's grandmother.'

'Well, I hope they back off your house,' Lissa said, over a yawn. 'Listen to me, I should be in bed.'

'How is Arlo sleeping?'

Lissa leaned forward. 'Sunday night, he slept for six hours straight.'

Ruby saluted her with her cup. 'That's fantastic!'

'Of course, I spent the first hour making sure he was still breathing and woke up four times to check he was alive, so it wasn't *that* restful. Last night was as bad as ever, he woke up three times. He's nocturnal.'

Ruby laughed. 'It's progress.'

Lissa finished her drink. 'So, what are you going to do about this man?'

'Jake? I suppose I have to confront him, find out what he's trying to accomplish for his client.' She had been holding off because, honestly, she had enjoyed speculating about him. 'He's an heir hunter for a big law firm in London. I don't even know if Mabel has a legitimate claim.'

'He's working for her. But won't you have to sell it anyway? You told me it needs a lot of work.'

Ruby stared out of the shop window, at people hurrying past the steamy window as the light faded. 'I think I'll have to. There's no money, it needs so much to repair it, heat it. It's slowly getting more damp and mouldy. And there will be a monster of a tax bill.'

Lissa stood up. 'Poor thing. But hopefully you'll be able to pay off your mortgage and maybe have a bit of money in the bank.'

After they said goodbye, and Lissa had disappeared into the stream of people outside, Ruby sat thinking about the house. She had once been desperate to get away, but that was from Fiona and all the artists watching her, asking her questions, worrying about her. It was like having half a dozen parents. Going to university and then finding a job had been liberating but isolating. She wasn't sure how much of her longing for the house was wanting to somehow find Fiona. She dabbed her suddenly wet eyes with a tissue and walked towards the door. Her phone dinged with a notification of a voicemail – she'd been getting them for an hour but didn't want to check while Lissa was there.

It was from Jake. There were several of them. *We need to talk* seemed to be the main message.

Yes, Jake, we do. Not until she'd dealt with the upset at his treachery, but they'd lost contact over the busy summer.

There was a text message, from Pony. 'Call me now.'

She walked along the high street, waiting for Pony to pick up the house phone.

'There you are. Ruby, you need to come home.' Her voice was more cracked than usual, and high-pitched.

'Pony, what's up?'

'I don't know what to do,' Pony wailed. 'You have to come home.' Ruby had to duck into an alley to hear her clearly, away from the traffic.

'What's going on?'

'Max – Max fell over, he had a fall. And I can't wake him up, and the ambulance is supposed to be coming but it isn't here yet...'

'I'll call Foxglove Cottage, get Zosia or Leon to sit with you,' Ruby said, snapping out of her melancholy. 'Don't worry, Pony, just sit down, take a deep breath.'

'He just fell over,' Pony sobbed, several times.

'Listen. Is he breathing?'

Agonising seconds passed while Pony checked. 'I think so. He's snoring.'

'Do you think you can put him in the recovery position? On his side.'

'I know what it is,' Pony snapped. 'I did it in Girl Guides in 1949.'

'I'm going to call Zosia, then I'll call you right back.' She cut Pony off and called the bed and breakfast along the road. Leon answered and promised one of them would be there as fast as possible.

When Ruby called back, Pony was crying, gruff little sobs she had never heard before, not even when Fiona died. 'He's too heavy, Ruby Roo,' she said. 'I can't turn him onto his side.'

Ruby could hear the wheezing grunts that Max was making. Still alive, then. 'Leon will be right there. It's going to be all right Pony.'

She could almost feel a presence behind her, supporting

her. Maybe it was Mum. By the time she had got into the car
and started driving out of the crowded city streets, it was gone.

24

MAY 1942

Clara walked into the garden of Laburnum Cottage, her calves still sore from the heavy pedals of the massive bombers she'd been flying back for repairs, some of them American. She had spent a few nights in an airbase hostel for WAAFs. She had missed the luxury accommodation Mrs Landscombe provided.

'I'm back,' she called through the house.

'Come through to the patio,' called Faith, from a reclining steamer chair that looked Victorian. 'We're lazing about in the sun for a change.' She lifted a glass of what looked like home-made lemonade. 'We have elderflower champagne.'

Marjory handed her a glass, and moved up to the end of the garden bench where she had been lying on cushions with a book.

'No missions today?' Clara asked, as she smiled a thanks for the glass. It was cool and slightly sweet, with the sherbet lemon scent of elderflowers.

'I've been away for two days. Faith came home late last night after being debriefed by the RAF.'

'I got chased by a Messerschmitt,' Faith said, and Clara gasped. It had always been one of her fears.

'How? I mean, what did you do?'

'I think he was expecting me to lead him home, but he could see I wasn't trying to engage him. He got really close. I waved.'

Clara leaned forward, her heart beating unevenly. 'But he didn't attack? Why not?'

Faith shrugged, but Clara could see how pale she was, how she couldn't meet Clara's eyes.

Marjory stood, and patted Faith's hand. 'Well, maybe he was out of ammunition. Or was saving it to get back across the Channel. I'll get some elevenses, we have fairy cakes somewhere.'

Clara noticed tears trembling on Faith's lashes. 'You must have been terrified,' she said.

'It's funny, I wasn't scared up there, but I was so upset once I landed. The engineer who came to collect the plane had to steady me out of the cockpit.'

They sat back in silence. Clara could distinguish the scents of lilac, the tree branches bent with the masses of mauve flowers. Beside it, a white rose was already in bloom. A sparrow fluttered down to the bird table, followed by another. In the distance, the occasional landing or take-off from the aerodrome broke through the birdsong.

In front of them, an overgrown rosemary bush sat in the border, covered with bees. Most were from Mrs Landscombe's hives, but the occasional bumble bee added a lower note. With the buzz came a deeper sound further away, a mechanical drone.

'That's not one of our Spits. That sounds like a Mosquito,' Marjory said, as she returned with a plate of little cakes. 'Tea's on its way.'

Clara could hear the whine of the twin engines, the familiar tone of one of the planes she'd been flying on her course. 'It does sound like a Mosquito. What's it doing here?'

'They have a few at Bristol,' Faith said, sitting up. She

cocked her head to one side. 'Listen. That sounds – odd. Are we expecting a Mozzy today?'

They fell silent as they heard the plane circle the base. 'He's not on a good approach for the aerodrome,' Clara said, worried. 'One engine isn't right.'

She could hear the puttering of an engine running intermittently. They all stood, and turned towards the airbase. Clara could see one of their new Spitfires coming in from the factory to the ferry pool, but she couldn't see the Mosquito. The twin-engine plane, famous for being mostly made of wood by a pre-war cabinet-making firm, must be beyond the hedge, but it was flying too low to be visible beyond the trees.

'Maybe it's running out of fuel?' Marjory said. They walked down the drive and to the field leading down to the river. 'There!'

Clara could see it now, circling a long way south of the quiet river, which was just a few hundred yards across. The pilot appeared to be looking for somewhere to land but it was slow – too slow – and the plane wasn't level. As they watched, one propeller stopped and a wisp of smoke trained behind it.

He's going to crash,' Clara said, in a low voice. 'The marshes! He's looking for the soft ground.'

'Could he make the aerodrome?' Faith stood on tiptoes, as if that would help.

'No time. He's about to stall,' Clara said. In her mind, she could see the fields sloping down the floodplain that bordered the river. 'He's coming right here!'

The other engine screamed with effort, then stopped. The only sound left was the whistling of air over the plane. Clara was already running towards the river, and she could hear someone back at the house shouting to alert rescue services.

The elegant plane was now gliding up the course of the river towards a big patch of mud known locally as 'the bog'. Many fishermen had got stuck in it.

It passed her, the pilot hunched over his controls, heaving at the stick to try to avoid hitting nose first. It landed flat on its belly instead, skimming for a moment, but then the nose dug in and the plane slewed sideways a couple of hundred yards to a halt in a spray of black mud. In the distance, Clara could hear the jangle of one of the base fire engines, but the plane was still and there was no fire.

With a struggle to open the canopy – at least the pilot was alive – a tall figure in a bulky flying suit and parachute pack stepped out and onto the wing.

'Stay there!' Clara shouted, waving her arms. 'Don't try and walk on the mud!'

To start with he didn't seem to hear, but he noticed her and shaded his eyes.

'Don't wade ashore,' she bellowed, watching as he walked to the wing tip. 'It's too soft, you'll get stuck. Are you injured?'

'Just my pride,' he yelled back. 'Is that... Clara?'

'*Giles*?' She ran down the narrow shingle beach. 'What on earth... Why are you here?'

'I'm supposed to be landing at Eastleigh but the engine kept cutting out. Then I remembered the ferry pool here, but I ran out of fuel.'

'Thank goodness you did!' she answered. 'Is everything out, there's no chance of fire?'

'I don't think there's any fuel left,' he said. 'I must have taken a hit low on the tank.'

A local farmer was walking down to meet her, scratching his head. 'I don't know how we're going to get *that* out,' he said. 'Pilot all right?'

'He's fine. How can we get him back?'

The farmer came back with a stack of boards, kept by the dinghies in the makeshift boatyard nearby. Clara laid the first one onto the mud, leaned back for another, then laid a short track through to Giles on the edge of the wing.

While she was looking up at him, she threw the last one. 'You'll have to pick it up and hand it to me as we go,' she warned. 'I don't think any of these would take both of us.'

They slowly made their way back, him retrieving the boards which were stuck, which only gave up with a sucking squelch. By the time they had retrieved the half a dozen boards, Clara and Giles were spattered with mud. It didn't stop him taking her in his arms once they were on the stony beach. She reached up to kiss him, shaking.

'I'm so glad you're all right. I thought... I can't believe you're really here,' she said, stepping back and trying to regain get her composure. 'Let me take you to the house, get cleaned up. You can call your base.'

'I thought that was it for a minute,' he said. 'Then I remembered sailing here with the sea scouts when I was about twelve.' He looked a bit shaken, and she squeezed his hand.

'It was a brilliant landing.'

'Belly flop,' he said, grinning at her. 'I hoped you would be here,' he said. 'I thought it would be a long shot, you're always away. It might have been my last thought.'

She looked away, swallowed down the dryness in her throat. 'Just got back from flying heavy bombers,' she said, as they helped each other up the beach and onto the grass. 'American mostly.'

'We've been piloting back-to-back missions for several weeks,' he said. 'I was hoping to catch up with you sooner, maybe for a weekend.'

Faith walked up, shading her eyes to look at the plane. 'They'll never get that out of the mud in one piece.'

Clara introduced him to Faith, and they shook hands after he'd wiped his on his flying suit.

'Clara said she was living with women pilots.'

'Well, she didn't say *anything* about you,' Faith said. 'Nice landing.'

'For a crash,' he said, turning to look at the plane. 'I hope they can salvage it.'

Clara introduced Marjory, who shook his hand cheerfully. 'And you're courting Clara? You kept that quiet, girl.'

'We're not exactly *courting*,' Clara said. 'We're friends.'

'Come up for some tea,' said Faith. 'It's up the hill, Laburnum Cottage. We have cakes.'

'They're very kind,' Clara said. She was still shaking at the drama of the landing, and especially since she'd discovered it was Giles.

The fire brigade and an RAF truck had parked by a slipway into the mud.

'Thank you, but I'll come up later, if I can. I've got to sort out this plane first,' he said, waving to them all. As he walked over to the fire engine, a man carrying a first-aid kit stopped to talk to him, and got him to sit on the steps of the vehicle.

Marjory and Faith turned to look at Clara. 'Well!' Faith said. 'You're a dark horse. I thought there was an ATA pilot writing to you?'

'He does,' Clara said, walking back up the hill, brushing ineffectually at the black, stinking mud. 'So does Giles, from time to time.'

'Both just friends?'

Clara couldn't answer for a minute – the adrenaline of the crash was making her wobbly. 'They are both my friends,' she said, holding onto a gate halfway up the lane. 'But this war makes everything so intense and romantic, it affects my judgement.'

Neither girl asked any more questions, but Faith took her arm and helped her up the hill.

'Well, he's a brilliant pilot to bring a Mosquito down safely in the estuary,' Marjory said. 'I'll tell Lizzie to put another plate out this evening, in case he can stay.'

25

PRESENT DAY, SEPTEMBER

Ruby's phone pinged, and she pulled over. A message from Leon told her to head to the city hospital, instead of the house. He said Pony had gone with Max in the ambulance, who looked like he'd had a stroke but was starting to come round.

It took ages to find a space in the car park, jog through to accident and emergency and enquire about Max. She was directed instead to a side room, where she found Pony looking shrunken and white, lying on a trolley with an oxygen mask on.

Ruby dumped her bag on the floor and flew over to Pony, who pulled off her mask and reached up for her like a child, arms shaking.

'Oh, Ruby, what's happened to Max? No one will tell me anything.'

'I'll find out,' Ruby soothed, hugging her then sitting in a chair beside her, holding both hands. 'They are looking after him. What's happened to you?'

'He's not dead?' Pony said, leaning forward with such an anxious look in her eyes, Ruby shook her a little.

'Not dead. Pony. It's a stroke. Are *you* OK?'

'I might have fainted,' Pony confided. 'Max had a stroke

before, you know. He didn't want anyone to know but I get his tablets, so I saw. But it didn't give him any big problems, except he gave up welding.'

Ruby's breath caught in her throat. 'He never said a thing! Are there any more secrets?'

Pony leaned back against the pillow, her clawed hand in Ruby's. 'I know he's a grumpy old so-and-so, but he's my oldest friend. Now Fiona's gone, it's just you and him, you're my whole family.' The phone in Ruby's bag chimed again. 'Don't you want to answer that?' Pony asked. 'It might be something to do with Max.'

'I doubt it...' Ruby turfed out her bag to get to her phone. 'No... it's Jake.'

'That man who visited with the American lady? The one who kept looking at you?'

'Yes, well, it turns out he was also looking at my house for his client – and perhaps he's putting in a claim to help her inherit it.' She looked away. 'He's looking into it for her.'

Pony squeezed her hand. 'They seemed like nice people.'

'You thought they were after the house from the beginning,' Ruby reminded her.

'You should ask what he's doing, though,' Pony said. 'Maybe he can explain.'

A nurse came in with a cup of tea for Pony. 'Hi. We're just looking after Penelope here after she felt faint in the waiting room.' She explained to Ruby. 'Are you her – granddaughter?'

'Close enough,' said Ruby, eyes misting up again. 'She's lived in my house my whole life.'

'Well, if you don't mind waiting outside, we're just going to run a few tests and do a chest X-ray, then you can come right back in.'

'Ring Jake,' Pony said, her voice muffled as the nurse put the oxygen mask back on her.

'Oh, all right,' Ruby said, pretending to be cross. She was

beginning to get a bit curious herself. 'I'll be back in a few minutes with all the news.' As she passed the nurse, she asked, 'Where can I find out about the gentleman who came in with Pony – Penelope?'

'Ask at reception,' the nurse said, pointing through the curtains to the front door. 'I think he's having a scan. You've got about ten minutes for the X-ray – we want to be thorough, she's a little out of breath.'

Ruby stood outside with a group of people on their phones, a few crying, one sitting down looking stunned. She felt much the same. Pony and Max, absolute staples of her life, both collapsing on the same day – it didn't bear thinking of the house empty, just the past drifting around the rooms, misting up the windows. Maybe she should just let it go, make it Mabel's problem...

For a moment, the knot of anger she'd been feeling was red hot. She took a deep breath and returned the call.

He answered straight away. 'Hello, Ruby.'

'I haven't got much time, I'm dealing with a medical emergency.' She had meant to be cool, professional, but it all slid away in her fear for Max and Pony. Tears caught in her throat. 'I met with my solicitor. Why are you trying to steal my house?'

'I'm not!' he said. 'I simply contacted the probate service to check on whether there was a will. I was just doing due diligence on Mabel's behalf.'

'But now they think she's an heir!' she stuttered. 'M-my solicitor had the information when I went in to see him!'

'No, it's not like that, it was the only way – I had to say I was representing someone who might be family in order to find out more about Clara and the baby. There's a special case number—'

'My case number,' she snapped back. 'For *my* family!'

'Yes, I realised that, I'm sorry about the confusion. Ruby,

you said there was a medical problem?' His voice sounded so concerned, it made her even more angry.

'You're the bad guy here,' she said, her voice breaking. 'I thought I'd found a friend.' She had never wanted to say anything like that, but somehow the words kept tumbling out. 'I liked you.'

'I liked you, too, which is why I would never hurt you,' he said, his words stronger. 'So, what's wrong? Who's ill?'

She wiped her eyes. 'Max had a stroke,' she said in a small voice. 'Pony found him, now they are running tests on her, too.'

'How bad are they?'

It was hard keeping the anger stoked when tears kept breaking through. 'I don't know. They are running tests. I have to go.'

'Ruby, let me explain. I simply enquired about the probate – which linked me to the case automatically. Mabel's not making a claim, she just wants to know who her mother was. We both want you to keep your house.'

'Well, I won't be able to,' she said, the tears starting to fall. 'Because I'll owe so much tax I'll have to sell anyway. I don't know where Max and Pony will go, even if they are all right. I don't have room.'

'I'm coming down,' he said, his voice strong and warm through the phone. 'Which hospital?'

'You can't just turn up! And I don't need your help.'

'You don't need it, but I want to help. They are your family, Ruby. You've already lost too many people this year.'

It was exactly what was whirling around in her head, and she was so grateful that he understood it. 'Don't come down. I'll call you in an hour, let you know how they are getting on.' Another wave of fear that neither would make it hit her.

She walked back into reception and asked about Max, afraid to find out what was happening. The news was better than she thought; the scan revealed a mild stroke and he would be moved to the ward soon for treatment.

'Ruby?' Leon was standing behind her, his arms open for a hug. He was the safest, most comforting person she knew. 'Are you OK? How's Pony?'

'Having tests,' she said, pulling away to be handed some tissues. 'I can't bear to lose either of them, but *both* of them...'

'Pony was fine this morning, this is probably shock,' he said, soothingly. 'And Max is being very well cared for.'

'And Jake...' She couldn't believe she had blurted it out.

'You really like Jake, don't you?' It wasn't a question really. 'I saw how he looked at you in the church.'

'I do. But he's...' His very reasonable explanation had started to sink in. 'He's acting for Mabel. She can have the house,' she said bitterly, 'then *she* can pay the bloody taxes.'

Leon rested his warm hands on her shoulders for a moment. 'It's always like this, after a death,' he said, his voice calm. 'But it all gets sorted out, in the end. This is grief, Ruby, everything is magnified. Fear, sadness, anger.'

She looked up through watery eyes. 'I shouted at Jake.'

'He'll understand. He lost his mother, too, didn't he?'

That was it for Ruby. She sank into a seat and sobbed.

26

MAY 1942

Giles was just in time for supper, washed and changed into his RAF uniform. Mrs Landscombe met him formally in the hall, the girls far less formally.

'It's lovely to have a cockerel in the henhouse,' Marjory said happily. 'Come and sit down in the living room. We've all dressed up for you, come and compliment us.'

He smiled at Clara, making her heart jump a little. 'You all look very nice. I don't know very much about fashion; most girls are in uniform these days.'

'I made this shorts and top set myself,' Faith said, and did a little twirl.

Clara tucked her arm into his and led him to the sofa. 'What we really want to know is, how's the plane?'

'They got it out of the water with a crane from the boatyard,' he said. 'The engines were underwater as the tide came in, but the rest floated for a while. They did used to call it the wooden wonder. I'm sure they'll be able to salvage it.'

It was a constant joke that the ingenious plane builders had made planes out of wood destined for fine furniture, but they really were lovely to fly and very effective. 'Is it really the fastest British plane?' Clara asked.

'It's fast. and it feels even faster,' he said. 'It's got a huge amount of power but it's so light. It glided very well, even when I lost the second engine. Thank goodness for all that mud.'

'I heard one engine fail from here,' Clara said as Marjory and Faith excused themselves to lay the table in the dining room.

'The second one stopped as I lined up with the river,' he said 'I didn't even get a bruise. I'm so grateful... I thought that was it for a moment.' He stared at her. 'All I could think was that if I was going to die, I'd be near you.'

'You idiot,' she said, though tears had sprung into her eyes. 'And if you'd landed over the last couple of days, I'd be out on deliveries. I'd much rather you didn't die at all.'

He took her hand. 'You remembered what I said.'

'And you remember that I said when this war is over, we'd talk.'

'Well, I can't see the point of waiting. Not if we're going to fly hundreds of missions. I'd rather get married now, just in case.'

'Please,' Clara said. 'I don't want to talk about it...' With Giles's long fingers holding hers, his disturbing presence making her falter, she couldn't think straight. *He nearly died.*

'Can we meet up?' he asked, standing up, pulling her with him. 'Please, Clara, hear me out. In private, somewhere.'

'I don't know...' William's face popped into her head, as it often did. 'There might be someone else.'

'That you like. You said that before.'

'That I have some affection for, he's a friend. More than a friend.' She could hear the girls moving into the dining room, calling her name. 'We ought to go.'

His fingers dug into her arm; it was both uncomfortable and exciting. 'What I feel is not *affection*,' he murmured, close to her ear. 'I don't want to just be your *friend*. I want you, Clara. I love you.'

She could feel her heart beating so fast she thought it must be visible. 'It's a strange time,' she said in a low voice. 'Everything is exaggerated. You could have died today. I could...' She struggled to keep her voice steady. 'I could have watched you die today.'

Marjory called again to say dinner was ready and Clara turned to the hall door. Mrs Landscombe was looking back at her. 'Come, my dear,' she said.

Clara managed a smile. 'Yes, let's eat. Everything will seem more normal after some food.'

Mrs Landscombe had called a neighbour who had a spare bed for Giles. Perhaps her landlady had seen how emotional they both were, had recognised that Clara wouldn't be able to ignore the tension between them. He couldn't stay on the sofa – she would never sleep. They said goodbye on the doorstep instead, formally, politely, and he walked into the darkness.

'Oh, he left this...' Marjory handed her the cap Giles had left on the coat stand. Clara ran down the gravel path in her bare feet to catch him by the gate, and fell into his arms. It was heaven to kiss him, it was so simple, they would marry and be together always...

It wasn't until they pulled apart that the world rolled back over her.

'You will be much more careful?' she whispered to him, breathing in the scent of his uniform, feeling the soft stubble on his cheek. 'If you make it through – if we both do – we'll talk about it, but I can't think about it now.' She looked up at his dark silhouette, the gleam in his eyes. 'I do love you, Giles. I really do. But I have a job to do as well. I can't just give it up—'

His arms tightened around her until her ribs ached. 'I know, I know. You're a pilot too, and this is a war we have to win.'

'Or die trying,' she breathed and he kissed her again.

'We have to survive,' he said, holding her. 'So we can make a great life together.'

'I'm not sure I could leave my mothers completely behind,' she warned, a tug in her heart at the thought of leaving the moor.

'I know,' he said.

After a long moment, she pulled away. 'You have to go. Up the lane to the top, then turn right. It's next to the church.'

'Will I see you before I go back?'

She shook her head. 'I have a job tomorrow right after dawn. I should be getting some sleep, it's a long mission.'

He kissed her swiftly. 'Fly safe.'

'You too.' She could barely let go of his arm. He turned and walked away, a small patch of gravel illuminated by his shuttered torch.

Slowly, the real world settled on her like dust. Life on the moor, the possibility of William flying combat missions, the sheer number – and condition – of the planes she was flying... Soon it would be autumn, mists over the airfields, clouds, rain. Flying wasn't even the problem, it was always the landing.

And with Will, and with Giles, the problem wasn't soaring in their arms. It was imagining coming back to earth.

27

PRESENT DAY, OCTOBER

Ruby helped Pony out of the car. Despite her treatment and a few days in hospital, she looked far from well, her skin parchment white and her hands shaking.

'I 'aven't slept for days,' she confided to Ruby. 'And I couldn't eat their food. I just wanted to get home.'

'And now you are,' Ruby said. She'd changed Pony's sheets and realised how dirty they were, how hard it had become for her to manage laundry and cleaning. There was now a stack of clean clothes in her chest of drawers and wardrobe, and the bed was freshly made and the curtains drawn back. But the stairs loomed over them both, looking like a cliff.

'I don't know if I can get up there yet,' Pony said. 'Let's have a cup of tea first, to give me a bit of energy.'

'I could always make up Max's bed for you,' Ruby said, dubious. 'Just while he's away.'

Pony laughed, a tired little cackle, as she moved along the hallway, bracing herself on the dresser and the coat stand.

'It's a long time since I was in Max's bed!' she said.

'Were you ever?' Ruby said. 'I mean, were you ever a couple?'

'Not really,' Pony said, putting a hand on her chest. 'Oh, lovey, I'm so out of breath, I need a rest.'

'I can get you a chair...'

'No, let's just go in the kitchen.'

Pony sat in Max's wing chair and closed her eyes. The room was cold, and without the spark of people living in it, it seemed dark. The shadows were deeper today, the presence of whispering spirits close by. 'I'll put the kettle on.'

'It's getting closer to winter now,' Pony said, making her jump. 'We're all starting to die.'

'It was an infection, that's all. You'll get better.' Ruby ran some water but it didn't warm up. 'I'll relight the boiler.'

'It's falling to bits,' Pony said. 'It's all dying at the same time.'

The boiler did light after a few attempts, and roared into life. Ruby looked up at it. The engineer always marvelled that it survived each service, and warned that parts were becoming scarce for the decades-old machine. *Like Pony, like Max.*

'They took me to see Max yesterday,' Pony said, as Ruby put cups out and the kettle started hissing. A movement out of the corner of her eye made her jump. More mice. 'He looked proper ill. White as them hospital sheets.'

Ruby thought of Max as she'd seen him in the hospital, silent as much from fear as from his stroke, lying still, sheets tucked in, not even letting her hold his hand. She hadn't been able to tell him anything cheerful, just that Pony had a chest infection but would get better. One tear had rolled down his face into the sheet.

'He is ill,' Ruby said, checking the fridge for milk. Fortunately, there was just enough for their tea. *I'll have to do an online order. And put the traps down.* 'But he's making progress. They've got him up on his feet, he's starting to eat a bit.'

'He's hardly been coping for months,' Pony said. 'He wets the bed sometimes. He can't get out quick enough.'

'He does?' Ruby was shocked at the state the two of them had got into. Before, she just trusted that with Fiona to look after them, that they would be fine and safe and there for ever.

'Maybe they won't let him come home,' Pony said with a dark tone. 'They'll put him in one of them homes, like the workhouse.'

'There's no such thing as a workhouse now, you know that.' Ruby filled up two mugs with hot water, then seeing how shaky Pony was even sat down, she poured a little out into the sink to make the mug less heavy for her. 'He might need to go into a special place for rehabilitation. To get him up and washing and dressing by himself.'

'They get you into those places, then you get worse, and you can't get out.'

Ruby stirred a spoonful of sugar into Pony's tea from the open bowl, hoping the mice hadn't been in that too. 'Their *aim* is to get him back home. They don't have enough beds as it is, that's why the hospital was a bit overcrowded.'

Pony watched her with bright, dark eyes, much like the mice. 'You'll go back to work soon and leave us on our own.'

Ruby had known she could not let Pony stay here by herself from the moment she saw her in hospital. 'I'm going to stay here for a while. My colleague is going to bring me loads of boxes of documents to catalogue and pack up for the archives. I'll have a good go at cleaning up the dining room, and perhaps we can put your bed down there. I know it will be awkward because Max will need to walk through it to get to the library—'

Pony cackled. 'It's not like he hasn't seen it all before,' she said.

'Yes, you said that. I'm trying to forget it.'

'Well, of course we slept together. There's really nothing else to do when you're snowed in, except work – and cuddle up. That was years ago, though. He was proper 'andsome then.' She looked down at her hands on the table. 'I'll miss my room. I'll miss my warm bathroom, I don't want to have a flannel wash in the kitchen like Max does.'

'Maybe we could put a stair lift in,' Ruby said, even as she knew it was useless.

'It's not worth it. You'll have to sell soon, anyway.'

'Maybe not for months, it could take a year,' Ruby said, thinking aloud. 'And it would help Max, too.' Max had smelled like compost for a few years, but recently he had been more acrid. 'He could have a shower.'

'You're beating a dead horse,' Pony said. 'We won't last much longer.'

Ruby tightened her fists. 'You're not giving up, not on my watch,' she said, through clenched teeth. 'I'm going to get some help, and we *will* bring your bed down.'

Leon and Zosia arrived with tools and cleaning supplies to help make the dining room into a bedroom. Their son, Krys, was put in charge of baiting and checking the live traps for mice, and caught three of the whiskery, boot-button-eyed rodents. Two of Zosia's friends turned up with children to help Krys, while they scrubbed the kitchen floor and work surfaces.

People talking and laughing reminded Ruby of her child-hood, the shadows driven away by the living. Leon dismantled the extra leaves on the huge table, and between them, they rolled up the carpet, releasing a thousand silverfish and woodlice, and clouds of dust. The parquet flooring underneath got scrubbed with wood soap and polished to a shine. The children were trusted with a biscuit tin full of grass for the mice, and to reset the traps.

Zosia brought a rug down from Pony's bedroom. 'We'll make it as much like home as we can,' she said.

Krys and his friends asked if they could release the mice.

'Careful on the road,' Ruby reminded them. 'You need to take them quite a long way.'

'I'll go with them,' Leon said, sneezing yet again. 'I could do with some fresh air. Then I'll help bring the bed down.'

Ruby was left with Zosia for a moment. 'I don't know what I'm going to do when I have to go back to town,' she confessed. 'They need carers.'

'We'll keep an eye on them. Carers are hard to come by on the moor, but Leon has a few contacts. We've borrowed a commode for night-times – someone will pop in and empty it, bring them a bit of food, when I'm not available. Come and help break down the bed.'

By the time Leon came back, Pony's Victorian metal bed was ready to bring down to the dining room.

'Should we help with Max's room?' Zosia asked.

'It's worse than Pony's,' Ruby confessed. Pony was right about Max's room – he'd been keeping people out for a reason.

Max's mattress was foetid, so Leon dragged it out in front of the house to get rid of it, and the carpet had been stained and bleached by Max's incontinence.

'I can't believe I didn't notice,' Ruby said, wiping her brow after rolling the carpet up with Leon. 'They always said they were fine. I feel terrible.'

Zosia put her head out of the door. 'I've just helped Pony to the loo, she could do with a lie-down now. All ready?'

'I'll bring her chest of drawers down in a minute,' Leon said, 'but Ruby's made the bed.'

'And I'll put the electric radiator on. She needs her antibiotics, too,' Ruby said. The ancient boiler had rattled a little warmth around the house to counteract the draughts, and once Pony was settled in bed, everyone retreated to the kitchen for hot drinks.

'She looks so tiny,' Zosia said. 'I always see her as such a strong person, but I haven't really noticed her out and about recently. What are you going to do?'

Ruby had been asking herself all day. 'I'm going to try and get a live-in helper,' she said. 'Or maybe visiting carers, just until—' She swallowed. 'Until she gets over her infection and is back to normal. She wasn't very mobile before – she used to go up the stairs on all fours and come down on her bottom. But she was much better than she is now.'

Zosia handed her a coffee, strong like she always made from a Polish recipe. 'You definitely have to sell?'

Ruby nodded, looking into her drink, hoping they didn't see the tears gathering. 'If I get probate – that's not certain – the death duties will be high. Mum didn't leave me any money. Even if I sell everything, I wouldn't have any money left over to fix the house up.'

Leon sat in the wing chair, and put his feet out in front of him. 'I'm shattered,' he said. 'But I think Pony is asleep, for now. She said she couldn't sleep in the hospital, it was too noisy.'

'Why isn't it certain you will inherit the house?' Zosia asked, sitting next to Leon and leaning against him.

'You remember Fiona was brought up by two mothers, Alice and Marissa? Well, she had a sister who died before she was born, who was Marissa's child.'

'Clara,' Leon said, 'who's got the big monument in the graveyard.'

'But *your* mum was Alice's child,' Zosia said.

'Well, Clara may have had a baby – we think she did, in 1944. When Marissa left the house to Fiona, she didn't exclude any other heirs. So Clara's child might have had a claim.'

Leon stared at her. 'There's another heir?'

'Possibly.' Ruby shrugged. 'Mabel Player, who you showed around the church. Jake's been making enquiries of the probate case, and he's now attached to the file as an interested party. My solicitor is investigating Marissa's will to try to get Mabel excluded.' She sipped her coffee. 'It's all nonsense, really. It's out of my hands and I'll have to sell anyway.'

'Maybe she could afford to take on the house, pay the taxes, fix the roof?' Zosia said.

Ruby thought about it but shook her head. 'Maybe – but that would mean the house would be Mabel's and I would still lose it. And that would make Max and Pony homeless. I can't expect a stranger to let them live here indefinitely.'

Leon raised an eyebrow and they waited.

'What?'

'I don't think the courts would overturn Marissa's will. And Jake and Mabel obviously like you,' Leon explained. 'They don't look like they're trying to steal your inheritance.'

'Maybe not.' She shook her head. 'But there's such a lot to do if I *do* inherit.'

'You still have the immediate problem of Pony and Max. Will your employers give you more time off?' Zosia asked.

Ruby looked out on to the yard. 'Maybe for a few more weeks if I work from home. I've got things I can do here,' she said, distracted by a chicken scratching under the raspberry sticks in the yard. 'I'll get the hens in.'

As she scattered grain inside their secure run, counting them in, she felt trapped. Trapped by this house, by her responsibilities, by the inevitable future where she would lose the two people she thought of as grandparents.

Tears came again. She had cried more over the last few days than she had over Fiona's death, but maybe some of the tears were for her mother, too. The wind lifted her hair off her collar, touched her shoulders as if in sympathy.

28

JUNE 1943

The next winter was difficult for flying, the weather wet and blustery. Spring came as a warm, dry surprise, perfect for flying multiple missions. Clara was competent on the first American fighters, powerful Mustangs, produced for the RAF. Except for their limited speed at high altitudes, she loved the sporty little planes as much as the Spitfires. The giant American bombers, the B-17 Flying Fortresses and B-24 Liberators, hugely powerful and normally flown by a whole team, were exhilarating and terrifying to fly in equal measure.

William was now training new pilots, doing intensive training of British pilots in American planes, and Americans in all planes. His letters had turned from chatty and friendly to warmer and emotional. He talked about the sadness of losing colleagues in combat or in accidents; he spoke with passion about the lakes and his parents' farm back in America.

Giles wrote too, but less frequently. He rarely spoke about flying but passed on news of mutual friends, and reported having stopped in at her mothers' house for a night on the way to somewhere. His words evoked a yearning for home that lasted for days, and a memory of his dark shape against the stars above the moors, the warm power of his kisses and the longing for him. But Giles wasn't the only one she loved, and she wasn't sure how she could love two men at once. She thought about Giles a lot, usually in the evening, whereas William she remembered in the sunshine.

She walked into the office with Faith. Marjory had sprained her ankle climbing out of a plane, so was on leave. 'I have a nice one for you,' the coordinator said. 'Just a short hop to Oxford with a shiny new Spitfire, and then take a slightly less shiny Blenheim back to Heston for repairs.' The Blenheim was a light bomber with a gun turret behind the cockpit, two engines but not overpowered. She'd flown one before. 'Faith, here's yours...'

Clara's heart skipped a beat. She might see William if he was available. She knew William was being deployed from Heston, a joint airfield with the RAF and USAAF

The Spitfire was a delight. She'd been instructed to fly high over cloud most of the way to Oxford, and she loved the approach to the city with its spires and mediaeval buildings. The Blenheim had had a heavy landing, and an engineer was still pulling shrubbery off the plane when she turned up for it.

'It's going to be a couple of hours,' he admitted. 'I don't know if everything is working, and I'm a bit suspicious about these machine gun holes.'

Clara had become quite knowledgeable about the anatomy of a range of different aircraft and where they could be seriously damaged, but she wasn't familiar with this type. 'I'll get some food, while you check it out,' she said, putting her kit bag over one shoulder and her parachute on the other. The ATA girls now had uniform trousers for flying, and they were both comfortable and flattering. She still carried a summer dress in case she could eat out or had to stay in a hotel.

She got almost to the hangars at Brize Norton, the mess building nestled between them, when someone hailed her.

'Clara!'

She turned and scanned the dozen or so people walking about. 'William? I thought you were at Heston.'

'I am, usually. I was hoping for a lift back.' He looked dapper in his blue uniform and he caught her up in a hug when he reached her. 'I hoped it would be you but I only get a glimpse at the ATA schedules now. Are you here for the Blenheim?'

'I am,' she said, staring at his regulation short hair, his cap tucked under his arm. 'You look like – such an American.'

'Well, I always was,' he said, laughing. 'Now I'm a sergeant airman as well.'

'Sergeant? It sounds like a soldier.' She couldn't stop staring at him, he couldn't stop gripping her hands.

'Well, technically I'm in the United States Army Air Force,' he said. 'Oh, I've missed you so much.' He pulled her towards him and she kissed him. There was no darkness in his kisses, just joy and love. 'Clara, you must marry me, you must,' he mumbled into her hair. 'I love you so much.' It reminded her of Giles's proposal.

Even remembering Giles's kisses felt wrong in William's arms, and she pulled away. 'The war, remember? We're going to think about us after the war.'

He took her parachute then held out his other hand for hers, and they strolled towards the mess. 'How's May?' she added. 'How's life in America now they are in the war?'

'Before I came here, I just assumed – we both assumed – that we'd pick our engagement right up when I got back. But now, with Pearl Harbor... She's changed. She's working at a hospital nursing some of the burns and explosion victims. She still writes, we both do, less often but longer letters.' He looked into her eyes. 'She's been my best friend since we were children. Now I can tell her stuff – things I couldn't tell anyone else.'

'Even about me?'

He lifted her hand up to kiss it. 'Even about you. But with you, I share something she would never understand.'

'Flying,' she said, smiling. 'It's still intoxicating.'

'Except that Blenheim,' he said, his forehead creasing into a frown. 'I'm not keen on you flying that.'

'But you're flying lots of American planes, that must be exciting. How are the Mustangs?'

'Great.' He smiled but dropped her hand to put both of his on her shoulders. 'Make sure it's safe, will you? I don't like the idea of you taking off and running into problems.'

'My friend had that problem,' she said, smiling at him. 'A bullet in the fuel tank, belly-flopped into the biggest mud patch in Hampshire. Saved the plane, too, at least for parts.'

'Was she all right?'

'*He* was, he's RAF.'

He put his head to one side. 'Is this your "friend"?'

She really didn't want to give him Giles's name. 'Can we talk about something else? I'm starving. How's the food?'

'Better since the Americans got here,' he said.

They ate well. She drank a couple of cups of tea and they exchanged news. She was able to rave about her accommodation in Hampshire; his barracks were less pleasant. 'But my rank gets me my own room,' he said. 'Which I know I will have to share soon, because we're running out of space.'

'And are you engaging with the enemy now?'

He made a face. 'I wish. I'm training our boys in everything from landing on your short runways, to etiquette and protocol with the RAF. But I hope to get into fighters to protect long-range bombers when we strike back at Germany.'

Her stomach suddenly felt heavy. Before she could say anything, they were interrupted by the engineer she had left with the plane.

'I can't find anything too wrong with it,' he said, tucking an oily rag into his pocket. 'It's got a bit of an oil leak but it's minor. You aren't going far.'

'Maybe I shouldn't give you a lift,' Clara said to William, and drank the last of her tea.

As the engineer walked away, William shook his head. 'If you're going down, I'm coming with you,' he quipped. 'It's not far, fifty miles. Half an hour, tops, with take-off and landing.'

She studied him. He had always looked too young to be flying, but now he had aged. Like everyone, the softness had been burned away by hard work and stress.

'I'm not going to crash,' she said, finally. 'I've even brought one down on a single engine before.'

'We could go out for dinner when we get there,' he said. 'Or we could stay in. I have my own room.'

She shook her head. 'Let's get the plane down first,' she said, smiling at him. 'Maybe we could go dancing, if there's time.'

Clara had never had a plane as difficult to fly as the injured Blenheim. It bucked constantly, as power either cut back or surged forward. Something was wrong with the fuel injection, she guessed, to the starboard engine. The other one seemed drastically underpowered.

'We should radio ahead,' he said.

'No radio, remember,' she said, wrestling to keep the plane level. The cockpit was cramped, the control column obscuring some of the instruments.

'What can I do?' he asked, his hands on the side of her chair.

'Sit back, check your parachute harness,' she said grimly. A glance at her watch and a quick look at the ground below, obscured by rags of cloud over the green fields, gave her an idea where they were. A smell of smoke made her look to the starboard engine. 'It's overheating,' she said unnecessarily. 'I'm going to have to put down. There's a map in my bag – we're over the Chilterns.'

He leaned over to see out of the cockpit, and even his movement made the plane lurch sideways. 'You're past Stokenchurch,' he said. 'Isn't there a good bit of road at Lane End? Long fields.'

She tried to remember. 'Yes, I noted it once before. Give me a heading.'

He did, and pointed out the road running towards Great Marlow. 'If the hay is very high, you'll crash.'

She smiled grimly. 'Most of the fields around here have had a first cut. I'm just worried about high wheat, or cattle.' The starboard engine was juddering now, making the plane shake and Clara's teeth rattle together.

She guided the plane lower, under the patchy cloud. The ground looked very hard and unforgiving – and uneven. She could see a little hill ahead – if she remembered correctly, there was a long stretch of grazing beyond. She prayed it wasn't full of animals... It was still going to be a short landing.

The starboard engine exploded at the same time as she realised the port engine was coughing.

'Oh, bloody hell!' she shouted, as much to herself. '*Brace!*'

29

PRESENT DAY, OCTOBER

Ruby had spent the last two weeks looking after Pony while working from Montpelier House. She had also become caught up in doing further research into her family tree for her own solicitor, to protect her inheritance. Pony had finally fought off the infection and was a little stronger now, though she still needed regular care. Volunteers from the local community were dropping in, enabling Ruby to get back into the office, though she'd return to Montpelier House each evening. Max had been moved to a care home in Plymouth for rehabilitation, but despite improvements in his mobility, he was wasting away.

In three hours' time she would have to go back to the house, with all its responsibilities and worries, but for now, she could focus on her work.

Lissa poked her head around the stacks, just as Ruby was trying to find a two-hundred-year-old will for a client. 'Someone to see you, Ruby.' Her eyebrows were raised, and she was making a face.

Ruby looked around the end of the shelves. 'Oh.'

It was Jake, in a smart suit, shiny leather shoes, neat haircut and black briefcase, and looking very much like he worked for a law firm. 'Could you spare me five minutes?' he said, formally.

'I suppose,' she said, handing the reference to Lissa. 'I think that has been misfiled under Bakewell,' she explained before stepping out. She was far less tidy: her hair was in need of a cut, she was wearing an apron to protect against the dust, and she was sure there were bags under her eyes. To add to all her other problems, Pony had started seeing ghosts and having night-mares, and Ruby had to go downstairs to the dining room several times a night to settle her. 'How can I help?'

'I've been studying documents from the time of Alice's death. Did you know Alice left everything to Marissa but in trust for your mother?'

She stepped back towards the office. 'I didn't know Alice had any money, to be honest.'

'Why wouldn't she? She was a famous society painter. Did you know she was commissioned to sail to New York a couple of times, to paint famous people?'

'I did.' Ruby was surprised. 'But how did *you* find that out?'

'American society newspapers loved her, even though they were scandalised by her relationship with Marissa.' He put his briefcase on a chair and pulled out a bulging folder. 'This was them in 1924.'

The picture was a newspaper quarter page, of a tall figure in a tailored suit which Ruby recognised as Marissa, with Alice on her arm. 'Wow. They were beautiful, weren't they?' Alice looked like a film star, her forehead covered with blonde curls and dressed in a long lace dress with an open back. 'They were so young.'

'I guess they left Clara at home with family.'

She couldn't get over the picture. 'Alice looks a bit like my mum, Fiona.'

'I suppose she would, as her mother. She looks a bit like you, too.'

She looked up at him. 'Mabel and I really are their grand-children,' she said, feeling it for the first time. 'We're all that's left.'

'I've been following the case. You're probably going to lose the house, even if you inherit,' he stated. 'I've looked into the tax you will have to pay. Your mother didn't leave you loaded, did she?'

'No,' she said baldly. 'By the time I've paid off all the bills, the funeral and so on, I'm broke. I'll have to sell the house and contents just to pay the tax. I don't have the resources to save it, to fix the roof, restore the original features. Does Mabel have that kind of money? If she is named as an heir, I mean.'

'Nothing like the amount she would need. She would be happy with a few mementoes; she never thought she would inherit the house.' He glanced at her. 'She's just so glad to have found her mother's family. At least, she will if she can prove it with a DNA test.'

Ruby didn't feel relieved, and the pressure settled onto her shoulders again. 'She wouldn't be able to keep the house either.'

He reached a hand towards her. 'I'm sorry about your house. This must be complicating things, your feelings about your mother.'

She stared at his hand for a long moment before taking it. 'I just miss her. My mother – living in the house reminds me so much of the life we had, before I ran away to college.'

'Your house has brought us together.' His hand was so warm, enclosing her shaking fingers.

She managed to smile. 'It has.' She sighed. 'Now it's just Pony and Max, dying in their own ways, in the place. My solicitor wants to get the valuation done, then put it on the market as soon as he is certain who owns it.'

'So I understand.'

She dropped his hand and shivered. 'It's hard to imagine

someone else buying it – maybe ripping it inside out to build flats or a hotel. It's a huge plot.'

'I know.' He looked away, out of her office window, over the square with a few sculptures and urban trees. 'The first time I saw the house, it felt like I was being invited in. By the place itself. It has been such a welcoming home for so long. It feels like it's full of people even when it's not.'

'I've always felt that way.' She patted a chair for him and sat down at her desk. 'My whole life, it's been like that. It sometimes feels like there are a couple of people whispering behind me, every time I'm doing something wrong.' She smiled. 'I used to hear a woman singing, when I was trying to go to sleep. Everyone said it must be Fiona but it happened even when she was out. I used to pretend it was Clara.'

'That's lovely. She didn't die there, though, did she? Isn't that how hauntings happen?'

She shrugged. 'I suppose ghosts could come back to places where they've lived. I don't know if I believe in spirits, but there was always that feeling at home. I think my mind created her to comfort me. I loved all the stories of her.'

'I'd love it if you told some of the stories to me.'

'I will, but not now.' She glanced at her phone. 'It's so late. I have to get going soon, I'm needed back at the house. Pony still can't manage by herself for long, and she falls over if she tries. Her infection really knocked her sideways.'

'So you're going back tonight?'

'I have to go back every night,' she said.

'Would you mind if I came with you? It's Friday – I don't have to be back in the office until Monday.'

She thought about her weekend, the visit she was dreading from the surveyors. 'I have some people coming tomorrow to value the house. An estate agent, an antique dealer and art expert, too. Do you want to help me with that?' She put her head on one side to look at him. 'I thought you were the enemy at first. I still only have your word for it that Mabel isn't going to go behind my back and try to steal my house.'

He shrugged. 'That's up to her, if she wants to try. But I really like you, Ruby. I don't want to lose you over your house.'

She looked into his dark eyes, feeling a pull towards him. 'I like you too,' she murmured. 'I hope to get our friendship out of this case, even when I sell. But what will happen to Pony and Max?'

'At some point you'll have to put your own needs first.'

She looked at him. He seemed so sincere. 'So, you *do* want to help me.'

'I'd be happy to. I thought I could at least be useful keeping Pony company and chasing the chickens out of the house.'

She laughed. 'Probably! But it would be good to have a catalogue drawn up of all the pictures and furniture for the auction.'

'Of your history.'

She nodded, her smile fading. 'Of my whole life,' she whispered.

30

JUNE 1943

For a moment, Clara felt like she'd fallen asleep in a peculiar position, but as pain spread from her forehead to her elbow, she realised she was lying on her side in the cockpit of a plane.

'Fire!' someone bellowed in her ear, and hands struggled with her webbing straps. She managed to unclip her parachute with one hand; the other one hurt too much. The creaking and a shot of cool air told her the canopy was being slid back. Fire. *Fire?* Panic made her heart race, her breath come short and fast.

She twisted, trying to pull herself up. The control column was folding into her stomach, she was pinned down. As she regained movement in her legs, she managed to slide under it. There was a smell of fuel and hot metal, but not smoke.

'Clara!' She recognised William's shouted voice, and he leaned over to help her from the outside. 'Get out, in case it catches.'

'I'm fine,' she said, wriggling some more, pushing up with her good arm. With a sharp additional pull from under her arms, she was free, standing on her seat. The plane was lying partly on its side. 'There's no fire,' she said, looking around, and finally at William. Apart from a trickle of blood from his nose and what looked like a swelling to one eye, he was standing and moving all four limbs. 'Let's get out...' The unthinkable could happen, an actual explosion, and her training kicked in.

The ground was close – she slid onto it and pitched forward onto her good arm, holding the painful one against her. The jolt when she landed made her feel faint and sick at the same time, a lightning bolt of agony shooting up into her shoulder.

'I guess we landed,' William said, staring at her, his uninjured eye wide. 'You landed us.'

'I guess I did,' she echoed, managing to kneel up. 'Where are we? I thought we were parallel to the road?'

'We were.' He looked back at the plane. 'But the wing came off – we spun into the hedge.'

The wing had exploded into a hundred pieces of wreckage around the fuselage, and there were painted metal fragments lying torn on the grass. 'But no cattle,' she said, gratefully.

The plane had ploughed into the soft bank and bushes, which had probably slowed them down.

She stood up with William's help, and checked all the switches were off. She didn't want a spark to catch any fuel. She looked down at her wrist, and supported it with the good arm. 'I think I broke it,' she said ruefully.

'Can you walk?' he said.

'Not on my hands, but my feet are all right,' she quipped, and finally he smiled.

'We're alive!'

He hugged her tightly, despite a muffled groan from Clara, trying to protect what felt like hot knives grating together in her forearm. 'At least we would have been together,' he mumbled.

She gently pushed him away. 'I would have settled for at least one of us surviving, thank you,' she said, trying to pull back her jacket sleeve without making the pain worse. The top few inches of her wrist looked purple and swollen. 'Get my bag, will you?' she asked.

'You're in a crash and you want your *bag*?' he said.

'Yes,' she answered, unable to explain. She felt so sick, the world was spinning enough that even a few feet away from the plane, she was struggling to keep her balance.

She grabbed a handy gatepost as he brought both their bags. 'In the top...' she said, spots floating in front of her eyes and a buzzing sound blanking out other noises. 'First aid.'

The next thing she knew she was lying on the grass with William's face beside her in duplicate, hazing in and out of focus.

'Concussion,' she said, before reaching up with her good hand. 'Find my scarf.'

While he rummaged through her clothes, she stared at the grass, at a crushed buttercup flower, anything to distract her from the nausea.

'Here,' he said, sitting behind her. 'Sit up, lean against me and I'll make a sling.'

It was a comfort just to feel his warmth behind her as she allowed him to wind the scarf around her neck and tie the two ends together under her broken wrist.

'Is it broken anywhere else?' he asked. 'Arm, shoulder?'

She felt down her arm, then gave a sharp intake of breath as she approached her wrist. 'Oh, it's just there,' she said, head swimming, sweat breaking out on her forehead. 'I feel horrible. I'm going to be sick.' When he looked confused, she elaborated. 'Throw up.'

'I'll wait,' he said, supporting her and mopping blood off his nose with a handkerchief.

After a couple of horrible paroxysms and the return of her breakfast, she felt better.

'Can you help me stand up?' she asked and he moved around to hold her by her good arm. 'We need to get help.'

He half lifted her to standing, and handed her a bottle. After a good rinse and a swig of stale water, she felt better, although the sky was still wheeling around every time she moved her head. A headache was competing with her broken arm.

'We need to get you to a doctor,' he said, guiding her as she staggered across the uneven ground. 'And tell our bases we are OK.'

'All I need is a plaster cast for my arm and a long nap,' she assured him. 'I did worse than this on the hockey field when I was twelve.'

He chuckled as they reached the gate by the road, to be met by a man running towards them.

'I've called an ambulance,' he assured them. 'I – who was driving the plane?'

'*Piloting*,' said Clara, with care as she felt dizzy again. 'I was *piloting* the plane.' Darkness rushed in like cold water and she fainted again.

She woke up almost immediately, but her fainting fit earned her a trip in an ambulance with William. X-rays at the cottage hospital revealed a fractured wrist, and two ribs on the same side, but no skull damage. Apart from a broken nose and a couple of bent fingers, William was fine.

It was getting dark when the doctor at the cottage hospital shone her torch into Clara's eyes for what felt like the hundredth time. 'I'm going to let you go,' she said, 'but only if your friend checks on you every two hours. We have a leaflet. You have a severe concussion.'

'I need to get back to my base,' Clara said vaguely, although she couldn't remember if she had planes to deliver or not.

'You can't go in an aeroplane for at least two weeks,' she said. 'And that plaster needs to be on for a month. Where's your family?'

'Devon,' Clara said, looking at her. 'I don't even remember hitting my head.'

The doctor took her hand and moved it to the matted hair on the side of her skull, above her ear. 'A bang on your posterior temporal zone. Can you feel the bump?'

The painful swelling under her fingers told the story. 'But no serious damage?'

'We don't think so,' the doctor said, then smiled. 'We'll know if you still want to fly beaten-up planes, I suppose.'

Clara laughed. 'It's my calling.' She waited alone behind the curtains, on the uncomfortable bed, and was just starting to doze off when William woke her up.

'Ready to go? I've got us a room at the local pub.'

That woke her. 'One room?'

'There was only one. I can sleep on the floor,' he said. 'I have to wake you up and check you out every two hours anyway. I told the landlady we were a couple.'

'Oh, my reputation,' she said, covering her eyes with her hand. 'Are you sure they don't have a spare room?'

'It's a busy time,' he explained. 'Haymaking or something. I can sleep in the dining room if you prefer, and if the landlady lets me. There's a kind of hard, narrow bench.'

She playfully punched his arm. 'Don't be daft. Just get me some clothes, will you? I seem to have ended up dressed in a sheet.'

Standing to get dressed made her dizzy, but a nurse helped, and she felt better with her clothes on. Her uniform jacket sleeve had been cut off, which was a nuisance – it wouldn't be easy to replace it without a trip to the tailor in London.

William was standing outside, waiting for her. He smiled and kissed her forehead. 'I'm so glad you're all right. For a minute there I thought you were a goner.'

'For a minute, I thought we both were,' she admitted.

'Oh. I forgot,' he said, letting go of her to search his pocket. 'I know this isn't the right time...'

'Right time for what?' she said, looking up at a miraculously starry sky. The blackouts had made the skies even more beautiful, or maybe she was still seeing double.

'You should wear a ring.' That brought her attention back to him. 'For appearance's sake. It doesn't mean – I know it's the wrong time to ask.' He pulled out a small box, and opened it. A slim band of gold with two sapphires and a small diamond caught the limited light at the doorway.

'Oh, William,' she said, taking the box. 'It's lovely. But...'

He took it out of the box. 'I know it's too early to give this to you, but we need to at least persuade the landlady that we're a couple.' He lifted her hand and slid the ring halfway on. 'At least you didn't break your left arm.'

'But she'll see it's just an engagement ring,' Clara stammered.

He rolled it around until just a slim, gold band appeared and slid it into position. 'Does it fit? I had to guess the size.'

'It's lovely,' she said, staring down at it. 'Oh, William...'

His eyes shone, and for a moment it was magical that they were both alive, and he was the most important person in the world.

31

PRESENT DAY, OCTOBER

Despite the awkwardness that she still felt towards him, Ruby was grateful for Jake's presence before the surveyor's team arrived. She had got Pony sitting up in a chair in the dining room, and put a heater on in there for her as Jake arrived from the bed and breakfast. He helped by chatting to Pony while Ruby ran around trying to get the boiler to work and tidying up a bit.

'They won't mind a bit of mess,' Jake said as she returned with a tray of hot drinks. 'They're valuing the house and contents.'

'I mind,' she said. 'I brought the chocolate biscuits, Pony – no point wasting them on the vultures.'

Pony's answer was vague; she was disorientated this morning. Jake leaned over to murmur in Ruby's ear. 'She doesn't seem to be getting any better.'

'No. I'm calling the duty doctor again to come out.'

Normally that would have got a response from Pony, but she had dozed off in the chair again. Ruby was halfway through her coffee when someone banged on the large door knocker.

The group of three men and a woman stood in the hall as

she shut the door behind them. They explained their roles –
Ruby immediately forgot which was which – and she empha-
sised that they couldn't disturb Pony without her being there.

As she pushed open the door into the drawing room, the
draught lifted her hair, whispering to her as if protectively.

'I don't want the picture moved,' she said, her voice coming
out sharper than she intended. 'It's by Alice St John, it's a
family portrait. I'll be in the room opposite if you have any
questions.'

Back in the dining room, she choked back tears. 'The beginning of the end,' she said, trying to summon a smile for Jake.
'This will determine the size of the tax bill.'

'How much is it likely to be?' he said. 'I hope you'll be left
with a decent amount. Property is expensive here.'

'I thought an American historian working in London would
be better off.'

'Ha!' he said, his face lightening considerably. 'My divorce
took any savings and my house.' He smiled at her. 'I don't mind
– not now. I just didn't see it coming, I thought we were happy.'

'Oh.' Ruby felt she needed to say something. 'I ended a relationship last year,' she said. 'I didn't realise how bad it had got.'

'Your mother told me,' he said, his voice soft. 'At one point I
think she wanted to fix *us* up...'

Ruby could feel the blush warm her face.

'My marriage had somehow become boring, *I* had become
boring,' he said. 'My wife was quite right to end it. I just wish
her divorce lawyer hadn't been so good at his job.'

'At least Oliver and I weren't married,' she said. It was the
only consolation; he had been bitter and vindictive over their
unhappy relationship. 'Splitting up pushed me into buying my
flat, though, which I love. Maybe I'll be able to pay off the mortgage one day.'

'Maybe when you sell this house.'

She looked at the cracked veneer on the edge of the dining

table, pushed into the bay window to make more room for Pony's bed. 'I hope so.' She looked around. 'When I come here, I hear them – the ghosts of my imagination, or the women that lived and loved in this place. I need to find my own home.' She looked across at him. 'It's a shame Mabel has found her family history just when I have to sell the house.'

'I know Mabel would buy a few mementoes of Clara and Marissa, even the painting if you are selling, so it won't be completely lost to the family.'

'It would literally be the last thing I could sell,' she admitted. 'It will take up most of the back wall in my living room, though, in the city.'

'I'd love to come and visit you there one day,' he said, his voice soft. His smile grew as she tried to find the right words to say how much she would like that, too. She jumped as someone knocked on the dining room door and opened it a crack.

'Do you have any keys to the outside spaces?' the woman said in a low voice. 'I'd like to look in the garage.'

'All the outside keys are on the kitchen work surface, next to the sink, in a bowl.' The bowl that Ruby had made at a pottery workshop her mother had attended, that she had painted with wobbly birds. She shut her eyes at the memory.

Jake reached out his arms, crushing her in a warm hug. 'I remember losing my home, too,' he said into her hair. 'Where we raised our daughter, where we were happy for so long. At least you're not losing your dog.'

She pulled back. 'Your wife got the dog?'

'Billy-Bob the incontinent spaniel,' he said, his eyes shining. 'I love that dog.'

She rested her head against him. For a long moment, they held each other, until her heart rate went down to normal and her breathing eased. 'This is hard, isn't it? I miss my mum.'

When she pulled away, he drew a hand over his eyes. 'I miss

mine, too,' he said shakily. 'There will be horrible days, and some good days, too.'

'I'm so worried for Pony and Max.'

His hand took hers. 'You can't worry about them more than yourself.'

'I've been trying to work out if I can fit them into a two-bedroomed flat overlooking the sea. With no lift.'

He smiled. 'Bunk beds?'

A cracked chuckle told them Pony was awake again. 'You've got to look after yourself,' she said. 'Like the boy says.'

Jake glanced over. 'It's been over twenty years since anyone called me a boy.'

'You're all just boys and girls to me,' she said, her voice facing.

'Where's that doctor?' Ruby hissed. 'She's getting worse, not better.'

'Go and ring the surgery, see when they are coming.'

Ruby caught some of the conversations between the surveyors, but couldn't distinguish anything useful. They didn't seem to be impressed or disappointed with the house and contents, but spent a lot of time studying all the pictures and artwork, taking photos and measurements and making notes. Ruby had to remind them some of the textiles were Pony's and the small maquettes were Max's.

'Most of the smaller works won't be valued individually,' one of the house surveyors said. 'It will be an approximate estimate, anyway. If you got a higher price in the next seven years for anything you sell, the taxman would want a percentage. It's going to be hard for our art expert to put a price on the picture of the baby in the living room. It's stunning.'

'That's my favourite piece,' she said.

'I recommend you don't sell it for seven years, then,' he said, eyes twinkling.

'How much is the house worth?' she asked baldly, reaching for Jake's hand. 'Ball park.'

'I would suggest marketing it as a development project,' he said quietly. 'You could ask for one point two or one point three million, but I don't think you'd get more. There are some big structural issues you may not be aware of, and I'm really worried about the drainage. You'll get a copy of our complete valuation from your solicitor once probate has been approved. You are the sole heir, I take it?'

'I think so,' she whispered, as Jake's hand squeezed hers.

'Absolutely she is,' he said, his voice firmer than hers.

The surveyor looked at them both. 'Look, I don't want to speak out of turn, but I do know a developer who might want to have a look *before* it goes on the market. They are looking for a place they can restore, sympathetically.'

The doorbell rang, and Ruby slipped out into the hall to usher the doctor in.

'Pony – Penelope – just seems to be getting worse,' Ruby told her, as the doctor set her bag down.

'Can we get a urine specimen?' she asked. 'And my colleague will be here in a minute to take blood. I don't want her to go back to the hospital. There's always a worry about them not being able to return home.'

'She's in the dining room – I know it's not ideal,' Ruby said, her hands clasped together. 'It looks like we'll lose the house at some point, and I don't know what to do to help them.'

The doctor patted her shoulder. 'It's not all down to you, Ruby. I'll let social services know, maybe together we can come up with a care plan for both of them. Max has a small window to fight back to health before he gives up and wastes away.'

'I haven't seen him for a couple of days,' Ruby said, feeling worse. 'I haven't had time.'

'Well, the rehabilitation unit are getting very frustrated with him because he won't do anything for himself. It wasn't even a big stroke.'

'Could I bring him home? Would he be able to cope?'

'That's what I'm hoping. If you don't have to sell straight away, we'll find carers. They have friends and neighbours who will help, too.' She smiled at Ruby. 'They could have another Christmas here, maybe get another summer before you have to move out.'

Ruby's eyes filled with tears as the doctor walked into the dining room.

The surveyor gently cleared his throat. 'Would you like me to arrange for these potential buyers to look around the house?' he asked. 'Mr Haydon thinks it might be a good idea.'

She took a deep breath. 'Next weekend, maybe, if they are available? Once I've got Pony coping better.'

The surveyor smiled at her, and she noticed that he had kind eyes. 'I think you'll like them.'

32

JUNE 1943

Clara's first thought when she woke in the morning was that her head hurt, and the rest of her right side was sore from her ribs to her fingertips. She lifted her plastered arm to look: the fingers were swollen and bruised. Behind her, William was asleep on the other pillow.

The memory of last night made her smile. He had woken her a couple of hours after she first fell asleep, and checked she wasn't unconscious or confused. He was still dressed then, sat in a small chair beside the bed.

'You must be exhausted,' she had told him, and patted the bed. 'At least sleep next to me. I trust you. Everyone thinks we're married anyway.'

Reluctantly, he took off his shoes and slid under the counterpane. 'Go to sleep,' he had said severely.

Later, Clara was jolted awake by a terrible dream. Her mothers were standing in front of their house, waving to her, but she couldn't control the plane which was heading straight for them. William was shouting to her too, and maybe the deeper voice was Giles as she wrestled with the controls, watching the house get bigger and bigger...

She had woken with the sound of the crash in her ears, and turned to William. He was asleep, his face so beautiful in the dawn light coming through the window, she couldn't stop herself touching his cheek. When he opened his eyes, she had looked deep into their luminous green lightness.

'I love you,' he said drowsily, and kissed her.

The rest of her memories were jumbled, but now he was asleep beside her, and still beautiful. The skin on his chest was a pale contrast to the tan of his face and neck, paler than her freckled skin. She rolled onto her back carefully, trying not to jolt her broken wrist or ribs, or her aching head.

She still wore the ring on her left hand, it had spun around and she could see the stones. *He loves me.*

She tried to move her legs, finding a few more aches and bruises from the crash, and managed to sit up on the side of the bed. The landlady had lent her a dressing gown with wide sleeves, just enough to pull over the plaster. At least she could get down the corridor to the bathroom.

'Mrs Carlson?' The landlady, still in curlers, leaned out of her room as Clara returned.

Clara jumped. 'Oh. Good morning.'

'How are you this morning?'

'Better,' Clara said, managing a smile. 'But I still feel like I've been in a crash.'

'Well, so you have! The ministry was here last night to look at the plane. It's a miracle you and your husband survived.'

Clara nodded. She was uncomfortable with the word *husband*, and even more so at being called *Mrs Carlson*. 'We'll get off home as soon as we can. I expect there will be a lot of paperwork.'

'Is it true you were driving the plane?'

Clara's head was buzzing and aching. 'Yes. I'm a pilot with

the Air Transport Auxiliary. William – he was with the ATA originally, but he's joined the American Air Force now.'

'Bless you,' the kindly, warm voice said, making Clara feel tearful at having deceived her. 'Both of you. I'll get some breakfast for you in about an hour, if that's a good time?'

'Thank you,' Clara said, the words coming out hoarse. 'It's probably going to take me a while to get dressed with this stupid cast.'

'Of course. At least Mr Carlson can help. I'll see you in the dining room when you're ready, there's no rush.'

Clara opened the door to the bedroom. William was sitting up in bed, yawning. 'There you are,' he said, his smile the widest she'd ever seen it. 'My darling.'

She sat down on the edge of the bed, with her back to him, and reached down to open her bag. 'I'm just glad we got through the crash,' she said. 'We could both have been killed.' There, the thought that caught in her throat and stopped her breath.

'But we weren't,' he said, and moved closer, to kiss her neck.

It was too much. She pulled away from his warmth. 'Which is why last night – what happened last night – happened,' she said, in as matter-of-fact a voice as she could find. She twisted the ring around her finger. 'I'll give you the ring back later – after we leave.' She couldn't look at him.

'It's yours, I bought it for you. After last night, obviously, I knew we would have to be married.'

'It's not that simple.' She shook her head, wishing it was. 'If we hadn't just survived an emergency landing, we wouldn't have spent the night together.'

'I don't understand.' There was a note in his voice that made her turn to face him. He caught her good hand in a painful grip. 'Obviously, I thought you wouldn't sleep with me unless we were going to get married some day.'

'You don't think the situation was exceptional?' she said,

with a snap in her voice that made a stab of pain shoot through her head. She softened her voice. 'This is a war, William. Why shouldn't we snatch some joy when we can? You can't judge me, surely? You were right there, you didn't seem to mind last night.'

'I'm so sorry, I'm being unfair,' he said, disarming her by kissing her hand. 'I bought the ring to ask you to marry me because I love you so much. Last night, I thought you felt the same.'

She caught one of his hands in her good one. 'William, I *do* love you. But that was not why we made love last night. Well, not just because of that. We could have been killed, we were exhausted, I was injured – I was so glad to be alive. And so very glad you were, too. I'm just not ready to get married.'

He looked down at their joined hands, at the gleam of gold and the stones in the ring.

'Will you at least be engaged to me, until you decide whether you'll marry me or not?'

'William,' she said. 'Please take the ring back. Keep it for a better day, when we're both thinking clearly.'

'I will never be more clear than I am now,' he said, meeting her gaze. 'It's your ring, do what you like with it. I'm not taking it back. Anyway, the landlady would be scandalised if you don't wear it.'

She sighed, closed her eyes against the pain. 'There will be breakfast waiting for us downstairs, once we get dressed.' She looked at the clothes in her bag. 'You might need to help me with this.'

'I'm not even hungry.'

She pulled her hand free. 'Well, we need to eat, and then I need to arrange transport to get home.'

'Back to the base?'

'No,' she said, rummaging through her open bag for clean underwear and something easy to wear over it. 'I'm going home to my mothers.'

33

PRESENT DAY, NOVEMBER

'Max is just in here,' said a nurse with the name Olivia on her badge. 'Are you his granddaughter?'

'Sort of,' Ruby said. 'He's lived in my house my whole life.'

Olivia stopped outside a door bearing a handwritten sign: *Do Not Disturb*. 'Look,' she said, 'he's struggling emotionally. He's actually recovering well from the stroke but he's given up. If you can cheer him up, get him out of bed even, it would be very helpful.'

'I'll try...' Ruby said in a low voice.

'He's hardly eating or drinking, he won't get up even to pee. We had to put him in disposable pants.'

Ruby put a hand on the door, afraid to go in. 'That's not the Max I know,' she said. 'He's been struggling with getting around recently, had had difficulty getting to the bathroom at home. But it's miles away, it's the outside loo, anyone would struggle.'

'He had a urinary tract infection,' Olivia said. 'And a couple of sores from sitting on a chair for too long. We'll get him a better chair for home.'

'He stays in the chair in the kitchen, because it's warm.' Ruby put her hand over her aching heart, and closed her eyes. 'I didn't see it I wasn't there. I was so busy looking after my mother. She had cancer.'

'It happens all the time to people Max's age,' Olivia said. 'Just talk to him, see if you can get him to help himself.'

Max was lying in bed under a heap of blankets, his face turned towards the window, leaves waving in the wind outside. He looked so small.

'I've come to see how you are,' she managed to say. He didn't reply so she walked around to the other side of the bed and sat in a chair there. 'I was so worried about you.'

'Don't worry about me,' he said, his voice so hoarse she imagined his throat was dry.

'Let me get you some water,' she said, jumping up. A glass of water with a straw sat on a locker. He took a couple of sips of water.

'How's Penelope?' he whispered.

'On the mend,' Ruby said. 'She had an infection, and hadn't been looking after herself properly. She's on new medicine now, she's much brighter.'

His deep brown eyes were sunk in nests of wrinkles. 'At our age, you can't always look after yourself any more. It's time to go, Ruby Roo. I don't want someone wiping my arse and force-feeding me baby food for the last months of my life.'

She grabbed a handful of the mattress and shook the bed. 'But you're not there yet! It doesn't have to be like that,' she said, more forcefully than she'd expected. 'And I never thought you'd go down to self-pity.'

The bed vibrated as he started to wheeze. For a long moment she thought he was having some sort of fit before she realised he was laughing. 'That's the spirit,' he cackled. 'But I still don't want to be here.' He laid his trembling fingers on her hand and squeezed. 'I'm a burden to you, and Penelope. I don't want to go into one of those homes. I might get a bit better but I'm still old '

'I need you to come back home,' Ruby said, her heart jumping at the thought of how impractical it was. 'Even though I'm not sure how we'll get you up the steps to the front door,' she added. 'But I need you, Max. I'm losing the house; I don't know what to do. I need you and Pony to help me through this last bit.' She put her other hand on top of his. 'And then there's Jake.'

'You like the boy, don't you?' he said.

'I do,' she said. 'But I'll deny it if you tell anyone. It's just – surveyors went around the house, putting a price on everything so I can pay tax on it all. And I might not even be the heir,' she said. 'We still don't know if Marissa's will can be overturned in Mabel's favour.'

'Is she fighting for that?'

She sighed, closed her eyes against the huge task ahead. 'No, but it still has to go through the courts. I don't want there to be a dispute over her claim later, so Jake is putting together the best claim he can for Mabel.'

'What can a knackered ninety-one-year-old do to help?' he said. 'I suppose I could die and leave you all my money...'

'But I don't want you to die,' she wailed. 'Or Pony! You're my family. I love you both so much.'

'You've just lost your mother, lass, of course you're clinging onto us now. But we're really just a burden, holding you back.'

She jumped to her feet, her heart pounding. 'You get out of that bed right now, and sit on this chair! I know you, you're tough as boot leather. You're not going to fade away, we'll have to beat you to death with sticks at a hundred.' She moved the chair to the side of the bed. 'What do you need to help you stand up?'

He beckoned at the walking frame. 'I'm only doing this,' he wheezed, 'because you threatened to hit me with sticks.'

She opened the door and called for Olivia, and the two of them helped him into the chair, padding it with cushions. He was quite out of breath and pale when he got there, but he gave Ruby a thumbs up.

'I'll come back after an hour and get you back into bed,' Olivia said.

'Promises, promises,' he rasped, with his eyes shut.

'He needs to get better because I'm taking him home. As soon as I can,' Ruby said. 'Before Christmas.'

'I'm all for it,' Olivia said, tucking a blanket over his legs. 'And we'll get help with providing carers and people to adapt the home. He needs a special mattress, too.'

He opened his eyes and looked at her. 'You just had to tell me that, before,' he said.

'We did many times.' Olivia exchanged looks with Ruby. 'You just couldn't hear it,' she said. 'But now you've got something to work towards.'

Ruby had got into the habit of calling Jake most evenings; this time she could tell him how she'd bullied Max into trying to get better. Pony was on a new antibiotic for a second infection, which had made her better, but she was now argumentative.

'She's enjoying one of her ready meals now,' she told Jake. 'She doesn't like my cooking, I fold her laundry wrong and I got her scented candles mixed up.'

'So you think you might be able to get Max back?'

'I think we're going to have to swap the rooms around. Max will need so much more space with a chair, commode and walker, but we can make the library nice for Pony. And we're going to need special carers, which we are only getting for a short time free, after that we have to fund it.' She sipped her glass of wine. 'I don't know how it's all going to work, but I couldn't just leave him there to die.'

'I'm never taking you to an animal shelter,' he said, far away. 'You'd come home with a dozen broken old animals.'

She looked out from the bedroom window. The light in the room made the sky look like it had been painted onto the window, deep inky black. 'I've had an email from my solicitor, about a potential buyer. The people the surveyor suggested. They are coming on Saturday.'

'I got a notification too,' he rumbled. 'I'm getting duplicates of everything for Mabel until this heir thing is resolved. I've seen Marissa's will, too. I think it looks sound, even if she wrote it herself.'

'It's not full of all the legal jargon I've seen before.'

'The main thing she neglected to do was to revoke any previous wills or heirs. She just gave it all to Fiona and then to you, when you were old enough to inherit. That's it. She didn't mention that she might have a biological granddaughter, living in America.'

She sighed, steaming the inside of the cold glass. 'And that could invalidate the will?'

His voice softened. 'Probably not, but the court has to weigh everything on Mabel's behalf. On a different note, I've got my daughter Emerald coming to stay. Emmy.'

She smiled. 'It's funny that she's called after a precious stone, too. Who's she like?'

'She's more like me than her mother. She studied conservation back in Wisconsin, living near Mabel, actually. She's a bit of an eco-warrior, she's just finished her graduate studies.'

Ruby smiled sadly. 'I suppose at some point, you'll want to go back to the States, with the rest of your family over there?'

'But at the moment Emmy's going to work in Europe, conserving wolves and bears in the Arctic Circle. Her undergrad thesis was on tracking polar bears through their faeces.'

Ruby couldn't imagine being in the polar night, surrounded by predators. 'Wasn't that dangerous?'

'She does carry – and knows how to shoot – a rifle. So far she's been OK, even in grizzly country in Canada.'

'Wow.' Muzzily, through the effects of the glass of wine, she wondered if she would ever meet his family.

'And to answer your question, no. I'm fixed in the UK. Because of you.'

She could feel the warmth in her belly spreading. 'That's – nice,' she said. 'I would really miss you.'

'Ruby, are you drunk?' His voice had lightness in it, a hint of laughter.

She stared at the empty glass. 'Tiny bit,' she admitted. 'I don't normally drink – on a school night. But every day's a school night at the moment. It's getting a bit difficult with work. There's only so much I can do from home.'

'Well, don't fall down the steps when you check on Pony,' he warned. 'I don't want to turn up and find you at the bottom of the stairs.'

Her heart quickened, even as she leaned against the chair in her room. 'It would be lovely if you do come.'

'I said I would help.'

'That's great,' she said, not caring about them, but feeling the pull to him. 'I'd love to see you and I could do with some moral support. I can't imagine anyone creating a family home out of it. Suppose they want to create flats?'

'The surveyor said they wouldn't. I suggest I drive down on Friday night, stay at the bed and breakfast, see you early in the morning.'

'You don't have to, you know,' she said. 'Stay at Foxglove Cottage, I mean.'

He laughed. 'That's the wine talking. Ask me to stay with you when you're sober.'

She could feel her cheeks warming up. 'I meant, I have a few spare rooms.'

'We'll talk about it, but I'll book a night anyway. We can have a go at sorting out that mess from the fallen ceiling in the drawing room. I'm sure we could make it look like the house is not actually falling down.'

She could hear him breathing down the phone and wondered what she would do if he turned up, right now. 'I miss you,' she said. 'That's not the wine talking.'

'I know,' he said softly. 'I miss you too, Ruby Roo.'

34

JULY 1943

Clara sat opposite a doctor with white hair at the ATA headquarters. 'I feel ready to go back to work,' she said, fingers clenched in her lap. 'My fracture has healed completely now.'

'You had to have it operated on four weeks ago?' He looked through her notes and held up the tiny film image to the light adjusted his glasses. 'It looks better now. How are your headaches? Any blurred vision or nausea? I understand you had a concussion.'

At least the nausea of the first week had passed, although she felt a little sick right now. 'I'm back to normal activities. I'd like to return to flying.'

'Are you driving a car?'

'Yes, for the last week. It's all been fine.'

'That's good. I can't find anything that would make flying more dangerous and difficult than it already is.' He looked at her over his glasses. 'How do you feel about getting back into the cockpit of a plane that could kill you?'

'I'll be a bit nervous at first,' she confessed. 'I will be delivering new planes rather than bringing wrecks back to be fixed. But once I get my collywobbles out, I'll be back to full duty.'

He smiled at that. 'Your "collywobbles", as you call them, keep you alert and alive. Never get complacent.'

'No, sir,' she said smartly. 'Am I fit for duty, Doctor?'

'You are. But ease into it gently. I'll give you a note for light duties for one week.'

Clara stood outside and breathed deep. Six weeks at home with her mothers had done her so much good, although she could see how much strain they were carrying. She had called them after the crash, just to let them know she was coming home, and she had seen how erratic Marissa's behaviour had become. Alice was anxious too, cleaning up as her love wandered around the house, talking fast and incoherently, and sorting and organising things randomly. Books had been arranged by colour, cushions were regimented in rows on the floor, and she had to feel Clara's forehead a hundred times a day.

'Has she ever been this bad before?' Clara whispered to Alice after Marissa missed dinner to sit outside in a shawl, counting stars in the summer night.

'Stress always sets it off, but it doesn't normally last this long. She was so shocked when we found out you had crashed... We both were.' Alice gripped her hand tightly. 'I wish you could give up flying, darling, I really do. If anything happened...' She let go, brushed a tear away. 'I think it would kill her. And that would kill me as well.'

Clara hugged her. 'Is she seeing her old doctor?'

'He's retired. He just said, don't let her drink, it would make her symptoms worse and he gave me a sedative for her if she needs it. His thinks she will come out of it by herself. But she's not eating, I'm afraid she will make herself physically ill, too.'

Clara forced herself to smile. 'Let's get her in and warm her up. And we really need to find her a new psychiatrist. Then I can go back knowing you've got some support for her until she recovers from this episode.'

Marissa had relaxed almost into a doze, sat on the front step gazing at the sky. She jumped when Clara sat next to her and put an arm around her shoulders. 'Come along in, darling Mother, it's cooling down.'

'It's not cold,' her mother said vaguely, before seeing Alice. 'I'm sorry – I'm being selfish making such a fuss.'

'It's not a fuss,' Alice said, taking her hand. 'Come in and let Clara tell you her news.'

Marissa walked in, Clara picking the shawl she'd dropped to the floor. Sat on the sofa, Marissa seemed to brighten up.

'What news, Clara?' she smiled a little. 'Is this to do with Giles?'

'No,' she said, a little taken aback. She had received a few letters from him, but he was away in the thick of the war. There had been a lot of letters from William but he, too, was flying most days and in challenging conditions, heading over the French coast to escort bombers to Europe. 'No, not Giles. I saw the doctor today and I'm all well again, my arm is working normally. I can go back to light duties.'

Marissa touched her pale, thin arm, weakened from six weeks of inactivity. 'Desk duties?' she asked.

'No, just easy hops with new planes,' she said, staring into Marissa's eyes, so much like hers but now she could see new lines. 'Hardly more work than driving a car. You must get better,' she said. 'Maybe go and see a new doctor, with more modern methods.'

Alice sat on the other side. 'This melancholy you've fallen into, it was all for nothing. Look, our darling girl is as good as new.'

'Until the next crash,' Marissa said, her eyes brimming with tears. 'I dream you are dead, you know. I dream it most nights.'

'But I'm not,' Clara said, squeezing her hands in hers. 'I am well, and will stay that way. And as far as Giles goes,' she said, wanting to leave them with something, 'we're going to talk about things after the war.'

'But there's someone else, isn't there?' Alice added.

Marissa turned to her. 'Is this the American boy?'

Alice shrugged. 'You left a letter in the living room. Mrs Goddings saw it and told us. He is an American, isn't he? I noticed the direction on one of your replies, USAAF.'

'He's a pilot, too,' Clara said, managing a wobbly smile. 'Surely *one* of them will survive the war.'

Alice laughed a little. 'Hedging your bets? But do you *love* either of these young men?'

Clara thought for a moment. 'When I'm with them, I think I do. But I love them both. I just don't think I'm in love with either of them. I can't choose.'

Alice nodded. 'Wait until you fall for one of them. Until you can't bear to be away from them.'

'But in the middle of a war, I don't want to feel like that about *anyone*. Not anyone who could be shot down, anyway.'

'Giles is a good match,' Marissa said abruptly. 'What is this American like, who are his family?'

'Mother, we don't think like that nowadays. He's a good man and a good pilot. He's kind and funny, his family are farmers.'

'What if he wants to drag you off to America?' Marissa snapped back, clutching at her hand.

'You've been to America, you loved it,' Clara said. 'If I married, I'd probably have to move away, whoever asked me. Even Giles would expect me to move to Hampshire, I suppose.'

Alice patted her arm and stood. 'It's time for bed, loved ones,' she said. 'I can assure you, you're not *in love* with either so it's a moot point. Or you wouldn't be able to tear yourself away from him.' She turned to Marissa, who took a hand and pressed a kiss into the palm.

'I suppose,' Clara said. 'I'm going to concentrate on doing my job well—'

'And not crashing your plane,' Marissa added.

'—and not crashing my plane,' Clara said, hugging them both.

Clara collected her bags to go back to her base. Mrs Goddings had the knack of folding everything so it would perfectly fit in the bags and minimise any creasing.

'I'm glad to have a word with you, Miss Clara,' she said, carefully laying a last silk blouse on top of her uniform shirts. 'I've noticed you've been a bit out of sorts.'

'I suppose I have,' Clara said. She could feel there was a bigger question there, from the woman she'd known since she was born. 'It was hard not being able to do everything I want. Drive, ride, carry things... fly.'

'But, to me, you seem different. I wondered if you've fallen. To one of your young men.'

'Oh.' The thought that had circled around the back of her mind, but never been allowed to come into focus, fell squarely. She touched her flat stomach. 'Oh, Beatrice, I don't know.'

'Well, you haven't had your monthlies, have you?'

'I just thought – the shock and everything, and feeling so low.' She looked down at her hands. 'It was just once, I don't... It was the first time.'

'It just takes one time, Miss Clara,' Beatrice said, sitting beside her on the bed. 'There's a clinic that can get you back into a good rhythm, if that's what you want.'

'Oh, no You mean, take it away? If it is anything.'

'People do,' Beatrice said. 'People who can afford these special clinics.' She looked away. 'My niece got into some trouble, she was just fourteen.'

'What, little Maggie? Oh no.'

'It weren't her fault,' Beatrice said. 'She was attacked in Plymouth. She thought he was a sailor but couldn't be sure. Some man in a uniform. Anyway, your ma sent her off to this clinic.'

'It's against the law,' Clara said, still shocked at the thought of Maggie being hurt like that.

'It was a kindness for Maggie, just a child. I suppose it is illegal, but it's possible, for people with money,' Beatrice said. 'Anyway, Miss Alice took her up to London one day and brought her home the next. She recovered really well, although it haunts you, that kind of thing.'

Clara shook her head. 'I couldn't do anything like that.'

'Well, maybe you can afford to have a baby. Before the war, girls used to go over to Switzerland or France, get the baby adopted, but you can't do that.'

'I don't even know if there *is* a baby,' Clara said. 'I just feel like I'm getting back to normal. I think – it must have been the shock, the crash.' She turned to Beatrice. 'Not a word to my mothers,' she said, in a rush. 'I need to deal with this myself – if it is anything.'

'You and the young man,' Beatrice said. 'You know, if he'll marry you.'

At least she had the answer to that, tucked into a corner of her purse.

35

PRESENT DAY, NOVEMBER

Ruby had expected a couple of men in suits and clipboards to turn up, to explore ways to destroy her family home for holiday flats or a wedding venue. Imogen Oldstock was about the same age as Ruby and accompanied by an older man using a stick, with a short, white beard and a flat cap. 'This is my father, Maurice Oldstock,' Imogen said, and he shook Ruby's hand with a strong grip. Ruby was instantly drawn to her; she seemed like she was full of energy, and was looking around at everything.

'This is a lovely house,' Maurice said, staring at her with dark, intense eyes like his daughter. 'I've always admired it from the road. Do you know much about its history?'

'Come inside, and I'll tell you,' Ruby said, pushing the door open wide. 'This is my' – she hesitated – 'my friend. Can you lead the way to the kitchen, Jake?'

As the pair walked down the hall they seemed fascinated by all the pictures and the assortment of oddments on the dresser. Maurice picked up the old riding crop. 'You keep horses?'

'We used to. It was my aunt Clara's. She rode a lot when she was a teenager, before the war,' she explained. 'Marissa kept

it after she died.' Turning to the Oldstocks, she explained.
'Marissa Montpelier bought the house with her partner, Alice
St John, in the nineteen twenties. Clara was their daughter, but
she was killed in the war.'

They walked to the kitchen. Ruby had spent a whole day
scrubbing it the previous weekend, and managed to get a coat of
paint on the walls. Just cleaning off the cobwebs, dust and
grease had brought it back to life. It had a large range cooker but
Pony hadn't lit it for a couple of years, and they lived off an old
electric cooker beside it, equally decrepit but after a good clean,
it still looked good. Ruby had made some cookies, and the room
smelled of vanilla and was warm.

'Oh, an Aga?' Imogen said, putting her hand on the cold
enamelled surface.

'It needs a service,' Ruby said, knowing it had rusted up. It
probably needed more than that. 'It used to keep this room
warm and heat the water.'

'This is a lovely room,' Imogen said, looking around and out
of the window. 'Oh, you have chickens! I've always wanted
some.'

'You probably have a hundred foxes, up here,' Maurice said.

'We have to get the hens in at night,' said Ruby, putting the
kettle on. 'Would you like to sit down? I can tell you some more
about the house. Or we could show you around first.'

Maurice stared at Max's multicoloured wing chair, then sat
down, leaning his stick against his knee. He was very thin, his
face pale and drawn, as if he'd been ill.

'I want to know how the house has been left, first,' he said,
as Imogen sat at the table next to Jake. 'I know there's more than
one competing heir. I don't want to try and buy something just
to have the other heir come along and scupper the deal.'

Imogen smiled and nodded as Ruby held up a teapot. 'Dad
and I were told about the house by our estate agent. They
helped value the property.'

'Yes,' said Ruby, 'but I don't know for how much yet. It's all in the hands of lawyers. But if you're worried about the heirs, it's just an American lady, Mabel, and me. Probate should be approved soon.'

'I work for an heir hunter firm in London and am acting on Mrs Player's behalf,' Jake explained. 'I know it sounds odd, but she intends to support Ruby's claim as much as she can. Mabel just wanted to find out who her mother was. There is a will which leaves the house to Ruby's mother – and then to Ruby.'

Imogen looked from one to the other. 'Would this Mabel be willing to sell the house, too, if her claim was stronger?'

'She would have to,' he answered, though a little wince told Ruby how hard it would be for him, too. 'She wouldn't be able to make the repairs it needs, nor pay all the death duties. She's asked me to represent her interests today.'

'She has?' Ruby asked.

'She has no interest in trying to inherit the house. She certainly wouldn't want to hurt you.' Jake's eyes met her gaze, and she smiled back.

'So, how old is the house?' Maurice said, as Ruby put out a milk jug and a sugar bowl with mugs and spoons.

'I think it was finished in 1856,' Ruby said. 'It was built by a Captain Marshall, he built what he called Heather House from the local stone. His daughters sold it to my grandmothers in 1920, just after my aunt Clara was born. They changed the name to Montpelier House.'

'You said "grandmothers"?' Maurice said.

'Yes. They were two quite famous artists in their day. Alice St John, my grandmother, and Marissa Montpelier, Mabel's great-grandmother. They lived here as a couple until their deaths, and worked from the house.' She filled the teapot and put it on the scrubbed kitchen table. 'I grew up here, but Mabel's mother was adopted by a family in America during the war.'

For a moment, Ruby poured out tea and politely displayed a plate of biscuits – Jake took two – before the bubble inside her grew too large to contain.

'If you are looking for a house to convert to flats—' she said, trying to keep her voice even. *Maybe it wouldn't be terrible if people actually lived here, if children ran around the wilderness at the back, maybe rode their ponies out onto the moor…*

'We're not,' Imogen said. 'We want to keep the house as it is. We understand there is a ground-floor extension at the back?'

Ruby was confused. 'The studios, yes. But who would need a house this size?'

Maurice looked at his daughter and nodded. 'We need you to understand what we're planning. You know the house best, you can advise how we would do it.'

'OK,' Ruby said, standing next to Jake's chair.

Imogen spoke first. 'We're looking to create a new style of retirement home for older people,' she said, in a rush. 'More like a hotel. I come from the care industry, I used to be the manager of a large facility. Big units can be so impersonal, so formulaic. They work out what the best plan for a room is, ergonomically, then pop them all out like pods. People aren't like that,' she said, in a rush. 'People get more individual as they get older, not less.'

Ruby could hear Pony's stick tapping slowly down the hall.

'What sort of thing are you planning? You do know this place has three storeys?'

'Our clients would be able to create their home in one room but have access to all the living spaces. They would pay for the room, laundry and food. But they choose the level of care they need to help them live as full a life as possible.'

Jake interrupted. 'We still have three levels, loads of stairs.' *We.* It made Ruby smile to see how attached he felt to the place.

'We would install lifts,' Maurice said. 'Wheelchair access, accessible parking. Some of our residents would be younger, more active.'

'But we're in the middle of nowhere,' Ruby said.

Maurice smiled at that. 'When getting out of a chair is difficult, the view out of the window becomes much more important. But we'd run a shuttle service for clients wanting to get out on the moor or go into town.' He looked at Imogen, then tapped his stick on the floor. 'It will be designed to suit me. I have Parkinson's. I will be its first resident.'

'Second,' came Pony's cracked voice from the doorway, over his shoulder 'That sounds like just the place I've been looking for.'

After tea and biscuits, and when everyone had spoken to Pony, Jake and Ruby took the Oldstocks through every room. Maurice was slow on the stairs but still managed to open every overflowing cupboard and look into the attic bedrooms.

'It needs a huge amount of work,' he said, finally, back in the kitchen. 'And it will take a long time to clear it all out, especially getting a van up that drive. Would you consider leaving the bigger antiques, like the dresser and dining table?'

'Of course,' Ruby said, having had a few stressful moments wondering how they were going to get all the big stuff out. 'The giant breakfront bookcase was built in the house, I know, as well as all the ones in the library.' Her heart lurched in her chest. 'They belong here.'

'We saw a bed in there,' Maurice said.

'I have another tenant,' Ruby said, for whom possibilities had been running wild ever since they went into the library. 'Max. He's the artist who made Leda and the swan, out the front. He's in hospital at the moment, but he's coming home soon.'

Imogen looked at her dad. 'Sorry, Penelope, but as sitting tenants, will you and Max give Ruby any problems, if she sells to us? If you have to move out and maybe can't move in here straight away? It looks like we would have a year of building work to be done. The wiring alone...'

'That was put in in the nineteen thirties,' Ruby said, cheerfully. 'The ladies paid for it to be installed, and the supply went as far as the nearby village, three miles away.'

'Yes, and the wires *look* a hundred years old, they need replacing.'

Pony cackled a laugh. 'As long as you're careful putting the outside lavvy light on, you're fine. I've got a few shocks off that one.'

Maurice laughed. 'I remember when you couldn't touch a light switch with damp hands, and I got shocks unplugging my mother's hairdryer.'

'The good old days, huh, Dad,' Imogen said, rolling her eyes. 'So, Jake, do you live here too?'

'I live and work in London,' he explained. 'Ruby has an apartment in Plymouth, but we get together when we can.'

Imogen asked again. 'So, Penelope...'

Pony looked across at Ruby. 'I'll do whatever's best for our Ruby,' she said. 'When she needs it. But you, Maurice. Where will *you* live while all this work is being done?'

'Well, here, of course,' he said. 'I have to sell my house to buy this one, but I have a buyer already, the paperwork is going through.'

'So *you're* going to be here, with your Parkinson's. Why can't I? I've lived through floods, hippies, births, deaths and dry rot. And I know this house inside and out.'

Imogen started to object but he put his hand up. 'You have a point,' he said. 'But you can't be a guest of the hotel until it's habitable. You could only be a tenant on the basis that Ruby rents to you.'

'One hundred a week, then,' Pony said, holding out her gnarled hand. 'If you go ahead. I can sleep anywhere, and I can still just about go upstairs if I have to.'

He shook it, smiling at last. 'Let's keep your suggestion on the table. After we've calculated an actual offer. And when we know who legally owns the place.'

Ruby felt Jake put a hand on her shoulder. It was a great idea, it might even create a home for Pony, and would solve all the problems of what to do with the house... She turned blindly into his hug.

She could hear him saying positive, congratulatory things to Maurice, but for a few moments, she vanished into the dark of his embrace and let the cold run down her spine. The house had seemed more precious since she knew she couldn't keep it. By the time she had found a fixed smile, a nod, and had turned around, she knew what she wanted from the deal.

Jake.

36

AUGUST 1943

Clara sat in another doctor's office in a private women's hospital, but the news was the same.

'About two months, I would say,' the doctor said, putting her horn-rimmed spectacles back on her nose. 'What are your plans?'

'I'm going back to work,' said Clara, a little stunned.

'I meant, for the baby,' the doctor said gently. 'Do you intend to marry the gentleman? Have you considered a discreet, private adoption? Or would you prefer to seek a medical solution to your – ahem – menstrual irregularity?'

'I understand you, I suppose,' Clara said. 'I don't really know. Is there a time limit before I have to decide? How soon will I start to show?'

'Any medical option would ideally be in the next few weeks. You'll start to show about then, too. It depends on the clothes, obviously. Many of our ladies manage to conceal their first pregnancy for half the pregnancy or even more. I can recommend a maternity corset for discreet support.'

'I need to think about it,' Clara said, even as she knew the 'medical option' was highly illegal and her mothers – what would they think? This was their grandchild. 'I need to talk to – uh, the father.'

'Exactly,' the doctor said, rising to her feet. 'In the meantime, you seem to be in excellent health, and I shall expect you to deliver a healthy child in seven months' time. We offer a very discreet maternity service if you choose that.'

After her appointment, Clara walked along the street to the station. Her first instinct was to go straight back towards Hamble, but the first train would also take her past Giles's accommodation. *I need to talk to a friend.* She suddenly wanted to see him desperately. She stopped at a phone box to call his group and leave a message.

The train was a slow one, stopping at all the little stations. She had almost decided it was too late in the day and he might be on operations anyway... when his face appeared in the window of the door. He opened it. 'Hurry up, old girl,' he said, a little out of breath. 'I had to run all the way down the train to find you.'

She grabbed her bags and stepped off into his arms as he hugged her fiercely. 'What's wrong?' he said, as she squirmed out of his embrace.

'We're in public,' Clara said, feeling her face heat up as a sailor whistled at them.

'No, I mean, after ignoring my letters, why did you want to see me?'

Clara's eyes filled up even as she looked away. 'I'm in trouble,' she said.

He understood at once; his face changed, his forehead wrinkled and his hands fell away from her waist. 'You're – in trouble.'

She stepped back as if repelled by his coldness. 'Yes.'

'Your American chap, I suppose.' His voice was different, angry, cold, but his face looked hurt. He stood tall. 'So why did you want to see *me*? Surely I'm the last person to come to.'

'You must know other people this has happened to,' she said, swaying with tiredness or emotion or maybe longing for him to hold her again. 'I'm sorry, I haven't been able to tell anyone.'

'Not your mothers?'

'Especially not them,' she said. 'Marissa is ill, she's struggling with her melancholia since my plane crash. Alice is busy looking after her.'

He stuck his hands in his pockets. 'So what do you want me to do? Help you get rid of it?'

Clara fell back a step. 'No! I know you're angry, I know you must feel hurt...'

'I'm not hurt, Clara, I'm jealous that you went to him, that you chose him. Go to Alice, she'll look after you. It's not like they haven't reared an illegitimate baby before. Go home.'

There was raw emotion in his voice, something she had recognised in William's voice after she had told him she wouldn't marry him. Jealousy.

'I'm going back to Hamble,' she said. 'My wrist is healed now, and I'm going back to duties.'

'Pregnant?'

She shrugged. 'I couldn't be more careful. If the worst happens, it happens. Anyway, the baby's just a blob or something. I looked it up.'

'What about later, when you're too big to fit behind the controls?'

She shook her head. 'I don't even know if I'll keep it yet.'

He walked to an empty bench and sat down, sighing heavily. 'This is *not* what I thought your call was about.'

She sat beside him. 'I'm sorry.'

'I thought you'd finally come to your senses and fallen in love with me,' he said, pulling out a cigarette case and offering her one. 'I keep forgetting, you don't smoke,' he said. 'I think I know everything about you, then I realise I don't know you at all.'

She sat quietly next to him. 'I haven't *fallen in love* with anyone,' she said. 'I think that's the problem.'

'Do you love him? Do you think you could marry him?'

'His name is William,' she said. 'And I do have feelings for him. But if we hadn't just survived a plane crash, we wouldn't have...'

Giles turned to look down at her. 'You keep your feelings locked up tight, don't you? You must have been thinking very oddly to give in to impulse.' He looked away. 'I just wish you'd done it with me.'

She smiled. 'I'd just had a bump on the head,' she admitted. 'But it wasn't that. We were alive and I didn't intend – I didn't know what I intended. It was dawn, he was there, we were *alive*. Don't tell me you didn't feel like that after the Mosquito came down in the river.'

'*In the river* sounds so much more romantic than on the mud,' he said, finishing his cigarette and stubbing it out under his shoe. 'But yes, that night, my senses were heightened, and you were there and beautiful... If you had agreed I would have taken you back to my bed. To celebrate being alive, and in love.'

'And *you* would probably have got me pregnant,' she said, the smile fading.

'It's not the end of the world,' he said. 'Just your freedom. Unless—'

'I'm not going to do that,' she answered. 'So there will be a baby.' The idea gave her a flicker of warmth for the first time. 'I'll just have to deal with it. My mother did.'

He looked across the tracks, then stood up. Before she could move, he went onto one knee.

'This is absolutely not the way this was supposed to happen,' he grumbled, fishing in an inside pocket of his jacket.

'Giles, no, don't...' He held out a box, and opened it to reveal a ring glistening on a cushion of silk. A diamond glinted in the low light.

'Will you marry me?'

She flinched, seeing the yearning in his eyes. 'But I'm having a baby, someone else's baby.'

'That's not the baby's fault, is it? I suppose your William's a decent sort or you wouldn't have gone with him. I'll do my best to bring him up as my son – or daughter. And to make you a good husband.' His mouth quirked into a twisted smile. 'I'll do my best to make you happy, Clara.'

'I don't know what to say,' she whispered. 'I want to say yes, because I know how you make me feel.'

He stood up, brushed his knee off, and tossed the ring box towards her. She caught it on reflex.

'No! I mean, you should keep this, hold onto it.'

'If I fall for anyone else – and I'm hoping I will – she'll get her own ring,' he said roughly. 'But until then, you're the only one I love. It's yours.'

She stood next to him, then put the box in her pocket. 'Thank you for asking, thank you for the offer – but I think you should take your time before taking on my child.'

His hands curved on her waist. 'Kiss me, even if you won't marry me. At least I know you'll do that.'

She kissed him, losing herself again in his arms. A train clanking and puffing onto the station made them pull apart. She checked the chalkboard with the times of the train. 'This one's mine,' she said, as he opened a door for her. 'Don't stop writing,' she said, leaning out of the window. 'Giles, don't forget! I do love you,' she said, helplessly, as he kissed her again. 'But...'

'Come back to me when you're in love with me,' he said, with his rakish smile. '*Just* me.'

37

PRESENT DAY, DECEMBER

Ruby had set up a small group of volunteers who could pop in on Pony while she went back to town to work, and help look after Max when he came home. He was improving, could now get out of bed and shuffle to the bathroom with a walker, and was eating better. He interrogated her during each of her visits to the care home about what these new people – the Oldstocks – wanted, how they were trying to rip her off. Finally, she went up to pack his things and bring him home.

She got a notification on her phone while she was there. It was the estimate for the valuation. she was so shocked she showed it to him, shaking. 'Everything adds up to more than one and a half million, Max. How can that be? How can I pay tax on all of that? They think the house won't sell for much more than a million.'

'Have these people made you a formal offer?'

'Not yet. Maybe they won't,' she said, gloomily, folding spare pyjamas into his case. 'It needs so much work.'

'What about your young man? What does he think?'

She shook her head. 'He thinks I'll end up with a few

hundred thousand after everything is settled. But then, where would you and Pony go if you don't stay at the house?'

'Never mind us. You'd get a tidy sum. Much better than if that woman Mabel inherits it all.'

She allowed herself to think about it. 'I suppose then I'd end up with nothing,' she said. 'And still have you, Pony and four chickens to find a home for.'

'We're not your problem, we're not helpless,' he said, reaching for a sandwich left for his supper. 'Pony and I can find something together, if we have to. We can share our resources.'

'It's not like you can move in with me,' she said, a spark of humour lightening her mood.

'Bunk beds,' he said, with a wheezy cough that turned into a laugh. 'Pony said your young man suggested that. How are you going to sort out this woman's claim?'

'Jake's taken bits and bobs that might have Marissa's DNA on. Letters and things, even a few bits of Clara's. Mabel has sent some specimens off for DNA analysis.' She smiled at Max. 'She just wants to find out about her mother. She died last year and… well, you look for something to hang onto. I found shopping lists in one of Mum's coats, old train tickets for journeys I didn't know about. It's like she's there for a moment.'

Max looked at her with such understanding she could feel tears welling up. 'I remember you wanted her to tell you who your father was,' he said, in his cracked voice. 'Before she died.'

For a moment, her heart jumped in her chest. 'Do you know?'

'I've had my suspicions, but she was seeing a couple of men at the time. One was a ceramicist with crazy metal glazes, Jim something. The other one was a strange man from Canada, liked to go up the land in the nude as I recall. I suppose he worked out why people on Dartmoor don't go barefoot.'

'Gorse, thistles, nettles,' she said, managing a smile. 'What makes you think he might be…?'

'Well, they had a really intense relationship over that summer. And Jim would swing by with his truck and take her off to a festival or whatever. I don't think she was sure herself, back then.' He grinned. 'She was a free spirit. You could be a little more like that.'

'I wish I was,' she answered. 'I feel downtrodden and dull, right now.' She turned an idea over in her mind. 'I might try a DNA test, see if it comes up with any matches. And if you could remember any names, I could research potential relatives and family trees, but honestly, I don't mind that much.'

'Give it a try. It might help this woman, not to mention adding her to your family tree,' Max said.

'I'd like that, I like Mabel,' she said. She stood up and grabbed her coat and bag. 'Love you,' she said, and kissed his bristly cheek. 'Let's get you into the car. I promised we'd get you home for Christmas.'

'You owe me some home-made biscuits,' he said. 'Pony tells me when you make them for her.'

'I'll make some more.' She got as far as the wheelchair by the door before she turned. 'What do you think of this idea to make a sort of hotel for older people?'

He shrugged. 'I think I'd like to ask them more about it.'

'I'll get them to talk to you when you've settled in. I'd love your opinion.'

She had sorted out a hospital bed and reclining chair for Max. She had been worried about the steps up to the front door, but Max was determined and was installed in his new room. Once Ruby had an hour to herself, she did some family research.

Ruby had always wondered about Clara's friend, or fiancé, Giles Ashton-Wilson, and searched for living relatives. His son, Sir Richard, was living at the family estate in West Sussex. He had published a book about his father's service and she was halfway through it.

Maybe Sir Richard didn't know much about Clara – he mentioned her only twice as a fellow pilot and family friend, when he recorded her death. There were no details, but Giles seemed to have thrown himself into his work, recording the most kills of his career in the months after she died, and being shot down himself, spending many weeks recovering.

On impulse, she emailed Sir Richard through his estate blog, and received a prompt answer and invitation to visit him. She arranged to meet Jake at the nearby station at Arundel, and drive there at the weekend. In the meantime, she worked through the week, sorting through more boxes of prints and paperwork from the house in her spare time.

Marissa loved photographing the moor in snow. There were hundreds of landscapes in blizzard, after heavy snow, and when it melted. Some were in colour, many done after Alice died, and labelled on the back with the name of the book or magazine that published them. Tourist boards took several, too. Ruby's favourite was one of herself, in welly boots, being lifted up by a younger Max to refill the bird feeders. She remembered it well – she must have been three, and she could see Alice at the side holding out a box of peanuts. On the back, a single line: *Darling Ruby*.

She covered her face with her hands, tears bubbling up as they did, often, since her mother's death. Now she felt like she was losing her whole past, along with the house. She often felt as if a photographer was watching her through a long lens, when she was in the garden, or almost heard an instruction to pose by a window or stand taller and look over her shoulder, one of Marissa's favourite poses.

She collected the few remaining personal items relating to Clara. She could imagine the distraught Marissa and Alice going through her belongings, looking for her, as she now was doing for Fiona.

She started sorting through her mother's old clothes, boxed up under the bed. She recognised the T-shirts Fiona had dyed, a pair of shorts she had worn for gardening, with bits of hessian string in the pockets. She searched every pocket as she went through, deciding what to keep, what to throw away and what could be donated. A receipt for flowers she must have bought for Marissa, who had a fresh vase every week. A shopping list on pink paper in Ruby's childish hand, asking for rabbit food for Arnold the grumpy bunny, and a chocolate flake. Fiona had drawn a heart around it, which brought on tears.

The light was going outside – the shadows seemed longer so close to the winter solstice – and she was comforted by the sense of a hand resting briefly on her hair.

38

SEPTEMBER 1943

Clara tried several times to tell William about the baby in a letter, but she couldn't. Instead, she invited him down to Hamble in between shifts. He chose the first offered date, which made her nervous. Perhaps he was making the same assumption Giles had made.

She met him at the station, having cycled up. Her figure was a little fuller; the pregnancy had done wonders for her bust but little for her appetite. She just hoped he didn't notice before she could explain.

His smile was as crooked and lovely as always, and her own smile responded even as her heart fluttered in her chest.

'Clara! You look lovely,' he said, kissing first her cheek then her lips. 'I've missed your letters. You must have been busy – I know we are.'

'Three planes a day, every day,' she acknowledged. Before she could take her handlebars he did so, balancing his bag on the seat. 'How's combat been?' she asked.

He took a moment before answering, a shadow coming across his face. 'Most of it is flying in formation, watching everything around us. Then there are these intense minutes where everyone is dodging each other and getting shot at – it was so confusing at first.' He looked across the field to the sunset, just starting to paint the sky with pinks and peaches. 'I met your friend,' he said, finally. 'Giles Ashton-Wilson. He's a marvellous flyer. He pilots like he'll risk anything to get his kill. He's flying with a load of Poles, they are brilliant.'

Her heart lurched. 'Have you spoken to him?'

'A little. He introduced himself to me, said he was your friend.' He looked down. 'He's the other man, isn't he? The one you are very fond of.'

'He is,' she said, baldly. 'I'm *very fond* of both of you.'

He held his bag as he bumped the bicycle down the lane. His smile had gone. 'Do you sleep with him, too?'

'No!' She walked behind him, having to speed up to match him. 'I wouldn't have slept with you, either, but...'

He stopped so abruptly, she almost ran into him. 'I'm curious. Why *did* you sleep with me?'

She stared into his eyes, noticing new lines on his forehead, around his eyes. Combat put a special stress on pilots; she had seen the same strain on Giles's face.

'I woke up,' she said, slowly. 'You were asleep, you were just so...' It was hard to put into words. 'We nearly died that day. I knew we might lose each other one day, that there might not be another day like that, when we got out of the plane.'

'And hobbled away,' he said, a hint of a smile creasing around his eyes. 'I suppose we were lucky there weren't any consequences,' he said, as he started walking away.

Clara stared after him. 'But there were,' she blurted out.

He stopped and looked over his shoulder at her, silhouetted against the now red sky. 'What?'

'That night. I'm having a baby.'

He turned and stared at her for a long moment. 'Is it mine?' he said, finally.

That hurt, like a thump to the chest. 'You know it is! You're the only person I've...'

'Not Giles? Really?'

She tried not to get angry, told herself he must be shocked, he was allowed to be upset. 'No. Just you.'

'Did you call me down here to tell me you would marry me after all?'

'No,' she snapped. 'That didn't cross my mind. Because after the war you're probably going back to America, to Wisconsin, and I'll never see you again.'

'I could stay,' he said, then turned back to the lane. 'I would stay for you. But I only want you to marry me when you love me so much you can't say no,' he said, pushing the bike on. 'Wherever *we* choose to live, we'll be together. I don't want you to marry me out of necessity.'

'If I wanted that, I would be marrying Giles. He already asked me,' she said, to his back. 'And he'll accept the baby as his.'

He stopped again. 'Big of him. Did you accept?'

'No,' she said helplessly. 'But he gave me a ring, too.'

That made him chuckle. 'You'll have to start a collection, cover the baby's college fund.'

She caught up with him. 'Please don't laugh at me,' she said. 'I'm so tired. I can't sleep, I worry about what I'm going to do every day.'

'But no answers?'

She shook her head. 'I want to keep the baby, but I won't be able to work, and maybe no one will want me further down the line...'

He took her in his arms. 'The right man will always want you,' he said. 'I just hope it's going to be me.' He stepped back. 'You're having a baby. *My* baby. When will you tell your commanding officer?' he asked, holding her as if he couldn't let go.

'As late as possible. I don't want to be put on ground duties or worse, sacked. The baby's fine where he is. Once he's born, I'll look into nannies and nursery nurses. My mothers will help, I know they will. But I don't know if I can continue to work if I'm living on Dartmoor.'

'I wish you would stand down. You've done enough for the war effort.' He sighed. 'I suppose you could fly to Bristol and back once a week if your flying club is still open.'

It was a good idea, she could see it working, if the runway were still kept in order. He kissed her again and the thought retreated.

'When will I see you again?'

He pulled away a little. 'Soon, if you want to. I'm still going to ask you to make an honest man of me every time I see you,' he added.

'Have you heard from May recently?'

'Most weeks. She's dating a student doctor from Connecticut called Harley.'

She smiled in the darkness. 'Will you tell her about the baby?'

'I expect I will. I'm in the habit of telling her things, and you know how close we are.'

Clara felt a pang of something like jealousy at his relationship with May. 'But she won't tell your parents?'

He patted his coat down as if looking for something. 'No, he said. 'We keep each other's secrets.' He pressed a note into her hand. 'I have her address written down. If anything happens – anything untoward – would you write to her? Explain what happened, that sort of thing. A notification telegram would go to my parents, she might not hear straight away and there won't be any personal details.'

'Of course I will,' she said, choked up. 'But you're going to be fine. You need to be careful, we all need you.'

'And I'm as cautious as I can be, but I need to do the job. *You* know.'

Remembering some of the shot-up, beaten-up American planes she'd taken for repairs, she did. 'I wish you weren't still flying,' she said.

'I wish *you* weren't,' he said, 'doubly, since you're carrying my child. Just keep my proposal in mind, won't you? You and the baby would be safe because you could resign, live with your mothers on Dartmoor. I could live in England, after the war, at least some of the time. And you might fall in love with America one day.'

The pull of the moor was powerful, and she could imagine growing her baby with her mothers' support. But it all seemed so far away, so far in the future. 'Maybe' was all she could say as she tucked the note into her purse, and kissed him. She wondered if she would see him again.

39

PRESENT DAY, DECEMBER

The weather on Saturday was bright as Ruby pulled her car into Arundel station to meet the London train. A striking young woman with flame-red hair was helping Jake with his bags.

'Hi,' he said, pecking Ruby's cheek. 'This is Emmy – Emerald. My daughter. She was so curious, she wanted to come. I hope you don't mind.'

'No,' Ruby said, a little breathless, holding out a hand. 'I'm glad you came, I wanted to meet you.'

'Me too I had to come,' Emmy said, shaking Ruby's hand then hugging her anyway. 'Dad's new case is such a great story, Clara the aviator. And Giles was good-looking, wasn't he?' She bounced on her toes. 'I hope he's nice, this Sir Richard,' she said, grinning. 'Shall I get in the back?'

Jake opened the door for her. 'I'm sorry if this is a problem,' he added. 'She's an unstoppable force.'

'I'm sure it will be fine,' Ruby said, as they got in the front of the car. 'I'm just not sure how he will feel about possibly having a new branch on his noble family tree. But it would be great for Mabel to fill in some of the blanks.'

'It must have happened before,' Emmy said, but her voice

was subdued. 'All families have their odd corners. My great-grandmother was pregnant when she got married, it was a family scandal.'

Ruby smiled. 'In my line of work, you see a lot of odd adoptions and late marriages. In a world before birth control, what else could they do?'

She followed her satnav's instructions for a couple of miles and came to a set of wrought-iron gates about twelve feet tall. In the distance, down a drive, she could see some high chimneys. 'It's a bit Downton Abbey,' she said, but at their approach, the gates swung open easily.

The house wasn't huge – a neat Georgian brick building with tall windows. As they parked in front of it, next to several vehicles, a tall man with a shock of white hair walked forward in a colourful jumper over shirt and trousers. He stood straight and was recognisable as Sir Richard from his website. Ruby knew his own military career had been as long and successful as his father's.

'Sir Richard?' she said, as she walked forward. He shook her hand with painfully strong fingers. 'You must be Ruby St John,' he said. 'And this is Jake Haydon?' he shook his hand. He stood back to stare at Emmy. 'And who is this young lady?'

Emmy took a step forward to clasp his hand. 'I'm Jake's daughter, Emerald,' she said. 'Emmy. I was just curious about Clara, it's such a romantic story.'

'It certainly is, come on in. We have quite a few pictures of Clara here.' He had long legs, and Ruby had to trot a bit to keep up as he led them up the steps and through double doors into a beautiful drawing room, with a thick carpet and a large television. He switched it off with a remote. 'Come in, come in. Don't worry about your shoes, this carpet's seen a lot more dirt that you can bring in. Sit down, shall we have some tea? Or coffee, since you're an American, Jake?'

Ruby and Jake sat on a sofa, and Emmy sat on a chair next

to Jake. As Ruby looked up, she saw a full-length portrait of a young woman, looking over her shoulder into the room. She had dark red waves rippling onto her shoulders, a silk dress with buttons all the way down the back, and exposed, creamy shoulders. Striking but not beautiful, her features a little large, her face a bit long, she was still stunning. 'Is that...?' stammered Ruby.

'Yes,' Sir Richard said, looking up. 'It's Clara. Alice St John painted her when she was in her early twenties, before Dad even met her. After she died, Marissa wanted to burn it, so Alice let my father have it. He treasured it in private, in his office, but he didn't display it until my mother died in sixty-seven.'

'I've never seen that,' Ruby said. 'Or even sketches for it, or photographs.' Clara was draped in a gown the colour of ripe wheat, almost gold. Turned to the viewer, she looked magnificent, and behind her soared the uplands of Dartmoor and the granite tors

'She was the love of my father's life,' Sir Richard said, turning to speak to an older man who had entered the room. He asked for drinks, while Jake stood and stared up at her.

'The love of his life. Was he the father of her child, too?' Jake asked.

Sir Richard stood next to him. 'He never said but I often wondered. He left a stack of letters that she sent over the several years they saw each other, but the only mention of a baby was in the year before her death. She made it quite plain that she didn't want to saddle him with a child, she would bring it up alone.'

'So, it could have been his?' Ruby and Jake stared at each other. 'I thought they were engaged,' she blurted.

'I think they were. At least, she still had the engagement ring he gave her when she died.'

He went to his desk and retrieved a small box. Inside were

two rings, one with a large diamond, one with a smaller diamond and two sapphires. 'She wore these around her neck on her final flight. My father didn't talk about them, but they were some of his most precious belongings.'

The rings were twisted at right angles by some terrible force, and when Emmy joined them, she gasped. 'How did she die? Ruby?'

'All I know is that there was a terrible incident, during the war.' Ruby looked away and sat down, shaking. The horror of the event was written large in the gold. 'Why are there *two* rings?'

'I never found out. He didn't tell me. I think he bought the big diamond one, though. The other one wasn't his style, it didn't cost as much.'

'Maybe – William's?' she said, looking up at Jake. He was still staring at the rings.

'Perhaps,' he said, reaching out a finger to touch them then drawing back. 'This makes it real,' he said, his voice thick. 'My client's grandfather adopted a baby, Wilhelmina, in 1945 in America. Clara's name was written along the top of the adoption certificate in pencil. Not official, but it was there.'

'My father tried to claim the baby, after she died,' Sir Richard said. 'My family assumed it was his, and wanted to find her a good home. But for some reason, it never happened. I believe the child went to America.'

Ruby slipped her hand into Jake's when he sat back down next to her. His fingers were cold. 'The dots are joined up,' she said. 'Mabel's mother must have been Clara's baby. With Giles probably the father.'

Sir Richard sat down opposite them, smiling at Emmy who was still enraptured by the picture. 'It sounds like she was a magnificent woman,' he said. 'And you know her granddaughter, is that right? I'd love to meet her, or her mother, Wilhelmina.'

'Wilhelmina just died recently,' Jake said. 'Mabel adored her, it was her death that got her interested in finding her English family.'

'What happened to Giles?' Ruby asked, as a tea tray was set down on a large coffee table.

'After Clara died, I think he struggled for a bit. He was given leave after an injury and went a bit mad. His words, not mine. When he got better, he went to Clara's family home to see the baby '

Ruby locked eyes with him. 'Why?'

'I think he had an idea of taking her if no one else wanted her. I don't know what was said, but he was reassured that she would be looked after and loved, anyway. I do know Clara's mother was completely prostrate with grief after she died.'

Ruby couldn't imagine how chaotic a house with two grieving mothers and a young baby would be. 'If Alice wanted to keep the baby, would she even have the right? She wasn't Clara's biological mother. I mean, legally she was just Marissa's *friend*.' She couldn't imagine the agony of losing both Clara and then her baby. She thought it had left a mark on Marissa and Alice, and also their home. Sadness and grief drifted around Marissa's part of the house to this day. 'You've been so helpful, so kind,' she said, eyes filling up with tears.

'I'm happy to talk about my father, any time,' he said, his own eyes shining. 'He met my mother and made a good county marriage. He became the local magistrate and they had five children, so it couldn't have been too bad. But he was never really affectionate with my mother, more like good friends who had a job to do, being Sir Giles and Lady Ashton-Wilson. They were brilliant at it.'

'But he hid the picture?'

'Alice gave it to him, to remember her, I suppose. It wasn't hidden, my mother just never came in his office. Once she died it came out and went up in pride of place. He said he wouldn't marry again and he never did.' His eyes twinkled. 'There were a few mistresses along the way, though. He died in his nineties, after breaking his leg falling off a ladder in the orchard. Let me show you around the property.'

Sir Richard gave them a tour of the house, and showed them several portraits of Giles from childhood to old age, until they were ready to go. He stopped Ruby at the door and offered his hand. 'Our families should stay friends,' he said, to all of them. 'And I'd love to meet Mabel. And I'd be happy to give DNA to see if I'm related to Mabel, if you like.'

He shook hands with them, and Emmy kissed his cheek.

Ruby walked out to the car, her eyes itching with unshed tears and her heart warm. 'He's lovely,' she said to Jake. 'That picture of Clara, though. I know he'll never let it go, but...'

'Oh, he will,' Emmy said from the back seat. 'Didn't he tell you? He said, when he dies, he'll leave it to you. He means to get to a hundred and he's only seventy-eight, though, so he says you'll have to wait. But you can visit whenever you want.'

Ruby caught Jake's eye for a moment and he laid his hand briefly on her arm. 'I'm glad we came,' he said.

'Me too,' she said, concentrating on driving him to the station. It was getting harder to say goodbye to him every time.

40

DECEMBER 1943

Clara had to give up flying at six months pregnant. The ATA, while ignoring her pregnancy at first, would no longer allow her to fly when she couldn't safely bail out with her parachute. Still quite slender, Clara was reduced to returning to Montpelier House to complete her pregnancy.

A month later, she felt enormous, as if the baby had inflated. She was less agile and her back ached from time to time. Marissa was going through one of her inspired phases, when she walked miles over the moor, often talking to herself, taking a sketchbook with her. Alice watched her from the house with a pair of binoculars, and occasionally sent a maid out to fetch her.

'Poor darling, she's quite manic at the excitement,' Alice said, sitting with Clara in the sun on the front terrace. 'She'll probably come down with a bump when she runs out of steam. Tell me, is this too small for baby?'

Clara looked at the lacy knitting. 'I have no idea. You have much more experience than me.'

'Twenty-five years ago I had an idea,' Alice reminded her. 'You have to remember, we were virtually children ourselves.'

'It must have been strange for you both,' Clara said, unable to imagine what life had been like for them, with no parents to support them. 'Why were you living on your own when I was born?'

'Well, Marissa was supposed to be living with a nurse who cared for fallen women. She was eighteen and her lover had been killed in the war. They were engaged. I think she thought sleeping with him would comfort him, before he went to the front.'

Clara knew the basic story but her mothers had never talked about the earliest days of their relationship. 'So where did you meet her?'

Alice smiled, finishing another tiny row and turning it. 'I know we always tell people we met at art school. I was there at sixteen because I'd been expelled from two "nice" girls' boarding schools already. For kissing the other girls, mostly, and running away. But I loved painting, so I behaved at St Ives – as much as I needed to. I dressed as a boy to clamber all over the cliffs and the beach. I used to go out with the fishing boats some-times, to get inspired by that gorgeous colour in the seas around the bay.' She looked over at Clara, her expression sombre. 'I met Marissa on the cliffs one day. I'd seen her there before, just standing, staring out at the sea. But this day she looked even sadder than usual.'

Clara stared back. 'Do you think – was she going to jump?'

'I don't know. She always says not, but... she looked so terribly sad. Anyway, I ran over to her, whooping to get her attention. She said I sounded like a goose flying overhead. I arrived, standing there in my boy's clothes, and she was in some beautiful dress and a sort of cloak over it. She looked an absolute picture, a heroine from a romantic story, I just longed to paint her. I blurted out that I was an artist and would she model for me?'

'What did she say?'

'She looked at me as if I was mad. She ran her hands over

her belly, like that would put me off. She looked like a goddess, her red hair rippling down her back, that wonderful profile turned back to the sea.' Clara knew that picture; Alice had painted it several times in different media. 'Then she asked me if I was really an artist. I told her I was at the school of painting and we walked down to the village together. She must have seen something hopeful in me. By the end of the week we had met every day, she had told me all about her tragic story, and I worshipped her. I started visiting the house, and that's when we started kissing. The woman paid to look after her threw me out, and Marissa packed up her bags and followed me to the cottage my father was renting for me. I had a maid, she looked after us both, even after Marissa's father, the earl, came and threatened us. But eventually he left her to "come to her senses".' She smiled. 'She hasn't yet, thank goodness.'

'But how did she have me? Did she go into a hospital?'

Alice put down the lacy cap. 'A woman visited, a midwife. Neither of us trusted her, although she was perfectly polite. She was employed by the earl – to spy on us, I presume – but he needn't have worried. We held hands sometimes and occasionally exchanged kisses, but never when the woman was there. My maid had been engaged by the art school – she was my age and enjoyed running our whole tiny household. Her name was Beatrice Goddings.'

'*Our* Mrs Goddings? I always thought she came here when you bought the house.'

'We sent for her especially when we moved here, later. She was the perfect maid for us, hardly twenty years old. She could cook, too. When Marissa started getting her labour pains, she didn't call for this London nurse who was waiting in a hotel. She sent for the local midwife, whose Cornish accent was almost indecipherable.' She paused, as if thinking back, remembering. 'We were so romantic, then. We saw ourselves as heroines in a fairy story, condemned to our doomed love. I had never seen Marissa naked until that day, I had never touched her in any way other than kiss her. She was my goddess. We were so innocent.'

Clara couldn't picture her mothers being anything other than deeply affectionate with one another, the way she'd always known them. 'How long did that last?'

Alice smiled broadly. 'Beatrice gave us some special oil to heal poor Marissa's bruised body. And lavender oil to massage her shoulders, and special cream for her sore nipples. We were lovers by the time you were weaned. Then the earl sent his servants to the cottage to collect Marissa. I was seventeen by now, and she was nineteen. She refused to leave without me. The servants were under orders to take the baby if she refused to go with them, so she went.' She looked down at her hands, turned the ornate wedding band she always wore. 'They were the worst four months of my life. And Marissa said you cried every day, all day, without me. Eventually, they sent her away to a seaside retreat and I joined her there. You settled for the first time in months, Marissa slept and we all snuggled every night in our big bed. We hatched plans for our future.'

'And my grandfather eventually agreed?'

'I don't know what Marissa had told him about me, but he visited one day and took me out for dinner. We must have looked strange. I wore a proper evening dress, kid half-boots, my hair up. I looked like a debutante, he looked like – well – as if I was his mistress. He was very uncomfortable.' She threw back her head and laughed. 'He asked me what my intentions were, as if I was her young man.'

Clara rubbed the spot where the baby was kicking, and Alice slid over to add her warm hand to soothe the baby. 'What did you say?'

'I said we were either going to bring embarrassment and gossip onto both our families, or we could move somewhere remote and live discreetly.'

'And he agreed?'

Alice nodded. 'He wasn't really the problem,' she said. 'It was her mother who insisted she go to social events, leaving you and me behind. She was hoping to catch a husband for Marissa. She even introduced her to Paul's brother, in the hope that she would take to him.'

'Paul?' Clara only knew that her father had died young, in a battle in the war. Marissa had carefully guarded his name.

'Will you promise me not to try and contact his family?' Alice asked. 'I shouldn't have said anything, but it feels like the time you should know.'

'Please tell me. I just want a name.'

Alice stood up and rummaged through one of the drawers in a bureau. 'I think you've seen this, haven't you?'

Clara took the tiny photograph of a young man in uniform, pale with dark eyes. 'That's my father?'

'His name was Paul Wyndham, he was a wonderful poet. He and Marissa were thrown together by his family, and they were a bit worried that he was too sensitive and artistic to be very – well, manly. But they were wrong. He led his men for four months with great bravery, before dying in a perfectly manly manner.' She looked down at the picture. 'They made love during his last leave, she was so sad and afraid for him. The war had haunted him. He only had one long weekend at home, bringing dispatches. She said she so wanted to make him happy, but she could never give him the adoration he seemed to need. She blamed herself a little for his death.'

Clara picked up the cap Alice had been knitting and turned it around in her fingers. It was so soft and tiny. She couldn't imagine the wriggling monkey in her belly being a baby in a hat. 'Love is complicated,' she murmured, thinking of Giles and William, each with their own terrible role in the war. 'I can't choose one of them over the other.'

'You don't have to. You're not head over heels with either of them, and you need that to go through a long marriage.'

'Will I never be in love, then?' Clara asked, longing for clarity.

'You will with the baby. We fall in love with our children,' Alice said softly. 'It's my one regret. No matter how much I love your mother, I would have liked to have another baby for our family. But I have you, my darling. And soon we will have your baby to adore.'

41

PRESENT DAY, JANUARY

They had a date for the probate hearing, at least, in February. Emmy had come down with Jake for New Year's, to help clear up the house after a quiet Christmas, ready for sale. Ruby had been too busy with Max and Pony to ask the Haydons to celebrate at the house, but she had wondered what it would have been like. The roof patch had been improved with a temporary repair, the scaffolding outside the back door providing perches for the chickens. Now there were no leaks, the floors and ceilings had started to dry out. The builders had also put a temporary piece of wood down to fill in the hole in the floor, and despite her reservations about rodents, the huge velvet sofa had been sent off for restoration. Ruby could imagine it in front of the big window in her apartment, overlooking the sea, but taking up much of the floor space. She could see how the picture of the baby might go on the wall behind it. It was so much part of her childhood, memories of her grandmothers and mother. She looked at the frame of it, screwed to the wooden panelling, the dust veiling the landscape around the edge. The dog was just a mound of black and tan fur.

'Jake, are you busy?' she called through to the hallway,

where he was packing up books. The Oldstocks had put stickers on anything they felt they would like to keep in the house, but the pictures still had to go into storage during the renovation. Ruby was moved to find they wanted to keep anything pertinent to Clara and Marissa that she didn't want. Marissa's old stick and Clara's riding crop would still be part of the house. But she had fought off all offers to sell the painting, either to the Oldstocks or to Mabel.

'Are you going to try to take the picture down?'

'I need some help,' she said, her face warming a little. 'I'm sorry, I know Mabel would like to buy it.'

He peered at the rusted screws and picked up a couple of screwdrivers. 'It's a gorgeous picture, and it should stay with you,' he said. 'But I hope to be able to visit it from time to time.'

She smiled and he kissed her. 'Any time,' she said.

He leaned closer to the painting. 'The more I see how beautifully painted it is, the more reluctant I am to risk damaging it,' he said, as he carefully started on one of the screws.

She tackled the one closest to the edge, afraid to scratch the canvas. The fixings were corroded and difficult to move, but she managed to get it turning.

'You really can visit it whenever you want,' she said in a rush.

He stepped back. 'It's *you* I want to visit.'

Her face curved into a smile involuntarily. 'We're so busy worrying about the family history and the house, we haven't talked about *us*.'

He turned back to the screw, winding it out of the wood and putting it in his pocket. 'I think it's time we had a heart-to-heart that didn't involve the house or Pony and Max. Can I stay for the evening? I'm happy to sleep in one of your many spare rooms.'

A knock on the door heralded one of Max's carers, and she

called through to let herself in, which gave Ruby a moment to think about her response.

'How about you and I go out to the Moorland Inn tonight for dinner, and talk about things, on our own?' she offered. 'I'll make up a spare bed for Emmy, too, if she doesn't mind keeping an eye on Pony.'

'About time!' Emmy shouted through from the hallways.

Ruby could feel herself going bright red. 'I'm not used to men with daughters,' she confessed.

'You get Emmy with me,' he said, grinning, a little pink himself. 'And you'll have to meet Fortuna, too, my ex-wife. You'll be a stepmother, of sorts, if you get tangled up with me.'

'I'm twenty-one, Dad, I don't need a stepmother,' Emmy said, putting her head around the door. She was covered with dusty streaks where she'd rubbed her eyes and nose, and pushed her hair out of her eyes. 'Can we agree that you two are head over heels, and move on? Glaciers move faster than you two.'

On impulse, Ruby stepped close to Jake and put her face up for him to kiss her. 'OK. Let's try going out properly.'

The next few screws were more difficult. One broke off and Ruby had to carefully drill it out. 'Last two,' Jake said, wiping sweat out of his eyes.

They wedged a side table and piles of books under the ornate frame, and worked together on the final fixture. Once the last one came out, they were able to lift the portrait carefully down.

'Emmy, come and see,' Ruby shouted. She tipped the picture forward, releasing decades of spiderwebs and mouse droppings, to see a decaying brown-paper backing. 'There might be a signature, or a note on the sitter,' she said. 'Shall we...?'

'You do it,' Jake said, bracing the frame and handing her a box cutter.

Very gently, she slit the yellowed tape holding the paper –

to reveal another picture. It was a man, very young and relaxed, his shirt open at the neck, sitting on a hay bale next to the other half of the dog.

'It's folded over,' Emmy said. 'Who is that?'

'I think... That looks like William Carlson, Mabel's grandfather,' Jake said. Together, they carefully opened the picture a little, to see the whole composition.

The dog sat between the two people, the baby smiling, the dog panting, the young man's hand just reaching behind the baby to steady her. The exposed part of the picture with his sleeve was so grimy Ruby hadn't noticed it before. 'I'll need to get this restored,' she said, as a piece of paper slipped onto the floor.

'What is that?' Jake said, leaning forward.

'It's the provenance,' Ruby said, tears rolling down her face. She ran her sleeve inelegantly over her face before Emmy handed her a tissue. 'It says: *William Carlson and Alissa Montpelier St John, child of Clara St John-Montpelier.* And it's signed with Alice's name.'

Jake held out his arms and she went into his hug. When she looked up, they were alone.

'I can't bear losing the house,' she said. 'Just when I feel so connected to it. But this is Mabel's grandmother – maybe she has more right to it.' It hurt to say so, but it helped, too, like taking a cast off a broken limb.

'This is the house where you grew up, where your mother grew up,' he said, and kissed her again. 'Your history is going with you, wherever you go. And I will be coming with you. The Oldstocks will appreciate this place and do something wonderful with it. And we'll be visiting Pony and Max regularly, so you won't be gone altogether.'

'How can you come with me? Your job is in London. How can we have a long-distance relationship?'

'I can do most of my work from home. Maybe I can stay

nearby when I come down to see you. Alternatively, have you got room for me to visit your flat?' he asked. 'I'd invite you to London, but my place is little more than a studio. Even Emmy has to sleep on the sofa.'

'I've got two bedrooms. But we'll only need one,' she said, a little dizzy, smiling at him. 'We can keep the other one for Emmy.'

42

FEBRUARY 1944

Clara and her mothers went up to London a month before the baby was expected. She was booked into the same discreet hospital where she had been offered an illegal 'medical solution', but there she could give birth in private. Before she went into labour, they stayed in a small hotel out of the centre of town, and took taxis to see exhibitions and plays that attracted them. As was her habit when going out in town, Marissa dressed in sharp, tailored suits and top hats at rakish angles, but when they returned to the hotel, they dressed dowdy and plain, so as not to draw attention to Clara. She wasn't ashamed, exactly, but she knew there would be a lot of criticism if the news got out that the illegitimate child of Marissa Montpelier was repeating her mother's scandalous story.

She had plenty of time to think about Giles and William. She arranged to meet William in a Lyons tea shop in Coventry Street, hoping she wouldn't bump into anyone she knew. She slipped on the ring he had given her, and turned it around so the stones tickled her palm. His letters had softened from demands and lectures to sweet, sad notes of how much he missed her –

and his home in the USA. He'd been in hospital twice, once with a burned hand and once with smoke inhalation.

She had covered her hair with a drab hat and he looked around for a moment before he spotted her. He walked over, staring down at the bump pushing against the table.

She was shocked at how tired and thin he looked. 'Sit down, you look terrible.'

'You look really well,' he said, sitting opposite her. 'Rosy cheeks.'

'Two months of home cooking and country walks,' she answered. 'Really, Will, are you all right?'

'As well as any of us are,' he answered, pulling out a cigarette. 'Do you mind if I smoke? It helps with the fatigue. We're flying almost every day and they are long missions.'

'Of course,' she said, looking around for a waitress. She caught one girl's eye, and beckoned her over. She ordered tea, but William wanted coffee and was grateful for a plate of sandwiches.

'We'll have a plate of cakes, too,' Clara said. 'Make a proper afternoon tea of it.'

'Afternoon tea,' he said, his voice derisive. 'Luncheon and hats at the races and tea and cakes. That's what we're fighting for?' She'd never heard him sound so cynical.

She stared at him, at the new lines on his face. 'If you like,' she answered. 'And British children growing up free.'

He shut his eyes as he took a drag on his cigarette. 'I'm sorry. I don't know how to talk to you any more. I mean, you're having my baby and you won't let me be part of it.'

'You know how important you are to me!' She lowered her voice. 'Please don't talk like that. I have to do this properly, concentrate on the baby.'

'The child who will be born a bastard,' he snapped. 'Unless you climb off your horse and marry me like any decent woman would do for her child.'

She wasn't taken in by his outburst – his eyes were brimming with tears even as they blazed with his anger. 'I'm guessing you have told your parents,' she said. 'And they are disappointed with you.'

'They are disappointed that I got mixed up with someone like you,' he said, then rubbed his eyes. 'Clara, it's so simple. I love you, you love me, and even if we didn't, we should still look after our child. Take responsibility.'

'Marriage is for life,' she said, then fell silent as the waitress arranged their drinks and food on the table. 'I was born out of wedlock. I managed.' There had been a few remarks that she had chosen to ignore when she was at school, and she had not been invited to be introduced to royalty or to come out into society, but her whole life had been full of love and adventure.

'America is different,' he said. 'My family are religious.'

'But this baby isn't going to *be* in America,' she said, pouring her tea and pleased that her hand didn't shake. 'After all this time at home, I've worked that much out. I'd be happy to visit, and those lakes of yours sound amazing. But my child will be born here and be a British citizen. A child of the moor, like me.'

'So, that's it, then? You're going to marry the rich baronet-in-waiting. Will he pretend the baby is his?'

She put her gloved hands in her lap. 'We don't need to make a scene, William. Please keep your voice down.'

'I should shake some sense into you,' he said, staring at her with anger in his face. Then his eyes softened. 'Except I could never harm a hair on your head.'

'I'm not getting married until after the war,' she said, looking away. 'I can't think straight when you could be killed any minute.' *Or Giles could be shot down.* 'I've lost too many friends to this war already.' She looked steadily into his eyes. 'You must give me time. Maybe I'm not ready to be a wife, but I'm definitely not ready to be a widow.'

He put out his hand to her and she saw the tip of his right ring finger was gone, just a pink step where it had been.

Tears came easily then as she reached out for it. 'Oh, *Will*.'

'It's nothing, stray bullet,' he said, taking her hand in his. 'Just tell me. Do you still love me?'

'Of course I do!' she choked. 'But I just want to get through this pregnancy in one piece.'

'What are you going to call the baby?' he said, his hand cold in hers. 'If it's a boy, would you call him William?'

She smiled through her tears. 'Our housekeeper, Mrs Goddings, says it's a girl. She has some daft superstitions. I thought I would name her after one of my mothers, if she is. If it's a boy... I thought Paul. I recently found out my father was called Paul.'

'I like the idea of naming him – or her – after family,' he said. 'I'm the third William in my family.'

She smiled as he poured his coffee. 'Would you mind if I gave him a middle name of William?'

His hand faltered for a moment. 'As long as you don't make it Giles.'

43

Ruby and Jake were exploring their new relationship. Emmy, even when she had to go back to her research, had loosened them up. Ruby found herself video-calling him every evening to share their days' activities, plan their next date, talk about their future. Emmy would ask questions that Jake would pass on to her, helping them get to know each other better. 'Where will you put the picture when it's restored?' was one.

Ruby had thought about it over the day, as she mentored a couple of new archivists and took delivery of a mass of Tudor writings, welded together by insect and rodent activity. She used her phone to show him the back of the room, overlooking the double-height windows that faced the sea. 'It won't be in direct sunlight there.'

'Your flat looks right over the sea?'

'Over the Hoe – that's a big green space that leads to it,' she said, in a rush. She didn't want to crowd him, but she was dying to have him visit. 'What about your place? What's your apartment like?'

'Come up to London and have a look for yourself,' he said. 'It's just me, Emmy's off again, surveying ancient forests.'

'I don't know if I can leave Max and Pony for long,' she demurred. But she did want to go, and found herself warming to the idea, not least because they hadn't been alone very much. 'I'll try and get a rota of people to pop in. If I did come to London, we could visit the painting at the restoration studio.'

'I'd love that. You said Pony and Max have managed better this week, too.'

'I'll take a couple of days leave, if I can get cover,' she said. 'And I'll go back to the house for the weekend when I get back, so Pony and Max can moan at me. Yes, Jake, I'd love that.'

A fortuitous phone call from the Oldstocks helped with the plan to get away. Imogen asked if she and her father could bring their architect to measure up and draw up rough plans on Thursday and Friday, and were more than happy to keep an eye on the tenants both days. Max had already struck up a friendship with Maurice, who was fifteen years his junior. He said their talks made him feel young again. Pony flirted with Maurice, but also loved chatting to Imogen about the artworks she had made that were dotted all over the house.

Ruby caught the train at Plymouth, changed at Exeter, and settled into a comfortable seat to get to London. They had agreed to meet at Paddington station, so they could go straight to the picture restoration studio near Hyde Park.

When they arrived, they were ushered upstairs to a light room where the whole painting had been mounted on a temporary frame. Ruby had been too scared to flatten the whole picture out at home – loose flakes of paint had fallen out from where it had been folded. Now they could see its size, and the colour contrast between the fresh-looking hidden part and the paler exposed part.

'Has it bleached terribly?' Ruby asked the conservator, Gemma.

'Probably a bit, but the pale part is just massively covered in dust. This was hung when it was still a little tacky – you wouldn't be able to feel it, but the picture was *new*. Oil paint can take months to cure and a year to completely dry. Dust and pollen would have got attached in that first year, then built up on that rough surface over the decades. It should have been behind glass, really. Which proves it was painted there, an Alice St John picture, one of her best, I would say.'

Jake leaned in to inspect the new part of the painting. 'He looks so young,' he said, a little in awe. 'Just early twenties, and flying combat missions. Mabel sent me a few pictures from that era, one of them has the baby at age three or four, on his lap.' He pulled up the image on his phone.

Ruby and Gemma leaned in to see the image. 'That does look like him,' said Ruby. 'He was at the house, getting his portrait painted. Was *he* the baby's father, not Giles?'

'We haven't had it confirmed yet,' he said, looking over at Gemma. 'We're waiting for the results of the DNA testing. There was another guy in her story.'

'But not in this picture,' Ruby said. 'Did you identify the birds flying overhead?'

'Oh, I don't think they are birds,' Gemma said, putting on magnifying goggles and moving a blue light over the sky area. 'I think they are planes. Single-engine, I think, but we'll know more when it's cleaned. One, I think, is a Mustang, one a Spitfire, from the war.'

Jake looked at Ruby, his eyes bright. 'A romantic gesture, for two pilots,' he said.

Gemma showed them through a magnifier the details of the planes, and they took photographs of the whole picture.

'There was a letter in the back. Is that enough to prove it was Alice's?' Ruby asked.

'She didn't sign the picture itself, but the letter is endorsed and looks completely authentic,' Gemma said. 'We have an expert on her pictures in the company, he's happy to do an appraisal and give you some idea of value, if you want to sell. And you need to insure it. It should also be authenticated for the catalogue raisonné, the official list of her works. Then if you ever do sell, you'll get the true value.'

'She's not selling,' Jake said, catching Ruby's eye.

'Will it always look like it was folded in two?' Ruby asked.

'I think it will come up great. There might be a tiny difference in tone, but it shouldn't be obvious. And it's such a talking point.'

'It's big, though,' Ruby said, touching the temporary frame.

'It's just under two metres wide and one point three high,' Gemma said. 'Nice proportions. I love it, it's got so much life in it, you almost expect the baby to laugh, or the dog to pant.'

Jake put his arm around her waist and kissed her forehead. 'Whatever the court says about the house, this is yours,' he said. 'You've seen it every day of your childhood. But I admit I'd miss the painting, now I know its story, from that room.'

'You will have to come and stay with me, then,' she said, smiling. 'Frequently.'

The days in London with Jake were easy. They walked along the river, arguing about favourite hangouts she had got to know at university. They talked about their previous loves, and he got angry on her behalf at her ex's cruel comments.

'My mother used to say I looked like a librarian,' she said, pushing her glasses lower on her nose and looking over them. 'He made me wear contacts and have my hair dyed so I wouldn't.'

'I would say you look *bookish*,' he said, stopping so he could put his arms around her. 'Scholarly. Intellectual.' As he added a kiss to each adjective, she didn't mind. 'Sexy. Seductive.'

She wound her arms around his neck. 'I'll take that.'

When they resumed walking, hand in hand, she looked back at him. 'Tell me about your marriage.'

'Fortuna? I met her at college. I did love her, everyone did. But she's a strong personality, she kind of told me I loved her and we got married.'

'Is that where Emmy gets her confidence from?'

'She is a gentler version of her mother. Don't get me wrong, we were happy for a long time, but I think she outgrew me. When I got this job in London, she sat me down and explained why this would be the perfect time for us to divorce. I didn't see it coming.'

'That must have been horrible.'

He half smiled at some memory. 'She told me it was just what I needed. She was right, there was some relief, too.' He looked at her. 'This is new for me, Ruby. These feelings are *mine*, how I feel about you is different from my previous relationship.'

She could feel the corners of her smile tugging at her ears, it was so wide. 'It's new for me, too.'

She tucked her hand into his arm as they walked.

'Are you ready for the court judgement on the will?' he asked.

It felt like a draught had found its way down her collar. 'I am trying to be,' she admitted. 'I'll be gutted if it doesn't all come to me, though, and the Oldstocks might not get it. I know it's a long shot that the court would overturn Marissa's will...'

'Until this year, Mabel didn't even know the estate existed,' he said. 'She just wanted to understand the story of her mother. She didn't want to make a claim against the estate, but the law won't give the estate to you until they rule her out. And you knew these people, you loved them.'

'Except Billie. She's the last bit of the family, the one I didn't even know about. I wish I could have met her. I'm glad to know Mabel, though.'

'I will be surprised if the DNA says she's not William and Clara's daughter,' he admitted.

'Maybe,' she said. 'But I haven't quite ruled out Giles yet. Do you remember the engagement rings?'

'Yeah. Sir Richard was sure the father wasn't Giles, and how many fiancés did she have?'

'The DNA will help with that,' she said, hugging his arm. 'This is lovely, being away from worrying about Pony and Max, away from work and the legal stuff.'

'I'm coming down to Devon for the hearing,' he said.

'Of course. Come down and stay, if you like.'

'House or your flat?'

'I have to be around for Pony in the afternoon, she has a doctor's appointment.' She pulled him around to face her. 'So, come to the house, whether it's mine or Mabel's.'

'Or the taxman's,' he said, kissing her.

44

MARCH 1944

Clara sat up in bed, the baby screwing up her face as she woke in Alice's arms.

'She's hungry,' Alice murmured. 'You used to look just like that when you wanted a feed.'

'I can't imagine Mother feeding a baby,' Clara said, staring at the baby, her starfish fingers, her pursed lips.

'She was eighteen. She could do anything,' Alice said, placing her little finger in the baby's palm and smiling when she grasped it. 'She was magnificent, even when she was feeding you. I, of course, bathed and changed you and did all your laundry.'

'Well, I'm very grateful,' Clara said, smiling at her. 'Now I know what a palaver it is.'

'You get deft very quickly,' Alice said as the baby squinted up at Clara with crossed eyes. 'Have you decided on a name?'

'Not yet. I'm rather glad she isn't a boy. I think it would be difficult not to name her after her father.'

'Which you aren't telling us just yet.'

'I can't... After the war. I'll tell you after the war.'

It took a little while to get the baby latched on and

feeding before Clara could look up again. 'It's just – it's private. I don't want to feel any pressure to contact him before I'm ready.'

'You remember how upset you were when we kept your father's name from *you*?'

'I know.' Clara bit her lip. 'I'll tell her as soon as she's old enough.'

'Will she ever meet him?' Alice's questions were exhausting, because they had taken up so much of the last two months of the pregnancy. Alice patted her knee. 'No, don't answer that, my darling. You do have a few letters of congratulations. I assume they are from your colleagues, since we didn't exactly put it in the society pages.'

'Can you open them for me?' Clara asked, sleepiness catching up with her as she shut her eyes. She hadn't slept more than three hours since the long labour.

'Should I read them?'

'Just from the ladies,' Clara said, quickly.

'Well, there's a lovely note from a Roberta, signed Bobby. That's your commanding officer?'

'She is.'

'*Many congratulations, Faith told us the news...* Lots of lovely messages relayed from your headquarters, too. Shall I leave them until you're ready?'

'Just read them, please. Is there anything I need to reply to?' Clara murmured.

'There's a little parcel.' Clara opened her eyes as Alice pulled out a tiny matinee jacket. 'From Marjory, down in Hampshire. Well, she'll grow in and out of that quick enough. You'll have to write a thank you note.' She paused over the end of the letter 'Bobby wonders if you have any plans to return to the ATA. Surely not.'

'Not yet.' Clara couldn't bear the thought of leaving the baby. 'Not until she's weaned, anyway.'

Alice opened her eyes wide. 'You can't go back now. You have the baby to think of.'

'It's a war. Very few people can do what I do.'

Alice looked up as Marissa pushed open the door. 'Do what?'

'Fly for the ATA,' Clara said, pausing to brush her lips over the red-gold hair on the baby's head.

'You've done your bit,' Marissa said, with authority. Until she started flying professionally, Clara might have bowed to that authority.

'If I am needed,' she said, softly but clearly, 'I will do my duty. To win peace for all of us. To win peace for *her*.'

'They have over a thousand other pilots,' Marissa said, sitting on the edge of the bed and her expression softening. 'There are many other ways you could help the war effort.'

'There's going to be an invasion,' Clara said. 'A push into Europe, to overthrow Hitler. They will have to move thousands of planes to the coast.'

'But not yet?' Marissa said.

'I don't know when it will be,' Clara answered, although the jobs were piling up. Faith and Marjory were exhausted, flying six days a week. 'I can live here, fly into Bristol for a few days a week, come home at weekends. If you will look after the baby. You will, won't you?'

Alice squeezed her foot under the blankets. 'Of course we will, darling. But – it's so dangerous. Think about the baby – oh, for goodness' sake, can't we give her a nickname or something?'

Clara smiled. 'I did have a name – but only if you both agree.'

'Try us,' Alice said, and Clara gently eased the nipple out of the sleeping baby's mouth and rested her on her shoulder.

'I thought – Alissa. Alice and Marissa.'

They both drew a little sigh and looked at each other.

'That's charming,' Marissa said. 'Don't you want to add some name reflecting her father, too?'

Clara shook her head. 'Please don't ask.'

Alice held up two opened letters. 'I'm assuming it's one of *these* gentlemen,' she said, her eyebrows almost in her hairline. 'I told you the name of *your* father. You must make sure the baby – Alissa – knows hers, too. Think about it.'

'You told her about Paul?' Marissa asked, her voice arctic.

'I did,' Alice replied. 'When she asked. When she needed to know.'

Marissa bowed her head once. 'Very well. But what happens if something happens to *you*, Clara?'

She smiled as the baby burped gently in her ear. 'In the very unlikely circumstance of something happening to me, you can ask the gentlemen concerned. *They* know.'

45

PRESENT DAY, FEBRUARY

In the foyer of the county court, Ruby got a huge hug from Mabel, fresh from the States to attend the hearing. She followed it up with a hug from Jake, who had driven Mabel down.

'We have news!' Mabel crowed, waving a thick envelope.

'Have you read it yet?' Ruby asked hesitantly.

'I have, but Jake hasn't. I want you two to discover it together.' She handed it to Ruby and they stood side by side to look.

'The DNA is a match,' Ruby said, feeling Jake's arm around her waist. 'Clara must have been Billie's mother.' *So Mabel does have a claim, after all.*

Jake guided her towards a bench. 'It's nice to confirm such a romantic story,' he said, as he sat down. 'I'm so glad for Mabel.' He beckoned to Mabel to sit beside him.

But she was too excited. 'Did you read the second page?' Mabel said, bobbing up and down on her toes. 'Read page two.'

'It says...' Ruby said, scanning the data and jargon on the form, 'that *the applicant Mabel Player shares fifty per cent of the subject with DNA identified as belonging to Wilhelmina Carlson, and twenty-five per cent of DNA identified as William Carlson.*'

'So, he really was my biological grandfather, not just my adoptive one,' Mabel said, tears making her eyes bright. 'And William was Clara's lover. Which feels odd, because I wouldn't have thought he was someone who would sleep around and get a girl pregnant. Even one as glamorous as Clara.'

'How on earth did your grandmother feel about that? Did she even *know*?'

'I don't know. Grandpa always said that he brought home the baby of a friend, who was half American. All true, I suppose,' Mabel said, sitting on the seat beside them. 'He said he told his fiancée, May, everything she needed to know. He never went into detail with his children about exactly *what* he was telling her.' She wiped away a tear. 'She was a wonderful woman. She was a loving mother and I didn't guess Billie was adopted until I was told. They did so many things together, you wouldn't have known they weren't related.'

'May sounds lovely,' Ruby said, feeling a twinge of grief at her own lost mother. 'So you might have a claim.'

Mabel caught her hand. 'I don't want your house, Ruby. I'll sign a paper to that effect, if it's needed. It's yours. I'm just so happy to know who my mother was. She came from a wonderful love story, I'm grateful for that.'

Half an hour later, Ruby and Jake left the courtroom with a piece of paper and a sense of disillusionment.

'Ten minutes to approve probate and name you the heir?' he said. 'After all this time and work on Mabel's behalf?'

'They acknowledged that she *could* have had a claim, but they gave probate to me because Marissa's will was sound.' She caught her breath for a moment. The weight of the responsibility of the house hit her hard. Part of her expected the court to open a new case for Mabel, for Jake to have to put in an appeal. Now everything – from the dry rot in the attic and the rats in the drains – was Ruby's. She couldn't wait to hand it over to the Oldstocks... Except... nowhere else had ever felt as much like home.

Jake was speaking again. 'I've booked Mabel in to the little place we were before, Foxglove Cottage. Is it OK for me to stay with you again?'

She could feel her insecurities gather like crows. 'Of course. I suppose I'd better get back, tell Max and Pony.'

'Ruby?' he looked at her, searching her face.

'It's OK,' she started to say, but the doubts were forcing tears into her throat. 'I've got to go,' she babbled, turning away.

He caught her arm. 'If you'd rather I stayed with Mabel, I can.'

'I just...' She couldn't explain and she didn't want to start crying. She tried to smile. 'I'm not sorry it went the way it did. But...'

'Let's go to the house,' he said. He smiled at her. 'All Mabel was looking for was her mom's family – and she found *your* family. She never wanted to steal your house. I wish you could keep it. For you. For all of you.'

She brushed a tear from her eyelashes. 'I know. I'm being silly. It's just, we only met because my mum died. It all feels so... random.'

'Life *is* random. But once I met you... you're a keeper, Ruby. You know that.'

His certainty made her feel warm from the heart out. 'I'm glad I'm related to Mabel through Clara. Even if not biologically, she feels like family.'

Jake said, 'I have the best of the family right here.'

He held her tightly, and kissed her while Mabel beamed, until Ruby got embarrassed. She held his hand as they walked out, Mabel holding his other arm.

'We can tell the Oldstocks they can start finalising the

purchase of the estate,' Ruby said. 'And I'm sure there will be a few bits of Clara's and Marissa's for Mabel, too.'

'Then we can move out anything you want to keep,' Jake said. 'We can put it in storage if you need to.'

She smiled at him. 'And I like the word *we*. As in, *we* might need a bigger house.'

Mabel chatted all the way across the moor, showing Ruby pictures of Billie growing up, while Jake drove. They rattled across a cattle grid which took them onto the moorland itself.

'I'll never get used to that,' he grumbled.

'It keeps the animals on the moor,' Ruby said. 'It works.'

Ahead, a small group of sheep were standing in the road, and he pulled up. 'Should I hit the horn?'

'It won't help,' Ruby said, undoing her seat belt and opening her door. 'I'll ask them to move on.'

It took a couple of minutes to persuade them to shift as they were quite unafraid of her. One of them stayed sitting in the road but when Ruby got back in Jake was able to drive slowly past it.

'I love sheep,' Ruby said, waving at the last of them. 'I used to help the local shepherd in the spring. Not these sheep, the ones from the farm nearest the house, the Dukes'. I was always given a few bottle-fed lambs to rear.'

'Oh, so cute!' Mabel said. 'What happened to them?'

'They grew about a foot a week and soon had to go in the field at the back. Then they went back with the flock, and then... well they would all be dead of old age by now anyway.' She remembered her worst night of lambing, trying to help the shepherd save the second lamb after the first was stillborn. 'I sometimes helped deliver a lamb,' she said. She looked at her fingers. 'The farmer said I had little hands, could grab feet that were folded back.' She remembered the scalding heat inside the struggling mothers, the bony wriggle of live lambs.

'Did it work?' Mabel put one of her hands over Ruby's.

'It usually did.' That had been one of those moments when she felt like someone was guiding her, as if she had done it before, as if someone was right beside her. 'I always thought there was some sort of spirit helping me,' she confessed. 'Of someone who knew what they were doing. I know that sounds silly.'

'What would a ghost know about lambing?' Mabel asked.

'Well, exactly,' she said, but she knew the answer. 'My grandmother Marissa once told me that Clara used to help with the lambing, too. She didn't approve but she was friends with all the local farmers, the Dukes and the Cawseys.'

'Who is it?' Jake's voice was soft and sombre. 'Do you think Clara haunts you?'

'*Helped* me. Maybe I did, when I was an imaginative child, when I was under stress.'

'You don't ever feel her now?' he asked. She could see his profile, his face a little strained.

'Sometimes I feel something, like someone just behind me, whispering. I'm not sure it's Clara. It could be my grandmothers. I suppose it could be anyone who lived at the house. Or my vivid imagination.'

'Someone who helped out with lambing?'

She laughed at that. 'Maybe. Why? Have you felt anything?'

He shrugged. 'Why should I?'

'Clara might like you,' Ruby said. 'She liked another American.'

'It's a house full of draughts and creaky floorboards,' he admitted. 'But I don't believe in ghosts.'

'I always hear it as whispering,' she said. 'And soft touches for comfort.'

'As I say, draughts,' he said, but he had a little waver in his voice.

46

NOVEMBER 1944

'It's just a routine delivery of a plane for repairs,' Clara shouted down the line to the house. 'Darling, just tell Baby I'll be back by bedtime, I'm going to Cornwall.'

'She's too young to understand why you're not here *now*,' grumbled Marissa.

'We need so many planes delivered to the coast to get to Europe, to follow up after D-Day,' Clara said. 'It's a quick hop, then I'm bringing back an American bomber which needs a new paint job,' she quipped. Hopefully it wouldn't be too badly damaged. Since the baby, she had been better at declining difficult flights. In the six weeks she'd been back to work, since weaning little Alissa, she had flown thirty-eight planes. While the exhilaration of flying was the same as before, take-offs and landings made her heart race more. There were days when she was hit by waves of yearning for the baby, even though she knew she was well cared for by Mrs Goddings and both of her mothers. Sleeping away was torture, so she did most of the flying in three days, with only two nights away. She tried to end her journeys close to Bristol so she could fly or drive home. She and Faith were stationed there now.

William was now flying missions from Europe; delivering fresh planes to the coast felt like the best she could do for him. She saw more and more of him in Alissa, as her eyes turned from deep blue to jade green, and her hair gathered in coppery curls. It made her long to see him, she missed him acutely. But it was Giles who had visited her in hospital after the baby was born, who had escorted her to register her birth.

'Are you sure you don't want my name on her birth certificate?' he had whispered into her ear, but she had been happy to name her Alissa St John, to at least make an effort to avoid the scandal of Marissa Montpelier's child having an illegitimate baby. The strange thing was, while she longed for William, she could imagine marrying Giles. From that day, she had started flying with both the rings on a chain around her neck, in the hope that it would help her decide.

'Here's your schedule,' Faith said, as she turned away from the phone. 'Easy hop to Cornwall, RAF Davidstow, but have a good look at the weather first. I would call ahead, there's some thick sea fog around the coast.'

Clara studied the office map of the area, noting landmarks. 'I don't know this area as well as Devon,' she said, making notes in her book. 'I might have to stay over, if the weather gets any worse. What's the forecast?'

'Winds getting up, so should help with that fog,' Faith said, sitting next to her. 'Did you hear about Marjory?'

'No. Is she all right?'

Faith smiled. 'Her engineer came back from France, asked her to marry him. She said yes, there's a party at Hamble at the end of the month.'

'That's lovely!' She could feel the tug in her heart. This was the security she was turning down. 'I hope I'm around for the party, if I can get away.'

'Bring something from your house on Dartmoor,' Faith said, laughing. 'A brace of pheasants or whatever your estate can spare.' Clara had frequently been teased about food from the country, and Mrs Goddings regularly sent parcels for the girls to share.

She grinned back. 'I will. Who knows? It is pheasant season.'

The final job was to study the notes for the aircraft.

'What are you flying?' Faith asked.

'A Bristol Beaufighter.'

Faith walked past with stacks of notes, and turned at the word. 'You know the RAF pilots wouldn't fly them at first. They had to put one through an aerobatic display before they would tackle them.'

Clara chuckled. 'Yes, with one of *our* female pilots at the helm. I like them,' she said, looking through the last page of the schedule. 'Not the most stable, and a bit heavy on take-off, but they're like a horse that rides up to his bit.'

'If the weather is manageable,' Faith said, peering out of the window. 'Call ahead before you leave.' She was standing next to Clara, and must have noticed her gold chain. 'Is that something to do with the baby?'

'Not really,' Clara said, pulling up the two rings. 'These are my lucky charms.'

47

PRESENT DAY, MARCH

Ruby and her friend Lissa went through boxes of stuff from the attic, ready for the auction house to take anything the Oldstocks didn't want to buy. Much of it was household items from the nineteen twenties and thirties, but a few tea chests contained older items. Lissa dragged another one out of the eaves cupboard onto the landing.

'Ruby, you need to look at this one,' she said, lifting out what looked like a huge gravy boat. 'Mid-Victorian plates and stuff. Is that – Minton?'

Ruby picked up a plate and brushed off newspaper so fragile it crumbled. 'Look at this, the date is eighteen something – 1891.'

'Who lived here then, before your grandmothers?'

'It must be from the time of the man who built the house, the captain. The rumour around here is that he married a younger woman, built this house for her and they lived happily ever after.' She logged in to a genealogy website and brought up her account. 'Here he is, mutton-chop whiskers and all.' It took a few moments to bring up the family tree. 'This is Mercy, his American wife, she came from Boston, Massachusetts. Maybe he met her on his travels. Oh, she was his *second* wife, she was pretty, wasn't she?' The greyscale couldn't disguise the twinkle in his eye nor the tilted head and half-smile on her portrait. 'She looks flirty.'

Lissa sat next to her on the floor. 'Is there a picture after she had a dozen children and hadn't slept for two decades?'

'How *is* Arlo sleeping?'

'We're clocking five hours between one and six at the moment.' She smiled as she thought of him. 'It's so much better. As long as I catch the odd nap in the week I almost feel back to normal.'

'Oh,' Ruby said. 'Look at this, there's a picture of her with the first two babies.'

A grainy picture came up, of Mercy, still smiling a little, with a newborn in her arms and a little girl at her knee.

'Why didn't the family stay in the house?' Lissa said. 'If there were multiple heirs, why didn't they inherit it?'

Ruby swiped through a number of records. 'Oh... they lost some of their children early.'

'That's horrible,' Lissa said, dusting off the plate and holding it up to the light. 'Wow, this mauve is gorgeous, really rich purple. I don't know what the flower is, though.'

'It's heather,' Ruby said, glancing at it. 'There are several really big patches in the back garden along with all the native varieties all over the moor.'

'So, how many children died?'

Ruby could feel her heart thumping, and the whispers she imagined when she thought of the family intensified. She pulled her jumper tighter around her neck. 'Several,' she said. 'And Mercy died of *general paralysis of the insane*. Oh no, she was only forty-four.'

'Was that a type of *dementia*?'

'Not exactly. Look at her history. Four children born close together, the first and second were fine. The third and fourth died very young, not unusual in that period. Then five, nearly six years with no living babies. Then three more, all dying in childhood. Then Mercy died young.' She looked across the hallway to her attic bedroom as the air grew cooler. 'It's a classic pattern you see with syphilis.' She searched through the records. 'Look at this death certificate. His first wife died at twenty-seven from "bad blood" too.'

'That's terrible. How could he do that?'

'He wouldn't necessarily have known, he might have thought he was cured. He could even have been born with the infection himself. But as a young man in the navy, travelling the world... It would have been common. Once he gave the infection to her, it would have been dormant for periods of time – during which she had two healthy children. Heather and Primrose.' She brought up one of the baby's death certificates. 'The next one, Samuel, died aged two months, from what they called *failure to thrive*. He died here,' she said, her eyes filling with tears as she enlarged the place of death. 'Only it was called Heather House back then.'

Lissa took the plate. 'He boxed up the china – her heather china – when she died.' She wiped her eyes with the back of her hand, smearing dust and newsprint over her cheek. 'That's so sad.'

Ruby unearthed a travel packet of tissues from her jeans pocket. 'Here,' she said, while wiping her own face. 'We look like a couple of Victorian urchins. The captain died just before Queen Victoria in 1901.'

'And the surviving heirs sold the house to a pair of crazy lesbian ladies. After the First World War?'

'Hardly ladies,' Ruby said. 'They were just teenagers in 1918. Marissa's parents bought them the house if they wouldn't make a scandal, just live quietly in the countryside with the baby. They both had allowances for life – they were still living on them when they died, as well as all their art sales.'

Lissa unwrapped another plate, then a cup, holding it up to the light, the purple colour glowing through the reverse of the bone china. 'You should really keep these.'

'I think they belong with the house,' Ruby decided. 'I'm going to clean them up and give them to Imogen and Maurice, if they want them. Something to go on the dresser in the hall, if they like.'

'Did Marissa and Alice live quietly?'

Ruby laughed, then sneezed with the dust. 'Alice's watercolours sold quite well locally. She used to paint sentimental pictures of babies and puppies – probably of Clara, I suppose. I should look out for one for Jake, we have a few around the place. But once she started painting in oils, she became so famous people started writing articles about the two of them. Then Marissa's photography took off, too. She only bought a camera to help Alice compose her pictures but she discovered a real talent for photography. Artists came from all over the world to see them and to work here.'

'Did that create a scandal?'

'I don't think it did,' Ruby said. 'By then no one cared. There's a book downstairs on Marissa. The biographer wrote how extraordinary they were as a couple, but no one cared about which bed they slept in, no one defined their relationship. They were extraordinary eccentrics. Marissa's photographs were exhibited everywhere. They used to display the pictures she took, and Alice's paintings that came from them.' She remembered one of Marissa's rare smiles, when Ruby had just taken a picture of a butterfly. 'It was all about recording the photographer's gaze, their thoughts, their feelings. Not just about having a level horizon or interesting points of focus.' She looked at Lissa, her eyes tickling with tears. 'It is hard, letting go of the house. It feels like losing them again.'

'Maybe you should read that book again. It might make you feel closer to them.'

Ruby nodded, then looked at her phone and typed in a search. 'The author is still alive,' she said slowly. 'She was quite young when she interviewed Marissa, I remember her visiting several times. I might have a chat with her, find out if she knows anything more about the family history.'

'You could catalogue Marissa's negatives and correspondence, to donate to the archive,' Lissa said. 'I didn't like to bother you so soon, but the board were going to make a formal approach, once you knew who owned them. Before you chuck anything priceless out.'

'Is that likely? I'm an archivist!' Ruby scoffed. It would be good to be so close to Marissa's work. 'Do you think they would like Alice's sketchbooks, too? Some of them are in museums and libraries already, but Marissa kept her favourites.'

'I think it would be lovely to create the St John-Montpelier archive, catalogued by Ruby St John,' Lissa said, smiling back.

Ruby wondered if the ghosts would approve, and follow her to the city.

Visiting Jake in London gave Ruby a chance to visit the war records of the Air Transport Auxiliary, and it was quite a shock to run into her ex-boyfriend at the National Archives. It shouldn't have been a surprise, as that was where they had met as he ran the British Civilian Gallantry Awards department. She had expected to be diverted to the military records, but once she and Jake had been directed to the correct department, her heart sank. His name was on one of the doors by the reception desk; he was standing with his back to them as Ruby approached.

'Uh, Oliver?' she said, her voice coming out as a squeak. She cleared her throat as he turned to face her, then his face changed. He shook his head, smiled at her and reached for a hug. She didn't hug him back, unsure what to do or say. He had left on such bad terms...

'Ruby, this is *great*. Are you here to look something up for work, or have you dropped in to see me?' He registered Jake standing behind her and his face hardened a little.

'I'm looking up details about a famous pilot, my aunt Clara.' She turned to Jake. 'This is my friend Jake Haydon, also a historian.'

'Oh, hi. Oliver Blythe. If I remember, you told me your aunt was in the ATA?'

'How do you two know each other?' Jake interrupted, his smile steely.

'We went out for a while,' Ruby said, withering under Oliver's sneering smile.

'We lived together for a couple of years,' Oliver said. 'We talked about getting engaged, didn't we, Rubes?'

Ruby found her voice. 'I think we realised in time that it would be a mistake,' she said, her pulse fluttering in her throat so hard she wondered if Oliver could see it. 'Ollie was so much more gregarious than me. Anyway, it's nice to see you looking well. I've got a few reference cards for our enquiries,' she said, holding them out to a young man at reception. 'If you could find the records, please?'

She could see Oliver bare his teeth like he did when he was annoyed, normally before he delivered a biting put-down. 'We prefer advance warning.'

'You had it,' she smiled back, starting to enjoy the moment. He was still tall, but a little stooped, and his hair was beginning to recede at the front. She had once thought he was so lovely, so intelligent. But never kind. 'Three days ago, it's on the booking cards.'

He managed a little smile. 'I'll set you up in the room. Sean will get your records – please look after them, they are originals.'

Ten minutes later, they were sat in front of logbooks and

personnel records, and Oliver had retreated to this office. 'Was he always mean, like that?' Jake whispered into her ear.

'At first I thought he was just strong, and I respected his opinion. But once the opinions started to be about me, things fell apart.' She shook her head. 'I took a while to get over him, but I am now.'

He put an arm around her shoulders, kissed her brow. 'Are you ready for this? It might be hard reading.'

'That is what I love about you,' she said, turning to the huge ledgers of missions. 'You are so kind.'

He took his arm away as she put on white gloves and opened the first book, carefully. 'You love me?' he said slowly and stared at her.

Her gaze met his and she could feel a blush warming her cheeks. 'I do love you,' she said, realising they hadn't really used the words before. They made her smile even more. 'I wouldn't ask you to come and stay with me, sleep in my bed and share my picture, if I didn't.'

'Oh,' he said, his grin stretching towards his ears. 'I love you too.'

She shook her head and turned back to the books. '*Missions, Hamble, September 1944.*'

His smile slipped away. 'When did she die?'

'November. In terrible fogs.' She skipped through the records until the fourteenth, fifteenth, sixteenth. There, lists of planes, airfields to pick them up from and deliver them to. Clara's name, underlined in black. She had to take a plane to an airport in Cornwall for repairs. There were no details, just a single line underneath.

Clara St John-Montpelier, RIP.

48

NOVEMBER 1944

Clara had a simple hop to Camelford from Bristol. The plane was dented and the paint was scratched but the engine looked in good condition and the engineer was happy with it. She tucked her bag and coat behind her in the Beaufighter and did an instrument check. All was well, and the plane took off easily, despite a natural tendency to drift.

She tucked her rings under her uniform shirt on their chain, against her skin, where they were a little cold. She could take the usual route over the top of the moor, over Tiverton and Okehampton towards Camelford, but preferred the straight route over Dartmoor. As the land rose, painted in browned bracken and purple patches of moor grass among the spikes of gorse, she wove her way between the tors, past Haytor, looking ahead for Combestone and Bellever, and south, facing the house on the hill.

The afternoon sun just touched the slates of the roof as low cloud drifted around. She flew through one, knowing after the house the village would soon be ahead, and as she came out into the light she saw another plane, not more than a few hundred yards away, flying parallel on her right flank.

As he peeled away she registered that the plane was German, and she banked left to avoid it. The ground was close – she hadn't wanted to spare too much fuel on gaining unnecessary altitude – but as she forced the plane down and forward, it gained speed. She heard the sound of the gun, but was able to spin away, praying she wasn't too close to the ground. Pulling up hard, she managed to recover the spin and gain a bit of height.

The guns spat again, and this time she could see him coming directly at her. She managed to clear him down her left flank again, but this time heard the thud of bullets hitting the fuselage.

She heaved on the stick but it was locked. The plane faltered under her as she realised that she was coming down the valley towards Hartford village. The school loomed straight ahead of her, her heart lurched as children in brightly coloured jumpers ran and played in the grass outside, just as she had done...

Anywhere but the school.

She yanked one last time to steer away, anywhere but the middle of the children. In the second before she overshot the school, narrowly missing the church and speeding towards the flank of the hill leading to the tor above, she thought of her love.

Alissa, laughing with that giggle she made when Clara lifted her from her cot...

49

PRESENT DAY MARCH

Ruby and Jake sat side by side looking at the faded ink on the folder. '*Accident report, 16 November 1944, 14:10, Hartford, Devon.*'

'That's right up the road from us,' Ruby said.

'Where we saw the church?' Jake asked.

'That's right. Why do I feel so nervous?' Ruby asked in a low voice. 'We know what happens, she died.'

'She's come to life for us now,' he whispered back. 'She seems real. The picture Giles had, the photographs, her records. The fact that she loved William Carlson enough to have his child, while she still had an attachment to Giles.'

He was right: knowledge had painted rich colours into her black-and-white imaginings of Clara. 'I don't know if I want to know the gruesome details,' she said, rubbing the back of her hand under her eyes to spare the archive gloves. 'The records were only released recently.'

'You can wait outside if you like,' he said, clasping her wrist briefly. 'I'll give you the highlights – as much as I understand, anyway. I'll get pictures for Mabel, too, when she's ready to see them.'

She looked up at him for a long moment, took a deep breath and laid her hand on the cover. 'No. We know so much of her story, we should know how it ends.'

He nodded, and she opened the folder. Inside, there were about a dozen black-and-white pictures of the wrecked and crumpled plane, and for a moment, Ruby thought she saw Clara's broken body as well. No, it was just her coat, laid in the cockpit. But the black splashes might have been blood.

A simple typed form described her death. A few words jumped out – *instantaneous, unsurvivable injuries, head trauma.*

She was five foot seven, nine stone three, her hair was reddish brown. She had recently had a child.

Somehow the details made Clara feel even closer to her, as Jake's arm went around her shoulders and squeezed. Her eyes were streaming but she read on. The pilot had lost altitude when an enemy plane attacked. In an attempt to avoid several houses and a school, Clara had swerved away and hit the rocky hillside, dying in the impact. There was no fire to spread to the cockpit, nor an explosion. She was recommended for a civilian bravery award.

She pushed the chair away from the table and took off her gloves, turning to Jake as he hugged her. 'It's real,' she whispered. 'Clara was as real as we are.'

Ruby had never felt closer to Clara than she did today, and even though they were not blood relations, Ruby's grief for her was no less diminished. She had known her story all her life, but she had never been able to research the details of the terrible crash.

'Did you see the list of personal belongings?' he murmured, as he stepped back a little to look at her. 'Two rings on a broken gold chain. The engagement rings we saw at Sir Richard's house.'

'Crushed and bent,' she said, tears building on her lashes. 'Like her.' She was shaking.

'Don't think about that now,' he said, pulling her back into his arms. 'We knew how her story ended, but it was a long time ago. *We're* here *now.*'

They kissed, and Ruby felt stronger, her tremors subsiding. When they moved apart, she noticed Oliver watching them from the doorway, then disappear.

'What happened with that guy?' Jake asked.

She shrugged. 'I liked him more than he liked me, at first. He used to tell me how to dress smarter, sit up straight, do my job better. I was a project for him but I had to get out.'

He smiled. 'Don't change a single thing for me,' he said, turning back to the table. 'You're wonderful as you are.'

After a lifetime of conditional praise and distracted love from Fiona, it was lovely to hear the sincerity in his voice. 'Is there anything else?' she asked, as he slipped on a pair of cotton gloves too.

'Just this,' he said, staring up at her, wide-eyed.

The copy of a letter was filed in its own folder. The king had awarded the British Empire Medal to Clara St John-Montpelier (posthumously) for her twelve hundred flights, her gallantry in the face of danger and her courage.

Underneath was a typed report of the day she died.

She read out the faded print slowly as she deciphered it.

'*On sixteenth of November 1944 at ten past two p.m. First Officer C. A. St John-Montpelier was coming out of low cloud at Dartmeet on Dartmoor in a Bristol Beaufighter, when she was engaged by a single German Focke-Wulf 190 plane. She was observed to immediately dive below cloud cover, which was low, at less than 200 feet to avoid engagement with the enemy. A number of shots were fired, two striking the engine. From the ground she was seen to swerve left, avoiding a school and several* houses, instead attempting to climb the hillside above Hartford village. The task was impossible, and the plane crashed into the rocky slope, then slid down some eighty yards. It is believed she died instantly. At the time, twenty-one children were present at the school and another eleven people in the surrounding houses. The FW 190 was engaged and destroyed shortly afterwards over Truro. First Officer C. A. St John-Montpelier is honoured for her courage in saving these lives, with the award of British Empire Medal, received by her mother, Miss Alice St John on 23 April 1946.'

Clara turned the paper over to reveal a photograph of Alice, in furs and silk dress, walking away from the throne room with her hand on the arm of a smart man in a suit, she imagined some sort of official. Her poise was perfect but her face twisted by grief.

'The end of the story,' Ruby said, in a hushed voice. 'Alice had to go home to look after Marissa, who was in hospital for three years with a complete breakdown.'

'Yes, but that wasn't the end of the story,' he said. 'A year later, Alice was pregnant by your grandfather and about to give birth to your mother, Fiona. Look at the picture again.'

She looked again at the man she assumed was an equerry. 'Him?'

On the reverse was Alice's full name and another name, Captain James Rushworth. He looked younger than her, maybe in his late thirties. She knew Alice would have been over forty, but young enough to take comfort in the arms of a man, even while she loved Marissa deeply.

'He could be my grandfather.'

'Maybe,' he said, carefully returning the documents to the folder. 'Do you think we can get these copied?'

'Ask at the desk,' she said, still staring at the old folders that somehow contained the death of Clara, the heroine she had dreamed about her whole life. She felt it strongly, then, the hug around her shoulders, and when she shut her eyes, a brush of something that might have been a kiss on her forehead.

MAY 1945

Alice St John stared at the young man Beatrice Goddings ushered into the parlour. He was younger even than Clara had been, fair-haired and green-eyed.

'Flight Officer Carlson, ma'am,' she said, and disappeared into the hall, sniffing her disapproval.

He stared at her, letting his bag drop to his feet. 'Miss Montpelier?' he asked.

'No. Lady Marissa is – indisposed.' How could she describe to this boy that Marissa was catatonic in a private clinic in London, destroyed by grief? 'I am Alice St John. Clara's other mother.' There wasn't time to pretend or obfuscate her relationship to Clara. 'The baby's grandmother.'

'Yes, ma'am,' he said respectfully, pulling off his cap. 'I was hoping to see the baby, if that was possible. She's mine, you know, if Clara didn't tell you.'

'She did not.' She could feel her reserve crumbling. Goodness, she could see so much of the baby in his eyes, his expression. 'I'm afraid she didn't have time,' she explained. 'But she kept your letters.'

His eyes filled up with tears. 'I hoped she would marry me

after the war,' he said, and after a moment, she waved at the sofa in the middle of the room.

'Mrs Goddings will get us some tea,' she said, afraid to show him the baby, as if he would run off with her. 'Or coffee, if you would prefer?'

'Tea would be fine, thank you,' he said, formally, sitting on the edge of the cushions. 'I was hoping we could talk about the baby.'

'Alissa is healthy, well cared for and as happy as she can be.' Her own eyes prickled. 'She misses her mother, of course, but she is surrounded by people who adore her.'

'She will be brought up by two grandmothers, rather than a mother and father,' he said.

Alice smiled. 'How old do you think we are, Mr Carlson? We are in our forties, and we have everything to offer – we brought Clara up ourselves.'

'I'm sorry – I saw an article in the paper last year, about an accident involving Lady Marissa.'

That dreadful day after they heard the news. Marissa had spent all night pacing the floors, muttering, then taken the motor at dawn and driven it up onto the highest point she could reach, across the moor, wrecking the chassis on boulders. Eventually, she had driven the car into the Cleave, a sheer drop of a hundred feet. The car's fall had been slowed by brambles and saplings, but Marissa had been badly injured. When Alice saw her at the hospital, she was staring into space, a bandage around her head and a broken arm. Months later, she was still staring into space, expressionless. She would allow people to feed her a little water or a few spoonfuls of food, but otherwise she was immobile and unresponsive. She only softened her posture when she was asleep, and Alice had spent many nights sitting with her, holding her, begging her to come back to them.

'Lady Marissa, naturally, took our daughter's passing very hard. We were all crushed.' Words faltered in her throat.

Mrs Goddings came in with a tea tray and for a few minutes, Alice was distracted by the ritual of filling the cups.

He spoke softly, his eyes filled with compassion. 'I understand Squadron Leader Giles Ashton-Wilson has visited.'

Alice nodded, unable to sip her tea. 'Actually,' she said carefully, 'he's staying with us for a few days at the moment. He and Clara were very close.'

'I know,' Carlson said bleakly. 'That's all – that's fine. All that matters is that we both loved her.'

'And she loved both of you,' Alice said.

He smiled then. 'Thank you for that. I will never forget her I doubt if either of us will. She was – wonderful. I don't know if she would have married me – either of us – after the war, but I like to think she might have chosen me. So we could bring our daughter up together.'

That brought tears to Alice again. It seemed she cried many times a day. She dabbed them away with a handkerchief. 'Clara would never have taken her daughter back to America. No matter how much she loved you.'

He nodded. 'You're probably right. I would have had to make my life here, with her.' Alice sipped her tea as she looked over the moorland beyond. He stood up to see better. 'That is a magnificent view,' he said, staring around the bay window. 'So wild. Maybe she took some of that wildness with her.'

'Everywhere she went,' Alice said softly. 'On all her adventures at school, in London, in Europe. Did you she tell you she went climbing in the Alps? She got frostbite, almost lost two of her toes.'

'She didn't tell me that.' He turned and looked down at her. 'I don't know if she would have chosen a homebody like me,' he confessed. 'She needed her freedom.'

'I don't think she would have liked being the lady of the manor with Giles, either,' Alice said. 'Judging flower shows and serving on committees.'

'You know what I've come to ask,' he said, standing in front of her, shifting from one foot to the other.

'I think so,' she whispered. 'And you know what I'm going to say.'

He rummaged in his pocket. 'Before I ask – and you say no – I'd like you to read this.' He handed her a letter, folded multiple times and crammed into an envelope that was too small. 'From Miss May Murchison.'

Alice frowned. *Who...?* She unfolded it slowly, afraid that it would somehow hold some vital information that would take Alissa away. *Don't be silly, there's nothing that can do that.*

She read, and read on. Four sheets tightly covered with neat handwriting, on both sides. She heard Giles come in, from riding Clara's big hunter that they absolutely must sell, only they were afraid he would go for horsemeat... She heard William stand and greet him – she didn't know they had met before – but carried on reading. Her hands were shaking by the time she ended the letter. She waited until they had both sat down before she folded the notepaper back, and handed it and the envelope back to Carlson. William, as she now thought of him, having read the letter.

'You'll stay for dinner,' she said, trying to find her composure while her heart raced at a hundred miles an hour. 'You can stay in one of the guest rooms if you like, while I consider... your letter.'

'Thank you,' he said, and sitting side by side with Giles she could see why Clara couldn't choose between the brooding dark giant with his blazing eyes, or the fair young man, with his kind look.

'I can go,' Giles said, half turning.

'I think it would be better if you stay to listen to what I have to say, too,' she answered. 'Tomorrow. I'll give you both my answer tomorrow.' She managed a thin smile. 'As it's tea time, our nursemaid Jenny will bring Alissa down to play. William – may I call you William? – you should meet your daughter.'

She watched him the next day, carrying Alissa around the stables, patting the horses' noses and naming things for her. Flower, hay, butterfly. The horses *really* would have to go; there was little chance that Marissa would be well enough to ride in the next couple of years, and they were all so old.

Marissa's mastiff was following them around with a look of adoration, as Giles pulled his ears gently and patted him. The sun was slanting around the side of the house, illuminating the whitewashed wall beside the stable, with a few bales of hay.

'William,' she said. 'Wait there, let me get a camera.'

She ran through the yard to the back door, and into the hall. Marissa's darkroom always had a couple of cameras loaded with film – when she could get it – for spontaneous shots. She walked back into the yard to find William sitting on a hay bale, with the baby babbling on his knee.

She caught a picture, his face turned in profile to answer a question; she realised he was speaking to Giles. Alice arranged a couple of bales to make a chair with a back at his side.

'Put the baby on there,' she said, looking through the camera at them.

'I'll have to hold her or she'll fall off,' he said, putting Alissa down, but keeping his arm around her back. 'How about that?'

The dog interposed himself between them and Alice caught one perfect shot. In her artist's mind she erased the mess on the yard floor, the dust in the air, the baby looking around. As Alissa looked up at Giles she smiled, a wide grin with two bottom teeth. Alice caught a succession of pictures as the two men played with her, then took the camera back in.

Giles had followed her. 'I'd like a copy of that photograph,' he said, his usually deep voice almost a rumble. 'To remember her by.'

'I haven't decided what to do quite yet,' she said, walking into the darkroom.

'What was in the letter?' he asked. 'Something changed when you read it.'

'It's from a young woman who loves William,' she answered. 'A young girl, really, who stood by him even when he fell in love with Clara, when he got her pregnant, when he was desperate to marry her. She offers to take the baby as their first child together, to bring her up kindly and with love. With brothers and sisters, if God gives them, she says.'

Giles snorted. 'What does she know about life?'

'She's been nursing through the war. She looked after sailors after Pearl Harbor, she's been caring for the pilots and soldiers that have been sent back to America. She says she's tired of war and wants to build peace.'

'But you don't know her! And what about Marissa, what will she say?'

Alice shook off the cold feeling she had whenever she remembered how ill Marissa was. 'She hasn't looked at Alissa since Clara died. At one point I was worried she would hurt the baby, smother her to send her to be with Clara. She's not sane right now, and when she comes home, I will have to look after her.'

'Even if she never gets better?'

'Even if she never gets better. She's my life, Giles, my love. Not my whole life any more, but she will always come first.' She gripped his forearm for a moment. 'You will love again. You will marry and have your own children.'

'But some stranger...'

'She will be with her *father*,' Alice said fiercely. 'We would have fought for Clara to keep her, why wouldn't we do the same for William?'

He looked down at the floor. 'How would he even get to America with her?'

'William is going to take Alissa with him when he goes. He's being repatriated, and leaving the air force.'

That made him look up. 'Why?'

'May explained in the letter... I don't really understand it. Some type of lung condition. But he'll be all right once he goes home.'

Giles looked at her, into her eyes. 'What about you? Are you just going to be a nurse to a madwoman for the rest of your life?'

She shook her head. 'She's had these spells before. I'll be there while she recovers. We have so many kind friends, I'll stay busy.'

'If she does recover.'

She smiled then. 'If Clara had been terribly injured in that crash, would you have waited for her?'

'Yes!' he said fiercely.

She wound the film to the end. 'I'll let you have the prints, when I do them. I'm not as deft as Marissa, but I can develop a roll of film. I want to do a painting of them both.'

'Will Marissa forgive you, for letting the baby go?'

Alice's heart jumped in her chest. 'Eventually,' she said. She hoped.

EPILOGUE

PRESENT DAY, JULY

Mabel had brought her daughters, both about Ruby's age, to the memorial ceremony. Jake and Ruby had agonised over the wording, and an unexpected donation from Sir Richard Ashton-Wilson had also helped fund a large wall plaque. The Oldstocks were there, and had brought Pony and Max, in matching wheelchairs to spare them the walk down to Hartford village church. Leon was dressed formally – it was odd to see him in full black vicar's uniform, but his smile was as warm as ever, and Zosia had organised the afternoon refreshments.

Jake, his warm hand in Ruby's, squeezed her fingers when she dabbed away a few tears. The memorial started with a reminder of the gratitude the whole village had for the men and women who had served in all capacities during the battle for peace in the Second World War. Leon mentioned the land girls, who were mothers of several local families, and had kept food flowing to the big cities. The servicemen who had fought for their country, from local hero Casimir Wojcik who had fought in the air force, to the many sailors from the area who had died, including the very youngest, Thomas George Fairchild, a cabin boy aged barely fifteen. Soldiers, marines, merchant seamen, police, firefighters and ambulance drivers, heroes focused on saving lives as Plymouth and the rest of the county was bombed. And finally, the Air Transport Auxiliary, who delivered planes for fighting or for repair, for more than five years, flying more than three hundred thousand missions. Many died. One of them was Clara St John-Montpelier of Montpelier House.

People stepped forward to remember her, or her final heroic deed. People who had been playing or living in the village that Clara had managed to avoid, at the cost of her own life. A child who was born that day in a cottage close to the school. The daughter of the vicar, who remembered her father's story of running to the crashed plane, and praying over the poor pilot he found there.

Leon stood at the front of the church to address the whole congregation.

'Without Clara's courage, the village may not have survived. The loss of a community's children can do that, as people move away from the constant reminder of their grief. Instead, we have something to remind us of her heroism, that binds us together in gratitude.

He beckoned to Ruby. She walked to the front, after a squeezed hand from both Jake and Max, sitting beside her.

'I'm really grateful to unveil this permanent memorial in the church, to Clara,' she said. 'She was my mother's sister, and although I never met her, I've been told stories about her all my life. She seems as real to me as if I *had* met her.' She took a deep breath. 'I know a lot of you have wondered about what we are doing with Montpelier House. Maurice and Imogen Oldstock are taking it on, to create a wonderful retirement home for the community. They are saving the house, and are restoring the original name, Heather House. I think it's going to continue to be somewhere wonderful and unusual, and it will fill up with great stories. Not least because Max is investing in the venture with the Oldstocks, and is going to stay with them as one of their first guests. Pony, who you all know and love, is going to be there, too, and they are keeping some of Clara's and Alice's and Marissa's history there.'

'And yours!' Jake shouted, and she realised tears were streaming down her face.

'And mine,' she said, 'because Dartmoor is the best place in the world, for me. Even though Jake and I are moving in together in Plymouth, we will be back all the time.' She pulled on the gold cord, and the velvet curtain revealed the plaque, as the congregation clapped and cheered.

When they quietened down, Ruby read the inscription aloud.

'*In grateful and loving memory of First Officer Clara St John-Montpelier of the Air Transport Auxiliary Ferry Pool 15, Hamble, lost to a crash in the pursuance of her duty, sixteenth November 1944. A daughter of Dartmoor, she flew hundreds of missions for her country. Her final action saved many lives in Hartford village. Vita data est in virtute.*'

In one corner were the two planes from the picture of the baby, which was now in pride of place at her flat. She touched her hand to the shiny brass, seeing the lines of the house in the background of the inscribed words.

People crowded around to see and she stepped back, to take Jake's hand, to smile at the many people who reminded her of Fiona and her own contribution to the community.

'All right, Ruby Roo?' Max said, leaning on a stick, out of his wheelchair.

'Definitely. How's the work coming?'

Max smiled at her. 'I'm getting one of the studios. It's going to be an en suite room off the yard, where I can work a bit of wire in the sunshine. I'm going small with my sculptures.' He allowed Imogen to take his arm.

'After he bought into the project, we couldn't deny him,

really. Pony's having the studio next door,' she said, 'and Dad is going into the front bedroom upstairs, with that brilliant view.'

'So you turned out to have some money after all?' Ruby said, speaking to Max. 'All those years at a hundred a week.'

'It's a solid investment for my heirs,' he said grandly. 'Well, that's Pony and then you, anyway.'

Pony shuffled up to them and grabbed her arm. 'Have you seen the line at the bottom?'

At the very bottom of the memorial plate were two names: William Carlson and Giles Ashton-Wilson.

'She couldn't choose between them, and we can't, even now,' Ruby explained.

It felt right, just the way Clara would have wanted it. Ruby was sure Clara would have approved of Jake, because she more than loved him, she was in love with him.

Jake put his arms around her from behind. 'Leon says they are having tea for everyone at the bed and breakfast,' he said. 'Are you coming?'

'I'll stay a bit longer,' she said, feeling wisps of touch, a wordless murmuring in her ear. 'I'll walk up in a minute. I want – I want to say goodbye.'

As people walked towards the porch and into the sunshine, she waited. Maybe she sensed one of her grandmothers or Clara. But on balance Ruby thought she had grown up with the motherly ghost of Mercy, and she would always be here.

'I'm leaving,' she announced to the empty church, the words echoing around the tin roof, off the scarred and scratched pews. 'But I'll be back all the time. And I have Jake now, and – you should be the first to know – I'm having a baby. And he or she will be christened here, so you can carry on blessing my family.'

There wasn't a word, but a feeling, of pressure around her, disappearing as quickly as it came, leaving the air in the church thick and warm.

Ruby walked out and into Jake's arms.

A LETTER FROM REBECCA

Dear Reader,

I'm so glad you found *Memories of Heather House*. I hope you enjoyed meeting Clara and following her adventure as a pilot for the Air Transport Auxiliary. For Ruby, the search was for herself after the loss of her mother, as well as finding love. If you enjoyed their journeys, you can keep in touch with future moorland stories by following the link below. Your email will never be shared and you can unsubscribe at any time.

www.bookouture.com/rebecca-alexander

I'm very fortunate to live near Dartmoor. It's beautiful but can be austere and inhospitable. You can get lost easily, weather sweeps in dropping you into dense cloud, heavy rain and then sunshine all in a few minutes. The many springs and streams follow into valleys then the slopes lead towards the overwhelming tors. The whole moor is covered in stones, some enough to turn your ankle, some too big to climb up. Old hut circles, avenues of stone from prehistory and stone crosses are everywhere. Nature surrounds you – skylarks, kestrels, rabbits and deer are all around. I get the impression anything could happen there.

I'm looking forward to writing more stories based on Dartmoor. Living in a small community where everyone knows everyone means secrets come to the surface eventually.

If you want to support me and the books, it's always helpful to write a review. This also helps me develop and polish future stories! You can contact me directly via my website or on X.

Thank you and happy reading,

Rebecca

www.rebecca-alexander.co.uk

𝕏 x.com/RebAlexander1

ACKNOWLEDGEMENTS

This book wouldn't be in your hands without the hard work and patience of my editor, Rhianna Louise. She is able to see the big picture, rather than the words and pages as I see them. Thank you, Rhianna, for caring for my characters (and their author) and helping me create a better book! Many thanks to the copy editor Angela Snowden who seems to know what I meant to say. And Jenny and Mandy and the rest of the team of book lovers at Bookouture, for continuing the process of polishing the novel and making the stories flow. They also design the lovely covers and organise the business end, which is a mystery to me. They are so knowledgeable and enthusiastic about books.

Much gratitude goes to my two beta readers, Carey Bave and Isabella Cousins. Both are great writers, full of stories of their own. I always look forward to reading their reports and suggestions.

As always, much love goes to my patient family, especially my eight-year-old granddaughter Lily. She always has an opinion about how the story should go, and names all the animals for me! I'm grateful for the support and patience from my husband, Russell, who knows when to drive me to a field by the sea, or to the middle of the moor, and leave me to write in my vintage caravan.

PUBLISHING TEAM

Turning a manuscript into a book requires the efforts of many people. The publishing team at Bookouture would like to acknowledge everyone who contributed to this publication.

Commercial
Lauren Morrissette
Hannah Richmond
Imogen Allport

Cover design
Debbie Clement

Data and analysis
Mark Alder
Mohamed Bussuri

Editorial
Rhianna Louise
Ria Clare

Copyeditor
Angela Snowden

Proofreader
Jenny Page

RAISING READERS

Books Build Bright Futures

Dear Reader,

We'd love your attention for one more page to tell you about the crisis in children's reading, and what we can all do.

Studies have shown that reading for fun is the **single biggest predictor of a child's future life chances** – more than family circumstance, parents' educational background or income. It improves academic results, mental health, wealth, communication skills, ambition and happiness.

The number of children reading for fun is in rapid decline. Young people have a lot of competition for their time, and a worryingly high number do not have a single book at home.

Hachette works extensively with schools, libraries and literacy charities, but here are some ways we can all raise more readers:

- Reading to children for just 10 minutes a day makes a difference
- Don't give up if children aren't regular readers – there will be books for them!

- Visit bookshops and libraries to get recommendations
- Encourage them to listen to audiobooks
- Support school libraries
- Give books as gifts

There's a lot more information about how to encourage children to read on our websites: **www.RaisingReaders.co.uk** and **www.JoinRaisingReaders.com**.

Thank you for reading.

hachette
UK

Printed in Dunstable, United Kingdom